BAD BOYS
ON BOARD

BAD BOYS ON BOARD

Lori Foster
Donna Kauffman
Nancy Warren

BRAVA

KENSINGTON PUBLISHING CORP.

http://www.kensingtonbooks.com

BRAVA BOOKS are published by

Kensington Publishing Corp.
850 Third Avenue
New York, NY 10022

All Kensington titles, imprints and distributed lines are available at special quantity discounts for bulk purchases for sales promotion, premiums, fundraising, educational or institutional use.

Special book excerpts or customized printings can also be created to fit specific needs. For details, write or phone the office of the Kensington Special Sales Manager: Kensington Publishing Corp., 850 Third Avenue, New York, NY, 10022. Attn. Special Sales Department. Phone: 1-800-221-2647.

Brava and the B logo Reg. U.S. Pat. & TM Off.

ISBN 0-7582-0428-0

First Kensington Trade Paperback Printing: April, 2003
10 9 8 7 6 5 4 3 2 1

Printed in the United States of America

CONTENTS

My House, My Rules

Lori Foster

Chapter One

He knew that damned aggravating little giggle anywhere. It was throaty and pure and never failed to set him on edge. He'd listened to it every Sunday for two long months when Pete, his baby brother, had been infatuated with her. That giddy laugh was often directed at him, instead of Pete, as it should have been.

With a heavy dose of dread and a visible grimace, Sam Watson slewed his head away from his whiskey and toward that annoying twitter. Shit. Sure enough, there sat Ariel Mathers. At the bar no less. And there were two men chatting her up.

What the hell was she doing in this dive? He glanced around but didn't see his brother anywhere. As to that, no one particular man appeared to be with her. Huh. The little twit was slumming.

So many times since first meeting her, Sam had wanted to put her over his knee. For leading his brother on at a time when he'd been vulnerable. For flirting with him, Sam, a man much too old for her. And especially for being so damned adorable, he almost couldn't stand it.

And now this.

His palm itched at the thought of it and his mind conjured

the image of her over his knees, her tush bared. He started to sweat, knowing that if he had her in such a position, punishment would be the very last thing on his mind. She was so petite that her bottom would be small. And pale. And no doubt silky soft . . .

Shit, shit, shit.

His eyes burned as he stared at her slim back. She had her hair up with a few baby-fine blond curls kissing her nape. Little gold hoops in her earlobes glittered with the bar lights. The heart-shaped tush he'd so often fantasized over, now perched on a bar stool, was easily outlined beneath the clinging silk skirt of her dress.

At twenty-four she was twelve years too young for him. His mind understood that. His dick didn't care.

She paused in whatever nonsense she'd been uttering to the hapless fool beside her. As she started to look around, Sam twisted in his seat to face the window. *Do not let her see me,* he prayed. He waited, pretending to be drunk when he was more alert than he'd ever been in his life. He'd nursed one whisky since coming into the bar, but he'd pretended drunkenness on his way in. Anyone who noticed him would assume he was there to top off an already inebriated night.

Fifteen seconds ticked by, then thirty, a minute—no one approached him. Sam relaxed, but kept his face averted, just in case. No way could he carry off his assignment tonight if Ariel got in the way.

He should have known better than to stare at her. People felt that sort of thing, just as he'd felt the big bruiser at the far booth watching him. He would have liked to order another drink, to call further attention to his feigned drunkenness. But with Ariel sitting there, it would be too risky.

Better to get this over with now, before he did something stupid. Like staring at her again.

Opening his wallet to show the bloated contents—two hundred dollars' worth—he pulled out a ten-dollar tip. He laid it on the table, stumbled to his feet and staggered out the door.

Once outside, he deliberately started across the street toward the abandoned, shadowed building where he would supposedly retrace his path home—and where his backup could clearly see him. Sam took his time, singing a crude bawdy tune about a woman from Nantucket, who according to the men, liked to suck it. It was a favorite limerick from his youth and he knew it by heart, but this time he missed some words, slurred a few others.

He pitched into the brick wall, laughed too loud, and started off again, only to trip over a garbage can, causing an awful racket. He gave a rank curse, stepped in something disgusting that he didn't want to identify, and dropped up against the side of a broken, collapsible fire escape.

Sam was fumbling for a more upright position when a meaty paw grabbed his upper arm, filling him with satisfaction. The perp had taken the bait.

"Give me your wallet."

Jolting around, Sam acted surprised, then spat in the big chap's face, "Fug off."

A ham-sized fist hit him in the side of the head and he saw stars for real. Jesus, he hadn't expected the fellow to get nasty so quick. Most of the thefts in the area—and there'd been plenty of late—had been done without any real personal damage.

Across a six-block area that covered three bars in Duluth, Indiana, more than twelve muggings had taken place in less than a month. It wasn't the best part of the city, so muggings weren't uncommon. But twelve? And all against men carrying substantial amounts of money. That smacked of premeditated, organized activity, and grabbed the attention of the police.

Sam twisted away, but was brought back around for another punch, this one in the gut. He bent double and almost puked.

Because he knew the guys would never let him live it down, he managed to keep his supper in his belly where it belonged. Just barely.

Where the hell were they anyway? Taking their own sweet time?

Before Sam could decide to take another punch or sneak in one of his own, a female banshee cry split the air, making his ears ring and his hair stand on end. Two seconds later his perp got hit from behind by a small tornado and the momentum drove him straight into Sam, against the side of the metal stairs. It felt like his damn ribs cracked.

Everyone started struggling at once and they went down in a heap, Sam on the bottom so that his head and back hit the hard, gravel-covered ground with jarring impact. The wind left his lungs in a whoosh.

While supine and wheezing, Sam got a good look at the familiar blond clinging tenaciously to his perp's hair with one hand while trying to use her purse like a club with the other. Sam couldn't quite tell if she was attempting to bludgeon him to death, or scream him into submission.

Wincing, the would-be robber reached back, caught her shoulder, and flipped her over his head. The next thing Sam knew, Ariel's behind was atop his face, her thighs pressed to his ears. Her dress had fluttered open and there was nothing more than a thin layer of silk keeping his nose from glory.

Damn it, why did things like this happen to him at all the wrong times?

He fought for air, breathed in her warm musk scent, and managed to shove her rump a few inches off his face. He was just in time to see the same meaty fist that had dazed him now headed straight toward her very tiny and very cute nose. Outrage exploded inside him.

He was supposed to be drunk, an easy mark.

He was undercover for the night.

But goddammit, no way could he let her get hurt.

Moving quicker than any drunk could, Sam caught the oversized fist in his own, gave one evil, toothy grin—which was somewhat smothered by Ariel's bottom cheeks—and twisted. Hard.

He heard crackling and then a loud pop.

The startled shock of pain on his target's face abruptly turned to one of sheer agony, accompanied by a guttural roar. Sam wanted to break his damn arm. Maybe a leg, too, just for good measure.

How dare he attempt to hit a woman?

Sam was still considering the possibility of doing more injury, when his backup finally charged onto the scene with a cliched, "Hold it right there!"

Hold it? They had to be fucking kidding, right? He had a woman straddling his neck, an unethical bastard trying to strike her, and they wanted him to hold it?

He gave the fist another squeeze, then shoved, causing the man to shout and recoil on the ground in the fetal position, cradling his impaired wrist.

Sam didn't have a chance to move Ariel before Fuller Ruth, one of the cops working the undercover sting with him that night, caught her under her arms and lifted her up and away. Sam got a bird's eye view of her more womanly parts in silky panties while her high heels poked him in the abdomen, the thigh, and damn near his groin.

"You okay?" Fuller asked her, while still letting her dangle in the air. Fuller was as big as the assailant, but unlike the assailant he had a very fastidious nature. He kept his brown hair well trimmed, his clothes wrinkle free, and he was always clean-shaven. His blue eyes were so pale, they reminded Sam of a Husky.

Ariel clutched at the front of her dress where it had gotten torn. "Put me down, you oaf. I'm fine."

Fuller set her on her feet, but then had to grab for her again when she turned in a rush, trying to get to Sam.

"Hey lady, easy now. Just come with me."

Fuller attempted to lead her away, but she turned on him, too, thumping him on the chest. "Turn me loose! I have to see if he's all right." In her fit, she forgot about the tear in her dress and the whole right side drooped down, exposing the top of one pale breast and a good bit of her beige, satin bra.

"Hey! Stop that." Fuller looked to be playing patty-cake with her the way he swatted at her flying fists. "Damn it, lady, you're spilling your purse. Just settle down. He'll be all right. Let the officer check him."

The officer he meant was Isaac Star, half Native American, half junkyard dog. People considered Sam dark, but that was until they saw him next to Isaac. Much leaner than Fuller, Isaac had the blackest hair and eyes Sam had ever seen. He was currently snapping handcuffs onto the giant, who yelled and complained of a broken arm. The big sissy.

"*Let—me—go.*"

It was a toss-up who made more noise, the perp or Ariel. Since he was supposed to be a drunken slob, Sam couldn't very well just sit up and explain to her that he was plenty fine, other than the damage *she'd* inflicted. He did, however, work his way to his elbows to mutter drunkenly, "Whass goin' on?"

Isaac grinned at him, making himself look like a pleased sultan. "I just saved your sorry ass, my man. This goon was set to roll you for your wallet."

Feigning confusion, Sam patted his chest, his front pants pockets and finally his ass until he located the pocket holding the packed wallet. He wrested it out, held it up, and said, "S'that right? Thank you, of'ser. Got my paycheck inside."

Isaac was lean, but his size was deceptive. He was strong as an ox. He pulled the giant to his feet with no effort. "Not too smart. Stay put while I stick this guy in the car."

Not more than twelve yards away, two official police cars lit up the block with flashing red and green lights. To the spectators, it looked as though the cops had just happened onto the mugging—not like the whole thing had been planned.

As soon as Isaac had the giant out of hearing range, Sam pulled himself to his feet. For the benefit of onlookers, he stood there weaving, but he gave one barely perceptible nod to Fuller, who then let Ariel go with a shrug.

She launched herself at Sam, big tears glistening in her hazel eyes, her mouth open to blast him with questions, with mothering concern that he neither wanted nor needed.

Sam grabbed her close, squeezed her so tight she couldn't say a single word, and growled into her ear, "I'm *working,* goddammit, so you better have a good excuse for this stunt."

"Working?" she squeaked out.

Damn, it felt good to hold her so close. He shook his head and tried to ignore the way her belly pressed into his crotch, how her breasts flattened on his chest, and how her soft hair smelled so sweet.

Better than half the customers from the bar were now out front to watch the proceedings. Sam had to keep his head, because he had to keep his cover. "That's right, and since you jumped into the middle of things, you damn well better play your part." That said, he slumped into her, forcing her to stagger under his considerable weight. She was five-two, maybe. He was six-three and outweighed her by damn near a hundred pounds.

The twit.

She grunted and nearly fell, until Fuller flattened a hand between her shoulder blades, pushing her upright again. Under normal circumstances, no cop worth his salt would let a drunk manhandle a woman. But these weren't normal circumstances, he wasn't really drunk, and his two buds had already figured out that she was an acquaintance.

Cops were notorious for trying to help each other get laid. If they thought Sam wanted her—which he did, but would never admit to anyone—they'd happily let him take advantage of the situation.

"Yer an angel," Sam said, leering at Ariel's breast with sincere interest. He'd seen more of her tonight than he had in the entire two months she'd been hanging around the family.

He rubbed his nose into her neck, making her lose her balance once more.

She tried to shove him away, but he snaked one hand down her back and grabbed her ass. *Oh, now that was nice. Real firm and plump. Not quite as generous as he liked, being he was a dedicated ass-man, but still nice.*

She gasped and struggled, but Sam didn't let go. Huh-uh. No way.

Fuller rolled his eyes. There was a limit to how much help he'd give in this particular campaign. "Here now." He dragged Ariel behind him, out of Sam's reach, then held Sam up with one outstretched arm. "You're drunk, man. I hope you weren't planning on driving home."

"Nope. Gonna walk."

"Well, you can thank the lady for being a good citizen and trying to help you."

Ariel stood there, her enormous eyes luminous in the dark night, her hair mussed in what Sam could only call a "just laid" way, and her makeup smudged. She smoothed her skirt with one hand while clutching her bodice with the other.

"That's quite all right, Officer. I did what anyone would have done under the circumstances." She looked at Sam with malice glinting in her golden eyes. "The poor drunken fool might have gotten killed otherwise."

Fuller choked on a laugh. "True, true. Now don't either of you take off, hear? I'll need statements from the both of you."

Ariel nodded. "I'll just wait over there." She pointed one manicured finger at the broken fire escape, then walked a wide berth around Sam on her way there. He noticed she was a bit wobbly on her heels, and concern struck him. Had she gotten hurt? She'd landed on his face pretty hard. He couldn't see her knees beneath the hem of her dress. Maybe she was bruised.

Playing it up, Fuller took Sam's arm and headed him in the same direction. Under his breath, he said, "Don't molest her, okay?"

"Don't be stupid."

"You're looking at her like she's the Christmas goose, but I need you to fill out paperwork, not be behind bars, resting on your lazy ass."

Sam grinned. "She won't be pressing any charges." Fuller pushed him to sit next to Ariel, causing her to scramble farther over on the rough metal step. "Ain't that right, sweetheart?"

She tucked her skirt in around her legs and smiled with false sweetness. "I won't press charges. But I might break your nose."

Fuller threw up his hands. "Young love."

He was gone too quick to hear Sam's rude snort. Ariel heard though, and she pursed her mouth, then slanted a look at Sam.

God, he hurt all over. All he needed was a boner to finish off the night.

Cautiously, every small movement enough to bring on a wince, Sam turned sideways and eased back against the brick wall, then sighed. "I'm too damn old for this shit."

Under her breath, but not under enough, Ariel muttered, "You're in your prime."

Sam stared at her, incredulous. "What was that?" Had she actually complimented him even while sending him dirty looks?

Without looking at him, she said, "Just because you're older than your brothers doesn't make you old, you know."

Sam grunted. Being six years older than Gil, his middle brother, and fourteen years older than Pete, he'd always felt old. Especially after their father had died three years ago with a heart attack.

Sam had tried to help his family cope as much as possible. He'd handled all the funeral arrangements for his mother, supported Gil in taking over the family business, and did his best to console Pete, who'd had the hardest time with the unexpected loss.

There was no denying that Pete had been a happy accident for their parents. Older and more settled when they had him, they'd doted on him in ways they hadn't been able to do with Sam and Gil. By far, Pete had been the closest with their dad.

"Does being on the downhill slide to forty make me old?"

"Hardly." Her voice was tinged with disgust. "And you're only thirty-six."

How the hell did she know that? "And here I thought all teenagers considered anyone over thirty ancient."

Apparently touchy about her age, she jerked around to face him. "Sam Watson, you know good and well I'm twenty-four, not a teenager. Wasn't that your big complaint about my friendship with Pete? That he was two years *younger* than me?"

Sam stared off toward the cruiser, wishing like hell they'd hurry up. He didn't want to sit this close to her. He didn't want to talk about her and Pete.

"Well?"

His biggest complaint? There'd been so many it was tough to pick a favorite. His baby brother *was* too young, far too immature, and entirely too unsettled to be getting serious about any one woman.

And Sam didn't exactly consider Ariel old enough either. She'd at least finished a trade school and was working as a beautician. But Pete had college to finish and he needed to do that without distractions of the female variety, which Sam knew were the very worst kind.

Worse than all that, though, Sam wanted her. It ate him up to think about Pete, who was a good kid but still a knucklehead, fumbling around in the dark with her. Sam wouldn't fumble. Hell no. He knew exactly where he wanted to touch and taste her—not that he ever would. Nope.

He changed the subject. "What the hell are you doing in the bar by yourself?"

"None of your business."

"Yeah?" Just what he needed to clear his head: a fight with the little darling. He spoke in a growled whisper that nonetheless expressed his anger. "Well I'm making it my business seeing as you damn near blew my cover."

Her whisper was every bit as quiet and fierce as his. "How was I supposed to know you were working?"

Sam eyed her. She had a death grip on her torn dress, pulling the material so tight across her breasts that he could see the outline of her nipples. It was a hot, muggy night, but her nipples stood out like diamonds as if she were freezing. Shock maybe? Or had she liked him playing grab-ass with her?

He groaned.

Immediately concerned, she leaned over him, her small hand on his brow, her sweet breath in his face. "Ohmigod, Sam. How bad are you hurt? Do you need a doctor?"

Not unless a man could die of unfulfilled horniness. "Back off, Florence Nightingale. I'll live."

At his insulting tone, she puckered up and smacked his shoulder, making him groan again. Damn fickle woman.

She sat hunched over, her shoulders rounded, her forearms on her knees. Sam asked, "Did you see me in the bar?"

"That's a stupid question." She hugged herself, staring down at her feet. "When you're in a room, you're *in* it. Of course I saw you."

"What the hell is that supposed to mean?"

Giving him a sloe-eyed look, she said, "Even as a miserable drunk, you're sexy. I spotted you the second I stepped inside."

He tried to close his ears, doing his best to tune out her stirring comments . . .

"Every woman in the bar noticed you."

"No shit?" Now that cheered him up. "I like that."

She went back to moping.

Sam looked around. The crowd had finally dispersed with only a few lingerers still standing around. Fuller was headed back toward him with a pen and pad, no doubt ready to take his fictitious statement just in case anyone should notice.

He stretched out his legs and bumped his big feet into her strappy, high-heeled sandals. She had her toenails painted pink. "So tell me this, Einstein. Have you ever seen me drunk before?"

A little wary, she said, "No."

"But you know I'm a cop, right?"

"Undercover. Lots of commendations. Heralded for being fearless by many, called careless by some, me included. But I know you're a good cop, Sam."

She surprised him with that string of mixed praise and censure, making him shake his head. "Yet you came charging into what could have been a very dangerous situation."

Her lips tightened; her shoulders hunched more. In a nearly imperceptible whisper, she grouched, "I thought you were getting hurt."

Sam's temper snapped. "And so you thought you, a pint-sized beautician, would dash to my rescue? Ha! Do you know what could have happened to you—what could have happened to me because you got in the way?" It took all he had not to shake her. "God save me from illogical women."

Ariel shot to her feet. "Shut up, Sam. Just . . . *shut up.*" Her entire puny body vibrated with anger, and she actually stomped one small foot. "You are so incredibly insufferable with all your endless harping."

Fuller said, "Now, now, kiddies. Let's play nice for the remaining spectators."

Pinning her with his gaze, Sam stared at her but spoke to the officer. "Ask me a question, Fuller."

"Right. Uh, how about . . ."

"Good enough. Here's my answer. Ariel, I want to know what the hell you were doing in that damn bar. And don't give me that garbage about it being none of my business because the second you blundered into things, it became my damn business."

Fuller pretended to write, nodding and smiling like a half-wit.

Mutinous, Ariel looked down her nose at him. "And if I don't tell you?"

A challenge. Sam almost rubbed his hands together. "If you don't," he said with a lot of glee, "I'll run your skinny little ass in."

Her mouth fell open and she sputtered. "For what, exactly?"

"Indecent exposure?" He dropped his gaze to her partially displayed breast so she wouldn't misunderstand.

She snatched the material higher. "Pig."

"Yeah, yeah. Real original insult for a cop. I've never heard that one before."

She turned away, came back, glared at him. "For your information, nosey, I was making sure."

His brows rose. "Making sure about what?"

As if awaiting the rest of her statement, Fuller looked at her. "Go on, Miss."

She huffed. "I was making sure there wasn't someone else who appealed to me."

Confused, Sam asked, "Someone other than Pete?"

Exasperation shown on her face. "Pete and I were never more than friends."

Sam's jaw locked. "That wasn't how Pete felt."

"And I'm responsible for that? I told him from the first day we met that I only wanted to be friends, and he agreed. When he finally admitted to me how he really felt, that he expected more, that's when I quit seeing him at all."

"And broke his damn fool heart in the process."

She swallowed. "I never meant to hurt him. He knows that. Besides, he's dating someone else now."

That was news to Sam. "He is?"

Nodding, Ariel explained, "That's why I was here. I waited until Pete found a girlfriend before . . ."

"Before?"

Her eyes narrowed. "Before making sure."

Sam threw up his hands. The woman just refused to make sense.

Fuller tilted his head. "I'm fascinated, really."

Sam turned to Fuller with a growl. "Officer, haven't you got enough there?"

"You never let me have any fun."

"Your idea of fun must be a toothache."

Ariel looked ready to spit. "If I'm such a pain—"

"You are that."

"Then I'll be on my way." Shoulders squared, her chin lifted in regal disdain, she started around Fuller.

Sam crossed his arms. "Just where the hell do you think you're going now?"

"Back into the bar."

"Like that?" He nodded at her torn dress.

"Oh." She stared down in dismay at the long rip. "Well, I suppose that might not be a good idea."

"But jumping into the middle of a brawl is?"

Her neck stiffened. "Brawl?" One slim brow arched high. "All I saw was you getting your butt kicked."

Insulted, Sam snorted, but not with much conviction this time. Surely, she didn't believe such an asinine thing. He'd been undercover, damn it, unable to fight back without messing up his cover.

But she looked serious, so he said, "You believed that act? Hey, I must be pretty good."

"Why wouldn't I believe it? I thought you were drunk."

She *was* serious. It was Sam's turn to shoot to his feet. Leaning forward in an aggressive stance, he poked a thumb into his chest. "Even drunk, I could take that guy. With one arm broken, I could flatten him. He was nothing."

She looked at her nails. "Uh-huh."

At the boiling point, Sam started to reach for her, and Isaac hurried over to them. "Are we putting on a damn show? There's enough melodrama over here to blow the whole damn thing."

Ariel again turned away. "I'll get on my way then."

Through his teeth, Sam said, "Grab her," and Isaac automatically obeyed, catching her arm and swinging her back around.

She almost toppled off her high sandals and retaliated by clouting Isaac with that lethal purse.

"There's another offense," Sam drawled while Isaac ducked. "Assaulting an officer."

Very slowly, she lifted her head to fry him with a seething glare, and if looks could kill, he'd have been writhing on the ground at her feet.

Sam grinned. From the first day he'd met her he knew she had a temper beneath all that good-girl, innocent blond pretense. "Before you hurt yourself or someone else, you can give me a ride home."

Like a doe caught in the headlights, she went utterly still. "Why me?"

Sam sent a telling look at Isaac's hand still wrapped around her arm. "You can let her go now."

"Oops. Sorry." He grinned, unrepentant. "I think I'll take our thug on in."

"Yeah," Fuller said, "as long as you have a ride, I'll take off, too. I've got everything I need." He winked at Sam.

"Hey," Sam said, "I don't suppose you guys would—"

Fuller raised a hand. "Consider it done. But you owe us, buddy boy."

"Yeah, I assumed as much." He watched the two men saunter away, Fuller speaking into his radio, Isaac assuring the remaining people that the fanfare was over.

The second they were in their cars, Sam again leaned on the brick wall. He realized his shoulder hurt, turned, and found out his shoulder blades were tender too. And his head . . . He didn't even want to know about his damn head. Ariel's attack had put him down hard. His brains were probably scrambled.

Truth was, he felt like he'd been run over by a Mack truck and standing on his own steam wasn't all that comfortable.

Ariel looked him over, forcing him to suck it up. "What are they going to do for you that you'll owe them?"

"Paperwork." Then, just to taunt her because he felt physically miserable and she looked as bubbly as ever, he added, "That, and they figure I might get laid if they leave me alone with you. If I did, I'd really owe them."

Rather than look offended, she blinked twice. "Laid by who?"

"You, sweets. They're assuming all your furious bluster has to do with sexual sparks, rather than honest dislike."

After a long, thoughtful moment empty of protests, Ariel nodded. "My car is this way. Should I pretend to help you or is the coast clear?"

After having her fanny on his face, he didn't want her hands anywhere near him. He had enough fodder for three wet dreams as it was. "I'll stumble my way there under my own steam, thank you very much."

Weaving this way and that, Sam trailed behind her, suspicious over her docile agreement to drive him home, and her lack of anger over his friend's crude assumptions. He was also aware of the sway in her hips and that delectable bottom he'd already manhandled.

Hell, half the things he wanted to do to that bottom were probably illegal in some states.

He forced himself to look away. He had to stop drooling

over her, for crying out loud. The woman was a complete and total pain the ass, only a year or two older than a teenybopper, *and* his baby brother's ex-girlfriend. He had to remember all that.

Sam was none too happy when she took the liberty of opening the door for him. Worse, the car was a beat-up, banana-yellow Pinto. "I won't fit," he complained, even as he folded himself painfully inside the cramped front seat.

She slammed the door after him, went around to the driver's side and got in. After she had the key in the ignition and the engine snarled and screamed to life, she leaned back in her seat with a sigh.

Sam waited for her to put the car in gear and when she didn't, he asked, "What's wrong? Are you hurt?" She'd told Fuller she wasn't, but she was stubborn enough to lie about it. He should have checked for himself.

That thought brought a shudder of excitement. Not a good idea. Not at all.

She stared up at the ceiling. "I can't drive and hold my dress up too."

"Ah." Forcing nonchalance, Sam shrugged and said, "Hey, I've seen every female part there is, hooters included, so unless you're unique in some mind-boggling way, it's no big deal. Don't worry about it."

Appearing stunned by such an outpouring of nonsense, she said, "Fine," and dropped the torn material. It fell completely below her breast.

Oh Lord. His nonchalance obliterated, Sam swallowed hard, looked away from her bra and how her nipple poked against the silky material. He did what he could to distract himself. He tried thinking about the job he'd just done, the repeat performance he had to put in tomorrow. He considered all the endless paperwork. He even tried thinking about Pete. It didn't help.

His aching body and splitting head should have been

enough to keep him off track, but there was no suppressing those pesky sexual urges. Whenever Ariel was around, they got a stranglehold on his libido.

"Let's play some music." Sam fiddled with the radio while she pulled off the side street and into the denser flow of traffic.

"Sure. Help yourself." Irony filled her tone since he'd already located an oldie station and turned up the volume to listen to, "Ohhhh, love to love you baby . . ."

Speaking loud to be heard over Donna Summer, she asked, "Mind if I come up for a minute when we get to your place?"

The way she said that, so casually, put Sam on edge. "Why?"

"Don't look so suspicious. I just thought I could find some way to fasten my dress, maybe a safety-pin or something. I know you have a house, but I live in an apartment and who knows how many people will be around when I pull up. I don't want to flash the neighbors and I don't want to start a lot of gossip."

He didn't want her flashing the neighbors either. As long as he got her in and out of his place in a hurry, it'd be okay. He could hold off that long. Maybe. "I have a sewing kit you can use."

"You're so gracious."

"Graciousness is hard to find when my head is splitting, thanks to your tackle."

She stopped at a red light and turned toward him. "And here I thought you were so macho. Let me have a look."

Without his permission she caught his left ear and turned his head. "Ouch," she said in sympathy. "It looks like you're bleeding a little."

Reaching to the back of his head, Sam located a lump, and a spot of blood. "Damn." No wonder his head hurt so much. "It's fine," he lied. When she started to protest, he said, "Green light. Let's go."

They were cruising right along, going about forty miles an hour when she suddenly said, "They were right, you know."

He'd been so busy trying to ignore her warm, softly scented body beside him, her words caused him to start. "Who's that?"

"The other officers."

"Fuller and Isaac?"

"I suppose. You didn't introduce me so I don't know their names."

She made it an accusation, setting his teeth on edge. "It was hardly a social affair, if you'll recall."

Silence reigned until he said, "All right, I give. What were they right about?"

Without him realizing it, they'd left the main road and were now in the suburbs, close to his moderate house.

She turned down his tree-lined lane. "You getting laid. That is . . ."—she hesitated, peeked a look at him, then forged on— "if you want to."

Several things happened to Sam at once. His stomach bottomed out, his eyes widened, and his dick gave a proud salute.

Well hell. What was she up to now?

Chapter Two

The silence was enough to squash her. Ariel didn't want to look at Sam again, not when her first glimpse had shown him to be anything but interested. Horrified, yes. Shocked, yes. But not interested.

Unfortunately, whenever he was around, she couldn't seem to *not* look at him. From the day she'd met him, he fascinated her.

It wasn't just his awesome physique that drew her, though that was pretty eye-catching. He was tall, muscular, mean, and lean. He had the attitude of a man in charge, spoke as if he expected to be obeyed, and had confidence down to a fine art.

And it wasn't just his incredible, look-into-your-soul blue eyes, so different from his brothers'. Sam had inherited his mother's eyes, while both Gil and Pete looked more like their father with chocolate brown eyes. They all had inky black hair though, and thick lashes. They were all handsome—just in different ways. Gil was sophisticated, suave. Pete was fun-loving and playful.

Sam was all basic male, rough-edged and rugged and keenly capable of handling any lethal situation.

He was also a pretty nice guy, though his gruff manner and burdening responsibility often hid that fact. Best of all, he was a bonified hero through and through. When his family needed him, he stepped up to the plate without complaints. On the job, he did what had to be done to make things right. His brothers looked up to him, his mother depended on him, and his fellow officers respected him. He was like Superman only real. And sexier.

Finally, with an uncertain laugh, Sam said, "Come again?"

Ariel cleared her throat. His tone of disbelief didn't exactly bode well, but she'd made up her mind. "You know when I said I went to the bar to be sure?"

"Yeah, right. Sure there wasn't anyone else—whatever the hell that means."

"It means I wanted to be sure there wasn't anyone else who appealed to me. But there isn't. That's the third bar I've been in this week."

A thundercloud would appear passive next to his darkening expression. "You've been hanging out in bars?" His teeth actually clenched, fascinating her. "Do you have any idea what's been happening around the area bars lately?"

She hadn't, but judging by what he'd done tonight, she assumed some muggings were taking place. Because she didn't want a lecture, she just shrugged.

His eyes turned red.

To pacify him, she pointed out her other visits. "I've also been to two nightclubs, the grocery, the park, and three concerts. Sorry, but there is no one else who appeals to me." She drew a long breath and admitted the stark truth. "You're the only one."

At that moment, Sam looked to be choking on murderous intent.

"Say something."

He didn't, he just sat there, steam coming off his head while his face colored and his fists curled. Ariel honestly didn't know if he fought the urge to take her or strangle her. Not that she was afraid of him. Never.

Sam protected people—he didn't abuse them.

Because she and Pete had stopped by his house once, she knew where he lived. She pulled into the blacktop drive and turned off the car. She didn't at first look at him, not when it felt like he was frying her with his gaze. When she finally worked up the nerve, she turned to him.

"Well?"

Through his teeth, he snarled, "Inside."

Oh good. At least he wasn't throwing her off his property already. She considered his grudging command a positive step. Slipping out of her car, she managed to hold her dress up, drop her keys into her purse, and close the door. Sam made no gentlemanly moves toward her, but then, he was badly beaten up.

She loved his old two-story house. It had a poured front porch complete with an overhang and wooden swing. The shrubbery was original and thick and outdated, but it made a nice contrast against the red brick. Enormous oaks lined the street and during the day, squirrels scurried everywhere.

At his father's death, he'd inherited a large sum of money. She didn't doubt that Sam could have afforded a posh, upscale home in an exclusive neighborhood. She was glad he hadn't moved.

When she reached Sam's side, he took her arm in an implacable grip and started her in a trot toward the front door. Some elderly neighbors in the house to the right hailed him, forcing him to stop.

"Evening Sam."

Sam groaned, slowly turned and waved at the two people visible by their front porch light. "Booth, Hesper. What are you doing up this late?"

Ariel giggled. It was only eleven thirty.

"The dog had business to take care of. Her old bladder just gives her fits."

Ariel's giggle got caught in her throat. She looked in the yard and saw the most hideous creature she'd ever clapped eyes on. An obese bulldog squatted by a bush, turned to sniff, and then lumbered back to her owners, who praised her as if she'd created gold.

"Who's your lady-friend?" Hesper asked with a nosiness reserved for the old or very young.

Sam leaned in close to Ariel's ear. His hot breath teased her when he growled, "Stay here." Then he moved away to the neighbor's porch railing. They spoke quietly so Ariel couldn't hear what was said.

Seconds later, both elders looked over at her with awe and horror. Ariel frowned. Just what had Sam told them? He returned, took her arm again and said, "Let's go."

"What did you say to them, Sam Watson?"

"Keep your voice down. This is a quiet neighborhood."

His walkway could use a good sweeping, she decided as her toes kicked through scattered leaves. Even the porch was littered with leaves and acorns.

As if he knew her thoughts, he said, "A recent storm blew crap everywhere. I'll get to it when I can." Using a key, he unlocked the front door and held it open for her.

She stepped into the inky darkness, then felt his hands close gently but firmly on her upper arms. With bated breath, she waited for a kiss, but got bodily moved out of his way instead, so he could turn off an alarm. "Wait here."

Left alone, Ariel tried to get her eyes to adjust to the darkness. When the lights blinked on, she squinted. "Why don't you have a wall switch by the front door?"

"The light's out and I haven't had a chance to change it yet. I've been working overtime on the bar muggings. Let's go to the kitchen. I have a feeling it might be the safest room."

"Why?" She trailed behind him.

He gave her a long look. "No place to get laid."

Refusing to let him derail her, Ariel grinned at his sarcastic wit. "There's always the countertop. Or the table. Maybe even the floor—"

His rough palm covered her mouth. "That's enough out of you." She mumbled against his palm and he lifted his hand. "What?"

"Tell me what you said to your neighbors."

His mouth curved in a sinful smile. "Sure. I told them you were a prostitute who'd ratted out her pimp, and I had to keep you close so he didn't kill you."

"Oh." He expected her to be insulted, so she asked instead, "Have you ever been with a prostitute?"

"*No.*" He didn't bother to hide his indignation at all. "Now behave for a minute so I can think."

While his back was turned, Ariel pulled out a chair, sat down and lifted her skirt to examine her scraped, bruised knees. They hurt, but Sam was in much worse shape than she so she tried not to complain.

"Now about this . . . what the hell?" He'd turned with a scowl on his face, only to pull up with a different type of anger. "You said you weren't hurt," he accused.

"Just a little. Nothing serious."

Muttering under his breath, Sam whipped off several paper towels, folded them, and doused them beneath cold water. He came to her and knelt down. "Hold still."

Despite his order, she jumped when the icy towel touched her raw scrapes. "Sorry."

"Damn." He dabbed at both knees, removing small bits of dried blood, gravel, and dirt.

Before Ariel could figure out what he intended, he flipped her skirt up higher. "Sam!"

When she tried to shove her skirt back down, he caught both her hands in one of his and held them up and against her breasts, almost shoving her out of her chair. "Shush. I want to see if you're hurt anywhere else."

She had to brace her feet apart to keep from toppling over. "This is outrageous!"

Blue eyes lit like the hottest flame, he glanced up at her. "You sitting on my face was outrageous. This is just concern."

Ariel gulped.

"Now be quiet."

Mortified, her mouth snapped shut. She *had* sat on his face. At the time, she'd been so worried about protecting him she hadn't paid much attention.

He found one large bluish bruise on her thigh. "How'd this happen?"

Ariel peered down at the mark. With both their heads bent, her blond curls brushed up against his silky black hair. "I don't know. Maybe when I jumped on that guy's back and we all crashed into the stairs."

"Anything else?"

Since he was on his knees in front of her, more caring than insulting, she showed him her elbow. It was raw and stung every time she flexed her arm. His mouth flattened in displeasure. "I ought to turn you over my knee for that damn stunt. Look at you. You're a mess."

So much for caring.

"Let me get some ice; then I'll fetch my first aid kit."

"I don't need you to doctor me."

He had his back to her, digging in his freezer. "Tough. My house, my rules, so I'm doing it anyway." Within minutes, he had ice crushed inside a damp dish towel and he pressed the freezing compress to her thigh. Ariel almost came out of her seat. The cold prickled so badly she tried to shove it away.

"Leave it," he ordered, keeping it firmly in place until she subsided. He took her hand and put it over the compress so that she had to hold it. His commanding gaze bore into hers. "I want to see it there when I get back, you understand?"

"Yes sir."

His eyes narrowed. "A show of respect from you at this late

date is beyond suspect, so stow it." Then softly, with exasperation, "I'll be right back. Sit tight."

Ariel leaned out of her seat to watch him trot from the kitchen, into the hall, and up the short flight of stairs to his bathroom. Once he was out of sight, she lifted the ice away and fell back in her chair.

None of this was what she'd expected. Not that she'd known what to expect, but worry over a few paltry bruises . . . She heard him returning and quickly replaced the ice pack, wincing at the bitter cold.

He eyed her when he reentered, his expression stern. "I hope you learned a few things tonight."

"Yeah, that you're surly when you're hurt and that you don't like women coming on to you."

He moistened a gauze pad with antiseptic and again knelt in front of her. "Wrong. I'm not all that hurt and I love when women come on to me. I just don't like little girls flirting when they don't know what they're getting into."

Seething, Ariel said, "If you don't stop accusing me of being a child, I'm going to—" She screeched when the antiseptic hit her scrapes, burning like a brand. Her legs stiffened and her hands gripped the sides of her seat.

"Sorry." For once, his voice was gentle, caring. Sam leaned forward and blew his warm breath over her knees.

A new ache filled her, one of overwhelming sexual hunger. She'd wanted him since the first time she saw him. She remembered that moment in vivid detail. Pete had taken her with him to his family's regular Sunday get-together. A storm had knocked a thick elm over in his middle brother's backyard, damaging a fence. Sam was there, shirtless, sweaty, tanned, and so sexy she'd stood dumbfounded for several moments while he swung an ax, cutting up the fallen tree alongside his brother, Gil. The muscles in his strong back had flexed with each movement. His biceps bunched and knotted. His hands were big, lean, his strength undeniable.

"Ariel? You didn't faint on me, did you?"

Taking a breath, she opened her eyes and locked gazes with him. He had one hand on her thigh, holding the ice pack there, the other gently touching her chin. The breath sighed out of her. "I want you so much."

He lurched back as if she'd kicked him, jerking to his feet in a rush. "You look besotted, damn it. Knock it off."

She couldn't reply, could only stare at him with all the love and hunger she felt plain in her eyes. *Please,* she silently pleaded, and got a wary frown from him in return.

"Here's a new rule. You have to be quiet while I finish this up. Understand?"

She stared.

"Answer me, damn it."

"Yes, all right."

He moved back to her cautiously. "Give me your elbow."

This time she bit her lip when he swabbed the remaining cuts and scrapes. She didn't want to be a wimp in front of him. She didn't want him to feel sorry for her.

He finished off by applying ointment and some bandages. Then he backed up. "All done. Now."

"Now what?"

"About this . . . wanting me business."

There was nothing she could do but wait and see what he had to say.

Sam floundered, but finally bit out, "Wanna tell me why?"

"Why what?"

"Why do you want *me?*"

Amazingly enough, when she came to her feet Sam backed up. Silly man. "Why wouldn't any woman want you?"

"Ariel . . ."

She took two steps toward him. He took one more back, then planted his feet and refused to budge.

"You're smart and dedicated and heroic and . . ." She shrugged, inching closer, more determined than she'd ever been about anything in her life. "You really are so damned sexy."

She'd gotten close enough to touch him. Lifting one hand, she reached for his shoulder.

He snagged her wrist, his warm, strong fingers wrapping around the delicate bones. "Don't curse. You're too young for that."

Enough was enough. She'd warned him, but he persisted in throwing her age in her face. With a smile of warning, she grabbed his neck with her free hand and went on tiptoe to reach his mouth.

"*Ariel*—" He tried to lean back, to turn his face away. But she'd backed him to the counter and there wasn't much room for him to maneuver. She knew he didn't want to hurt her and that gave her an advantage in their wrestling match.

Her mouth landed on his throat first and she licked the salty taste of his skin, groaned, and bit his chin.

"Goddammit . . ." He sounded very uncertain, pained, and he grabbed her other wrist. "You little—"

Her mouth smashed up against his. They both froze, but only for a second. Slowly, deliciously, with a purr of excitement, Ariel licked his lips. Her heart threatened to break through her ribs, it drummed so madly.

He brought her arms behind her back, but that only pressed her breasts to his chest, and since her dress hung open, she could feel his heartbeat, as wild as hers. She caught his bottom lip in her teeth and nibbled, all the while breathing hard with excitement, expectation.

And then he exploded. From one second to the next he'd been held immobile by her brazenness. But it wasn't in Sam's nature to be docile, to let anyone else take the lead.

Ariel found herself plastered against him from groin to breasts while his mouth opened over hers in ravenous demand. His tongue thrust in and he groaned low in his throat, the vibrating sound thrilling her.

He slanted his head and drew her even closer, still holding her hands behind her, straining her shoulders, almost lifting her off her feet. Her head was pressed back, leaving her mouth open and vulnerable to his. His whiskers scratched her chin, his erection pressed into her soft belly, and he tasted so good she didn't ever want him to stop.

But he did. She was limp in his arms, merely accepting the onslaught of his kiss, unable to do anything else with the controlling way he held her. With a visible effort, he raised his head a mere inch and stared down at her. An incandescent hunger burned so brightly in his eyes, it almost frightened her.

He looked at her mouth, breathed hard for a moment, then growled low in warning, "You shouldn't push me, little girl."

The way he said that, it wasn't an insult so much as an endearment. Getting enough breath to speak wasn't easy. "You . . . You kept ignoring me."

His hands tightened on her wrists, making her wince. He immediately loosened his hold, but didn't release her. Every muscle in his big body was bunched. His eyes were bright, his cheekbones flushed, his mouth hard. "You were my baby brother's girlfriend."

"No, just a friend," she gently reminded him.

"He still cares about you."

"Not anymore. He's seeing someone else."

"You're only twenty-four-fucking-years old."

He sounded desperate, giving her hope. "I'm a grown woman, Sam. I know what I want. And I want you."

His head dropped forward, almost touching her shoulder. She could feel his angry, hot breath against her throat, sending chills down her spine, building her sexual excitement to a fever pitch.

Necessary arguments crowded her brain. She had to convince him. "Sam? Look at it this way. It's only sex, and you're known for wanting sex."

His head jerked up. "What the hell does that mean?"

"You have a reputation."

"Several actually." His eyes narrowed. "Which reputation are we talking about?"

She wanted to shrug, to act cavalier. It was well beyond her. "For mind-blowing sex."

For three heartbeats he didn't move; then he gave a rough guffaw. "I hate to break it to you babe, but I only give run-of-the-mill sex."

"That's not what I heard."

"No? Who you been talking to? Besides me?"

That made her smile. Sam *was* prone to bragging. She'd heard him once when she'd come to visit Pete. He and his two brothers were in the backyard and didn't hear her approach. Sam and Gil had been teasing Pete, accusing him of being a virgin, which Pete vehemently denied with a red face. Gil offered advice, but Sam told Pete he should come to a pro if he wanted to learn how to make a lady squeal in pleasure.

The graphic details she'd heard then had held her immobile in fascination. Even Gil and Pete had looked awed.

When Pete mentioned Ariel, Sam had froze up and changed the subject.

"Your family goes on and on about what a lady's man you are."

"Yeah, well they have to sing my praises because they're family. Ask any lady, and she'll tell you I'm a pig."

"A cop."

"No, I meant in bed."

Ariel shook her head. "I'm not buying it, Sam. Especially not after that kiss." Her voice went husky. "That almost did it for me right there."

"Don't." He tightened up again, and then, slowly, a new light entered his eyes, one of challenge and determination. "So you want to get laid by the best, is that it?"

A trick question, if ever she heard one. "I want you."

He looked down at her mouth. "I think you need to learn a few lessons."

A shiver of alarm slipped up her spine. "A lesson?"

"On why you shouldn't taunt bad-ass cops with ugly attitudes."

"You do not have an ugly attitude." She couldn't really deny the bad-ass part. But she hated for him to downplay all he did for the community and his family. "You're a good man—"

"And you assume I'm a good man in bed. Is that it? You want to use me to get your jollies?"

She started to say she wouldn't care if he wasn't good, but it'd be a lie. She wanted him, all of him, in every way, and fully expected him to be as excellent in bed as he was out of it.

He locked both her wrists in one hand and used the other to softly stroke her cheek. "You tired of twenty-something boys groping you, never quite getting you off?"

When Sam decided to be crude, he was a pro.

Those taunting fingers moved down her throat and across the top of her chest, just gliding, teasing. "Is that it, Ariel?"

She swallowed hard. What could she say other than to keep repeating the truth? "I want you."

His long, rough fingers dipped lower, nudging the edge of her exposed bra cup. "So be it. But my house, my rules."

At his agreement, her knees almost gave out. "What rules?"

So much wickedness and triumph filled his slow grin that she started to shake. "Rule number one, no one ever knows but us. I won't have Pete hurt."

Ariel was pinning all her hopes on the fact that once Sam quit denying his physical attraction to her, he'd quit denying his emotions, too. She was head-over-heels in love with the stubborn cuss, but telling him that now would blow what little progress she'd made, so she nodded. "All right."

Rather than look pleased with her acceptance, his expression hardened even more.

While he stared intently in her eyes, his fingers curled into the top of her bra cup—and then stripped it down, leaving her breast bare. Ariel gasped.

He didn't look down, but that big hot palm closed over her, kneading steadily, rasping her nipple while he continued to intimidate her with his molten stare.

The only sign he was affected by the touch was the flare of his nostrils, his increased breathing. "Rule number two. You do only what I say, when I say." She started to protest and his fingers closed around her nipple in a tantalizing grip that silenced her in an instant. "I'll make you come ten times, Ariel, but my rules stand."

She nodded dumbly, but finally found her voice. "One thing."

"You don't get one thing. You do as I say."

"It's just a . . . a question."

He considered that for far too long before nodding. "One question."

"Do you want me?"

He tugged gently on her nipple. "I won't have any problems keeping it up, if that's what you mean."

"No, it's not what I mean." She loved him. She wanted him to love her too only he had so many walls in place, so many responsibilities and he'd die before ever hurting a member of his family. She had a wealth of emotion in store for him, but she wouldn't be used. If he didn't at least want her, *her,* not just any woman, then she'd make herself walk away.

His hand was still at her breast, still teasing and taunting her nipple making it near impossible to think and speak clearly. "You . . . You've insulted me many times."

"When?" He looked genuinely puzzled.

"You've made it clear that you consider me a nuisance and not too bright."

His hand paused at her breast and his black brows pulled down. "If you're talking about that little stunt you pulled back at the bar, you're damn right—" He stopped, ground his teeth together, then admitted roughly, "You don't own an ounce of caution, but I didn't mean to say you were stupid. I don't think that at all. But I was scared shitless for you. I don't ever want to see you or any lady hurt."

Relief made her weak. "I didn't mean to scare you."

"Great. Don't ever let it happen again. Now is that it?"

"Not quite." He rolled his eyes, so she hurried through the rest. "You've insulted my body . . ."

"I *never*—"

"You said I had a skinny ass!"

He turned his face to the side and for one horrified moment, Ariel thought he was going to laugh. But when he looked at her again, tenderness filled his eyes. "You have a spectacular ass and once you quit trying to stammer out your explanation, I intend to devote about an hour to it."

"Oh."

"Enough said?"

"Yes."

He turned her around, gave her a stinging swat on the butt, and said, "Go upstairs to my bedroom and wait for me there."

"What are you . . . ?"

"No questions. My rules. Just go."

She started to recover her breast but he saw her and said, "Leave it."

She nodded and, feet dragging, made the climb up the stairs. Her belly churned in excitement and uncertainty and so much more. Finally, Sam would make love to her.

She'd give him her body and her heart, and hope he accepted them both.

The second she was out of sight, Sam turned to the sink and slumped against it. Jesus, he was only a man and not all that sterling a man to begin with. How the hell was he supposed to tell Ariel no when he'd wanted her for months?

He opened his right hand and looked at it, then curled his fingers in, reliving the feel of her young, firm breast. Fucking her would be so sweet, so hot.

And very wrong.

But Ariel was set on having her own way, so he knew he had to do this, and do it right, or she'd never leave him in peace. If he didn't take ultimate control, she'd have his balls in a ringer. Before long, he'd be on his damn knees asking her to marry him.

No. *Hell no.*

Pete would be hurt and he'd been hurt enough since their father passed away. He couldn't do that to him. And if Pete was really over her, as she'd suggested? Well, she was still too damn young and far too innocent. Where he was dark, his work and his lifestyle ugly and edgy and uncertain, she lived a carefree life of sunshine and smiles. He couldn't take that from her.

He gave himself ten minutes to get a grip on his control and to let her stew. While he kept her waiting, he took two aspirin and used an antiseptic swab to clean the cut on the back of his head. It burned like a son-of-a-bitch, making him wince in sympathy for Ariel. Her knees, her elbow . . . She could have been hurt worse, even killed if the asshole trying to rob him had had a weapon.

She was a danger to herself and to him, a giddy young woman with more bravado than common sense. What the hell did she think, putting herself in danger for him? If he let her hang around, she'd be forever underfoot, forever taking risks that no woman should take.

With renewed conviction for his quickly formed plans, Sam stormed up the stairs.

He found her sitting on the side of his bed, her feet together, her hands folded in her lap, her breast still uncovered. She looked wary and uncertain and flushed with excitement and so . . . ready, he broke out in a sweat.

Sam forced himself to stop in the doorway. Watching her, he began unbuttoning his shirt, then gave a grimace of pain as he pulled it off his wrenched shoulder.

"You're hurt!" She shot off the bed in a flash, her soft hands fluttering all over him, finding bruises and swollen muscles, her damn tender touch setting him on fire.

"Sit—back—down."

She blinked at his tone. "But you need the ice worse than I did. That ape hurt you. We should take you to the hospital . . ."

"*Sit,* Ariel." She drew back, hurt and confused. "One of the rules," he drawled, trying to soften his command. "You don't touch me unless I tell you to. Now, don't look like that. I'm fine, really. My own brothers have put worse bruises on me just horsing around. Trust me, I'm not being macho. It's nothing that won't heal in a day or two."

She looked undecided, but fell silent when he dropped into a chair and unbuckled his ankle holster.

She stared at his small off-duty weapon, a .38 caliber five-shot revolver. He always had it on him when working undercover because his primary weapon, a .40 caliber Glock, would be too easy to detect. "You carry a gun?"

"That's a . . ." He started to say stupid question, but caught himself. He really didn't want her to think he considered her dumb. "I'm a cop. Of course I carry a gun." And then, when he retrieved the lethally sharp knife from the other leg, he added, "Among other things."

Her eyes were huge when he crossed to the nightstand and opened the bottom drawer. He lifted out a metal box, turned the key in the lock, and opened it. Once the gun and knife were safely inside, he relocked the box and pocketed the key.

Under normal circumstances, both weapons would have sat atop the box, but then, this wasn't a normal circumstance—not by a long shot. And Sam never took unnecessary chances with safety, especially with his gun.

Shirtless, in his bare feet but with his pants on as a deterrent, he went to her. She looked adorable sitting there, all mussed and nervous and he felt like a conquering hero ready to ravish the innocent. It wasn't at all an unpleasant or inadequate perception.

Using just the edge of his finger, he stroked her exposed nipple. It was puckered tight, a pale pink, and he wanted to draw her into his mouth. Why not? he thought. This was his show.

He caught her hand and pulled her to her feet. "Stand still." With no preliminaries, he bent and covered her with his mouth, curled his tongue around her, and sucked.

She jerked hard and stepped back, almost falling onto the mattress.

Sam looked at her. "I said to be still."

"Reaction." She blinked hard. "I . . . I didn't mean to—"

He again took her into his mouth and this time she moaned, stiffened her arms and her back and held as still as a statue. He suckled at her, loving her taste, the way she trembled, the desperate little sounds she made. Using his tongue he stroked her, teased, then sucked hard.

"Sam!"

"Shh." He straightened to look at his handy work. Her nipple was now ripe, reddened, and wet. "This is cute," he managed to say, his voice little more than a rumble as he flipped the material of her ruined dress, "but I think I'd prefer you naked."

Her chest rose and fell, both from what he'd been doing and what he would do.

"I'm going to undress you, stretch you out on the bed and taste you like that all over."

Her lips parted. "All . . . ?"

"Over. Don't move." He reached behind her for the zipper to her dress.

Disregarding his orders, she leaned into him and breathed deep. "You smell so good, Sam."

He grunted at that, but didn't push her away. It felt nice

having her lean into him. "You find the smell of sweat and alcohol appealing, do you?"

"Your sweat, yes."

He stripped the tiny sleeves off her shoulders and let them drop down to her elbows. He reached for the back fastening of her bra. The position put his cheek over her shoulder and he could feel her silky blond curls touch his ear, his jaw. Shit, now *he* was trembling.

"You don't smell like alcohol though. Just like a man, like you. I've always thought you smelled good."

"Another rule," he said as he peeled the bra away, leaving her naked from the waist up. "No talking."

"But . . ."

"No talking. You're distracting me." *And making me crazy and I won't be able to do this if you don't quit.*

She covered her breasts with her arms, making Sam lift a brow. "Change your mind?"

She shook her head.

"Then don't hide from me." He waited, wondering if she'd call it quits, half hoping she would, half praying she wouldn't. "Make up you mind, Ariel. Anytime you want this to end, all you have to do is tell me. I'll walk you to the door."

She swallowed hard, drew a fortifying breath and let her arms hang at her sides.

He admired her courage. "It's only going to get harder you know. If you've changed your mind—"

"I haven't."

But she would. Eventually. How far would he have to go before she cried uncle? No matter, he had to carry it to the bitter end. He had to ensure she wouldn't test him again, because he wasn't at all certain of his ability to resist her.

"All right, then." He pulled the dress over her hips and let it drop. It pooled around her feet. "Step out of it."

She did, accepting the hand he offered for balance. Left only in panties and sandals, she blushed bright pink. But Sam paid little enough attention to her face when her body was all but bare. His hands at her waist, he stroked her, from her hips to her ribs and back again. She was a little too slim, her curves understated. "Damn, you're beautiful."

He didn't get a reply, but then, he didn't expect one.

He glanced up at her face. "You blond everywhere?"

Her color deepened.

"No, don't tell me. I want to find out for myself." Then, smiling into her shocked face, he whispered, "Take them off."

Chapter Three

Ariel had never felt so exposed in her entire life. She gulped and tried to find a little courage.

"I'm waiting."

He just stood there, his arms crossed over his hairy chest, his feet braced apart. His silky dark hair was mussed, hanging over his brow and beard shadow darkened his jaws and upper lip. His long black lashes hung low over his piercing eyes, direct, taunting. Watchful and expectant.

She wanted to throw him to the floor and drag his slacks off his gorgeous body and kiss him all over. But he wanted to do things his own way and she knew Sam well enough to know it was his way or not at all.

"All right." Feeling awkward and unsophisticated, she hooked her thumbs in her panties and pushed them down. Sam held her left elbow as she tried to step out, but she caught her stupid sandals on the leg bands, getting her panties twisted. She should have removed the shoes first but she wasn't exactly an expert at stripping with an audience.

When she finally got them free, she dropped the panties on the floor with the rest of her clothes and started to sit down to take off her sandals.

Sam had other ideas. "I like the look." His voice was gruff, raw. "Leave them on."

She peeked at him, but he stared at her belly, or more specifically, below her belly. She nearly jumped out of her skin when he reached out and stroked his fingers through her pubic hair.

"Part your legs a little."

This test of his was a killer. If he'd only kiss her again, hold her . . . but he wasn't going to. She knew he wanted her to shy away, to run home scared. To prove she wasn't a mature, experienced woman.

The experience part . . . well, hopefully he'd forgive her for that. But she was a woman, *his woman,* if he'd only stop being so pigheaded. She forced her chin up and set one foot several inches from the other.

"You're not as blond here," he said while still fingering her curls. "But then your brows and lashes are a few shades darker too. It's pretty."

Never in her twenty-four years had she expected such a conversation to take place. He was complimenting her on her . . . well, on something very private. This wasn't at all as she'd assumed lovemaking would be. She thought there'd be a lot of reciprocal touching, breathless loss of control, and a simultaneous agreement to move forward in intimacy.

At the same time, being here with him like this was so wildly exciting, she knew she was wet and she feared he'd know it too in just a moment.

He stepped away from her. "Turn around."

Her mind went blank. What in the world did he have planned now? Breath rushed in and out of her lungs. Feeling wooden and clumsy in the stupid shoes, she forced herself to move. When her back was to him, he said, "There. I want to look at you."

She tried to stand straight and tall, but more than anything she just wanted to crawl into the bed under the covers and then convince Sam to crawl under them with her.

The touch of his breath on her nape raised her awareness another notch.

"I love your ass," he whispered, and then both his hands covered her there, squeezing and cuddling. Her eyelids grew heavier and heavier until her eyes closed. Without thinking, she reached back for him. Her fingertips just grazed his fly long enough for her to feel the straining power of his erection.

"No." He caught her hands. "No touching from you." He placed her hands alongside her thighs.

"I want to touch you," she said. "The same way you're touching me."

"Yeah? Like this?" His hands came around her and he caught her nipples in his fingertips.

Her back arched. "Sam . . ."

"You like that, don't you?" He tugged, plucked, and rolled. He opened his palms and grazed them over her, then covered her breasts, gently holding them while he kissed her shoulder, her nape. Every damp warm touch of his mouth brought her temperature up another degree.

"Answer me, Ariel."

"I like it, but . . . I'd like it more if I could touch you, too."

He laughed, the sound masculine and satisfied. "I just bet you would. But then you'd be breaking the rules and we can't have that."

He went back to tormenting her nipples and he took so long she wasn't sure she could stand it. Her every nerve ending was alive, sizzling. Stars danced in front of her closed eyes, her breasts ached and felt heavy, and between her legs she throbbed and burned.

And still he just played with her breasts and kissed her shoulders and back and neck.

In desperation, she whispered, "Sam, *please*." She honestly didn't know how much more she could take. An imminent explosion skirted through her, almost there, but not quite. Her hips moved, embarrassing her, shaming her but she couldn't seem to hold still.

"All right," he whispered. But he didn't turn her to him. Instead, those tantalizing hands coasted down her ribs, over her belly, and between her legs. "Open them more."

Trying but unable to get her legs to cooperate, she whimpered.

He helped her, putting one large foot between hers and nudging them open. "More. I want to be able to get to you." *Oh God.*

"How I teased your nipples? I'll do that here, too." His fingertips brushed against her clitoris and she cried out at the electrifying sensation—then felt his smile press to her shoulder. "Yeah, right there," he said in deep triumph. "It'll make you crazy Ariel and if we're both lucky, you'll come for me. I want you to, you know."

Horrified by the thought of standing and performing to his demands, she stiffened. Surely he didn't expect her to do such a thing with him detached, manipulating her but uninvolved?

"Don't stiffen up on me." Gently, using only his fingertips, he opened her. "We'll get to the bed, I promise. No way in hell will this be it. Unless you tell me to stop." Carefully, holding her open with one hand, he circled her clitoris again. She felt his fingers, his rough, warm fingers, moving over her and she couldn't seem to get enough oxygen into her starved lungs. For one brief instant, she thought she might actually faint.

"Breathe, Ariel." He held still, waiting, leaning over her shoulder to watch her face. She did, gulping air and shaking from head to toe. "You're close, aren't you, baby? I wonder if you can do this standing up. Some women can't you know. That tidal wave of melting pleasure washes over you and your legs go weak and . . ." He shrugged. "I'll hold you though. Don't worry."

Staring straight ahead at the window opposite his bed, Ariel bit her lip, fighting the urge to plead with him again.

"You'll tell me if I hurt you."

"Yes."

He opened his mouth on her neck, giving her a soft love bite—and pushed his middle finger into her.

Her head fell back, a deep, shuddering groan escaping her. He gave an answering growl of pleasure and pressed deeper and it was the most amazing thing, a little embarrassing, very arousing. Her hips moved again and this time she didn't care.

"You're small. And hot. And you feel so damn good."

Ariel was well beyond words. She hung in his arms, her legs open, all her attention on his hands and how he touched her and the expanding pleasure that would ebb and then grow stronger as it rolled through her.

With his finger pressed deep inside her, he found her clitoris with his thumb and he began an incredible slick friction that sent her right over the edge. She cried out, stunned at what she felt, at her total loss of control. She couldn't be quiet, couldn't hold still.

True to his word, Sam wrapped one muscled arm around her waist and held her upright while he continued the press and retreat of his fingers, kept the pleasure flowing until indeed, her legs gave out and she slumped into him, boneless, exhausted, replete.

His arm stayed locked around her while he lifted the other hand. Ariel roused herself enough to turn her head and look at him. She saw his eyes close, saw him suck his fingers into his mouth, taking her taste, her wetness.

Their eyes met. Looking far too serious, he pulled his fingers out and touched them to her lips. She shuddered, but was too spent to pull away.

Gently, Sam lowered her to the bed on her stomach, then stretched out beside her. He stroked her head, found the few pins that still held her hair and pulled them out to flick them across the room. With an open hand, he combed out the curls, spreading them over the pillow.

"Sam?"

"Mmm?" Propped on one elbow, he continued to pet her, down her spine, over her bottom.

"Will you make love to me now?"

He slanted glittering eyes at her and said, "You just can't be quiet, can you?"

Ariel felt hurt. He'd just done the most amazing thing to her and still he was apart from her. It wasn't easy, but she got her sluggish limbs to work and turned on her side to face him. He stared down at her body, his gaze concentrated, hot.

She stared at his chest. Among a smattering of older scars randomly dispersed over his torso, there was a fresh, dark bruise coloring his ribs, evidence of the night he'd just had. Stricken, Ariel thought of how many times he'd been hurt, how much he must have suffered in his efforts to protect. Maybe, she thought, he physically wasn't up to making love with her. Old wounds, new wounds . . . Was she being selfish?

He'd already given her pleasure without intercourse. She could do the same, sparing his sore body.

Wanting to make him feel as good as she did, Ariel leaned forward and brushed a butterfly kiss over the nearest scar, a small bullet wound that grazed his shoulder. Sam froze, not even breathing.

Encouraged, she spread her hands over his chest, tangling her fingers in his dark chest hair, stroking him as he'd stroked her.

Ariel noted a thin, light line near his collarbone, about two inches long. It looked like it might have been a deep cut, perhaps with a knife. Appalled at the awful risks he took, she kissed that, too.

This close, his scent was twice as potent. Those odd turbulent feelings roused in her again.

She kissed three bruises, one on his shoulder, his temple, another on his ribs. "Sam," she whispered, and opened her mouth on him. His skin was deliciously warm and sleek, his flesh firm. Turning her head, she moved closer to a flat nipple hidden beneath his chest hair. Her tongue touched him.

Sam grabbed her shoulders. In a heartbeat, Ariel found herself flat on her back with Sam straddling her hips. "I said no touching, Ariel."

She blinked up at him, unable to move, confused by how quickly he'd reversed their positions. He sounded so stern, looked so dangerous. "I'll try . . ."

"Too late."

Her eyes widened. Oh no. He was going to tell her to leave. He would throw her out and she hadn't had a real chance yet to make him understand how perfect they'd be together.

He stretched her arms high until they nearly touched the slatted headboard, then reached across her for the nightstand and jerked open the top drawer. Ariel twisted, trying to see what he was doing . . . He pulled out handcuffs.

"*Sam.*"

"I haven't had much chance to use these since going undercover." He let them dangle in front of her face, waiting, she knew, for her to protest, to insist he release her.

They stared at each other, his expression lethal, hers uncertain, but neither of them backed down. Sam leaned over her.

One metal bracelet clicked around her wrist, then clicked and clicked again when he tightened it to fit her small bones. She had room to turn her hand, but she couldn't slip it free. Her stomach fluttered in apprehension.

He glared down at her. "You ready to call a halt?"

Damn him. She wasn't a criminal he could intimidate so easily, because she knew Sam would never hurt her. No matter his games, no matter his intent, she knew him, loved him, and trusted him. "No."

His mouth tightened. "Make sure, Ariel."

She would not let him scare her. She would not let him off the hook that easily, either. One way or another, she'd get through to him, even if that meant showing him her trust first by playing out these bizarre games of sexual dominance.

She stared him in the eyes. "I'm sure."

Sam wanted to howl, to curse the moon and punch a hole in the wall. Ariel had taken his control and turned it back on him, openly sharing her pleasure, then kissing his injuries—old and new—as if she wanted to heal him.

Like a few stupid marks on his body really mattered to her.

He was so damn hard his guts clenched and his brain cramped. Watching Ariel come had been something he'd never forget. She was so sweet she made him break out in a sweat just by smiling.

Would she taste as sweet as she looked?

Jesus. Before he could change his mind he caught her other wrist, aware of how tiny her bones were, how delicate. He slipped the chain connecting the handcuffs through a slat in the headboard then snapped the cold steel around her.

Breathing hard in both regret and shattering lust, he looked down at her pale, slim body stretched out beneath him, shackled in place. He didn't want to think about anything, he only wanted to devour her, to take everything she had and give her another mind-blowing orgasm.

He plumped up her breasts in his hands, thumbed her nipples roughly, watched her squirm.

"Not a word," he warned, knowing if she started telling him what she wanted again, he'd lose the fight. He moved off her, opened her legs wide and repositioned himself between them, on his knees so he could drape her legs over his. "That's better."

Those beautiful hazel eyes of hers, now more topaz than

brown, watched him without blinking, conveying some silent message that he damn well didn't want to hear. Her mouth looked puffy and soft and kissable. Her small chin quivered, but not because she might cry. No, he knew Ariel wouldn't do that.

Probably it quivered with stubbornness.

"I like to see a woman, all of her, when I take her," he explained. Her legs draped his, white against his dark slacks, sleek and lightly muscled. He looked at her breasts. Earlier her nipples had been velvety soft, but once he'd touched them, they'd stayed puckered, begging for his mouth.

She lightly licked her lips, luring him. Bracing his hands on the pillow at either side of her head, Sam bent down and savaged her mouth with ruthless hunger, kissing her hard, thrusting his tongue between her teeth. She didn't fight him or pull back. No, she accepted his tongue, sucked on it, returned his kiss with equal passion.

He groaned, aware of her straining up to him, trying to get more of him. Her thighs were tensed, her belly lifting into him.

He pulled himself away and took his pleasure at her breasts. He loved suckling a woman and could be content to spend an hour on her nipples alone. But not this time. As soon as Ariel started writhing, he moved lower, nibbling on her ribs, then lower still until he could dip his tongue into her navel.

She held her breath, anticipating what he might do, he knew. Did she like oral sex? Had any man ever kissed her between her thighs? He hoped not. He wanted to be the first.

"Wider," he said as he pressed her legs farther apart and held them in place when she would have automatically brought them together again. He glanced up at her still face, flushed but uncertain. "Keep them that way."

Using his fingertips, he opened her lips, exposing her glistening pink flesh. Her clitoris was swollen from her recent climax, extra sensitive. Gently, he kissed her, heard her shocked, eager gasp, and he closed his mouth around the tender bud.

With a hoarse cry, she nearly lurched away, but he cupped her hips firmly in his big hands and held her secure. Because he knew her nerve endings were already tingling, still alive from her last orgasm, he was very careful not to push her too fast, to cause her any discomfort. He suckled softly, easily, taking his time, stroking with his tongue. When she was ready for more, her legs stiffened and her arms pulled tight against her bonds.

"Sam," she said, all breathless and low. "Sam, Sam, *Sam*..."

Her cries were raw, real, and he loved it, the way she responded, the pleasure he gave her so easily. She didn't hold back at all, didn't try to temper her response. He replaced his mouth with his fingers and raised his head to see her face.

Her neck was arched, her teeth clenched, her breasts heaving. "Beautiful," he breathed, ready to come just from looking at her. After endless moments, she quieted, and Sam moved up beside her, smoothed her hair from her face, placed a kiss on her open lips.

"That was nice." He waited, but she didn't open her eyes, didn't reply. Sam smiled. "For a youngin', you come with a lot of energy. I like it."

Sweat glistened on her chest, the tops of her cheekbones. A rosy flush covered her body and her heart still raced. With an obvious effort, she licked her lips, swallowed, and said, "Shut up, Sam."

He grinned, fighting off a chuckle. "You're not supposed to talk."

She cast him a wanton look that nearly did him in. "No? I've never been handcuffed before, Officer. What should I be doing?"

Sam lowered his hand to her belly and felt it hollow out when she dragged in a breath. "Rest. You're going to need your strength."

"I am?"

"Mmm. I'll give you a few minutes before we start again."

Her eyes widened, darkened. "Start . . . ? Sam, no. I . . . I can't."

He pushed his hand lower until he cupped her mound. She was slick, very wet and pulsing with heat. "Yes you can." All the teasing left him. "I'll see to it."

She squeezed her eyes shut. "Sam . . ."

"Crying uncle?"

A sob almost rose in her throat, but she managed to swallow it back. Sam watched her closely, waiting for the words he needed to hear, waiting for her to tell him to fuck off, to get out of her life once and for all.

"No. I'm not crying uncle."

They watched each other, at a stalemate, until finally Sam cursed. "Fine. Have it your way." His fingers curled against her, his middle finger sinking past her creamy wetness, into her up to his first knuckle—and someone rang his doorbell.

They both jerked to a breathless, astonished standstill. Their motions were frozen.

Ariel gasped, "You have *company*?"

Sam shoved himself off the bed and stalked to the window, barely moving the curtain aside to peer out. "Ah fuck."

A loud knock sounded.

He turned to Ariel, took in the sight of her handcuffed naked to his bed and knew he'd just screwed up royally.

"Who is it?" she whispered in a fearful voice.

Sam rubbed his face. "It's Pete."

"Ohmigod." She began jerking and twisting. "Let me loose!"

He walked past her. "No, just be quiet. I'll get rid of him and be right back. I promise." He snatched up his shirt and pulled it on.

"Sam!" Her face went white. "Don't you dare leave me here like—"

He held a finger to his lips. "Shhh. You made a deal, Ariel. Now keep it. If you're real quiet, Pete will never know you're here." He pulled the door shut, aware of her distress—and aware of his own regret. But she did fall silent, thank God.

He closed the door and trotted quickly down the stairs. His brain churned, trying to think of what to say, how to explain Ariel's car in his driveway, how to get rid of his baby brother.

Pete knocked again, growing impatient.

"All right already, give it a rest." Sam threw the door open. "What the hell is the matter with you?"

Pete, looking healthy and happy and in something of a hurry, burst in and said, "I need the keys to Gil's boat."

"What?"

His black hair was mussed, his shirt untucked and he had a hickey on his neck. "Gil's out of town, but he said I could use his boat only I don't have a spare key and you do."

"Gil's out of town?"

"Yeah. Business—don't you remember? He's been gone all week. Forget that part. Just give me the key."

Suspicious, Sam leaned around Pete to look out the door. His brother's sporty little Focus was at the curb, still running, and in the passenger seat was a cute blond. "Ah. Big plans?"

Pete bobbed his eyebrows. "Is she hot or what?"

Amazed that Pete apparently hadn't even noticed Ariel's car in the drive, Sam went to the kitchen for the spare key to Gil's houseboat. "Yeah, she's cute."

"Cute? You've gotta be kidding me. She's in my statistics class, smart as hell and sexier than that."

"And willing?"

With a sly look, Pete said, "Oh yeah."

At twenty-two, Pete was a good-looking kid with an athlete's body that had yet to finish filling out, sincere brown eyes, and a sexual drive exclusive to young male animals of the human variety. Sam loved him so much that it sometimes hurt and in the three years since their father's death, he'd felt more responsible for him than ever.

He held the key out of reach. "You got protection?"

"No, you wanna loan me a gun?" He grinned.

Sam didn't take birth control lightly. "You know what I mean, Pete."

"She's got it covered."

Scowling, Sam grabbed him by the ear and lifted him to his tiptoes. "*She* does? How many times do I have to tell you—"

Laughing and wincing at the same time, Pete pulled a condom from his pocket and waved it under Sam's nose. "Hey, I was teasing, all right! It's covered. Literally."

Sam turned him loose. "That's it? One?"

"With three more in the glove box."

"Then don't exceed four, you hear me?"

Pete snatched the keys from his hand. "Yeah, four." He held his heart and pretended to stagger. "Four."

Sam laughed and walked him back to the door. Not for a single moment was he unaware of Ariel upstairs, naked, waiting. "You like them blond, huh?"

Pete shrugged. "Or brunette or redhead or . . ."

"Well, I meant because both she and Ariel are blond."

"She," Pete emphasized, "is a lot more fun than Ariel ever tried to be."

Sam's knees locked. "Yeah? How so?"

"You kidding me? All Ariel could ever say was no, no, and no. No real dates, no kissing, and definitely no sex. Got to where I thought my name was No-Pete."

Sam's heart gave a heavy thump. "She cut ya cold, huh?" Now why the hell did that thrill him so much?

"She cut everyone cold, not just me. She told me she was waiting till she got married." Pete rolled his eyes.

Dropping back against the wall, Sam said, "No shit?" His head started to pound.

"Yeah, real old-fashioned attitude, right? I think she just liked to lead guys on. You know, like a tease."

Anger roiled up, making him want to take Pete by the ear again. He didn't, because it shouldn't matter to him what was said about Ariel. But as a big brother, he could say a few general things, and did. "I hope like hell you're not repeating that to anyone but me, because if I hear of it, I'll be royally pissed."

"I know." Pete winked. "Preserve a woman's honor no matter what. I remember."

Sam caught his arm. "I mean it, Pete."

He looked down at the hand holding him with marked confusion. "No sweat. I liked Ariel a lot, still do as a friend. But she made sure it was never more than that, end of story."

"You were really hung up on her."

"I thought I was. Gil told me I was suffering lust, not love and I have to admit he was right. But hey, I'm not bitter and I'm not out to trash her." He tipped his head toward the door. "I am out to have a good time tonight though, if this impromptu lecture is over."

Sam opened his fingers by force of will. "It's over. Just be careful."

"I'm twenty-two, Sam. Not fifteen."

"I remember. Make sure you remember it, too."

Rolling his eyes again, Pete playfully punched him in the ribs—causing Sam considerable pain, which he managed to hide—and then Pete trotted out to his car. Sam propped himself in the doorway, waved to the young lady when she laughed and lifted her hand toward him, and once the car pulled away he closed and locked the door.

Ariel had wanted to wait till she got married.

His pulse raced, causing a wild thrumming in his ears. Breath held, he looked up the stairs at that closed bedroom door. Surely to God she wasn't a virgin?

But even as he thought it, his balls tightened and his blood boiled. He could be her first. That upped the stakes even more, made the temptation nearly impossible to resist. He had a choice to make—take her and give himself a fantasy to last a lifetime.

Or send her innocent little butt packing while he still could.

There was really no choice at all.

Chapter Four

Ariel was livid by the time Sam walked into the room. Her wrists were raw from the furious pulling she'd done when she heard Pete spewing such nonsense about her. She hadn't gotten this far with Sam only to have his youngest brother ruin it with exaggerated nonsense.

Frowning, Sam sat beside her on the bed and caught her arms to hold them still. "Stop that," he said, "you're hurting yourself."

"That miserable little cretin." She tried to jerk again, but Sam was too strong for her, keeping her immobile.

"Who?"

"Pete, that's who." Ooh, when she got hold of him, she'd box his ears. "I can't believe you let him stand there and say those awful things."

Sam leaned back, his expression guarded. "You heard?"

"Every damn word."

"And you're jealous?"

"Jealous?" Ariel sputtered at such a ridiculous notion. "I'm furious!"

Sam's scowl was black enough to straighten her hair. "Because he's taking his new girlfriend out to Gil's boat for some privacy?"

She gasped so hard, she nearly choked herself. "Don't be an idiot. I couldn't care less who Pete sleeps with, as long as it isn't me. I'm mad that he stood down there and spoke about me like I was some ice princess or a . . . a . . ."

"Cock tease?"

Fury rolled through her. "Let me go. Right now."

Sam scrutinized her. "I don't think so. You look violent."

Digging her heels into the mattress, she pulled and tugged and thrashed—until she saw Sam holding the key in front of her face.

"You're destroying my bed."

Ariel arched her neck, looked upside down at where the chain for the cuffs had gouged the smooth wooden slats of his headboard, and she smiled in evil satisfaction. "Good," she practically spat at him. "I'll tear the whole damn thing apart if you don't unlock me."

Sounding very put upon, Sam sighed. "I give you two orgasms and all you can do is threaten me."

That was true enough, so she grudgingly muttered, "Sorry. I do appreciate what you did."

That made him laugh and shake his head. A second later the key clicked in the lock and the cuffs opened.

Sam drew her arms down, held her wrists loosely in his hard hands and gently rubbed. "Look what you did. You had enough scrapes and bruises without deliberately adding to them."

For the first time that night, he sounded calm, completely detached. Ariel got worried.

"Tell me something, will you, Ariel?"

Uh-oh. She didn't trust this new mood of his at all. In the time she'd known him, she'd become accustomed to his sarcasm, his sharp wit, his merciless teasing—but never indifference. "What?"

He snared her gaze with his and wouldn't let her look away. "Are you a virgin?"

Well damn. She started to pull her hands away but he resisted and Ariel didn't think it was worth a struggle. Silence stretched out, more uncomfortable by the moment. She felt pinned to the mattress with the way his unblinking stare penetrated her confidence. Stalling, hoping for an out, she asked, "Do you mean, like, *technically?*"

His eyes narrowed at her avoidance. "Have you ever had intercourse?"

She squirmed, chewed on her bottom lip. "Well, if you mean—"

"Sex, Ariel. I mean sex."

"There's like, sex, in the general term as in touching and—"

"Have you ever been fucked, goddammit?"

She nearly jumped out of her skin at his abrupt blast of outrage; then her own temper ignited and she jerked her arms away from him and came up on her knees to face him head on. Poking him in the chest to emphasize every word, she said, "No, all right? No, there's been *no one.*"

His eyes widened over her attack and he leaned back out of reach.

More softly and with a little desperation, Ariel explained, "I only ever wanted you."

Looking equal parts pained and provoked, Sam started to rise from the bed. He'd turned halfway from her when resolve overrode her anxiety, and Ariel hurled herself at him, tackling him hard from the side.

Unfortunately, her surprise attack sent him right over the edge of the bed. Unprepared, he had no way to stop himself. Arms flailing, he crashed to the hard floor. Ariel landed on top of him with an "omph," forcing a loud grunt from Sam.

For five seconds, he just stared up at her, his face blank in shock at what she'd done. Ariel quickly took advantage. She grabbed his ears and kissed him.

When he tried to turn his head, she bit his mouth.

"Ow!" He wrenched back. "Damn it to hell—"

"You have a foul, but delicious mouth, Sam Watson." She kissed him again, licking her way past his teeth, rubbing her breasts against his naked chest. When he stopped fighting her, holding himself in a sort of suspended indecision, she ran her hands all over him, over his sleek hard shoulders, his wide, hairy chest, down his sides and back up again. She couldn't get enough of him and let him know with the way she touched him, how she crawled over him.

Sam groaned and in the next instant, his hands opened wide over her behind, gripping her tightly, grinding her into his erection. Thrilled, Ariel opened her legs to straddle his hips, and threw her head back with a triumphant moan. Beneath her mound, even through his slacks, she could feel the thick rise of Sam's erection. She had thought herself long done, half dead, uninspired toward anything else sexual.

But it took very little for Sam to have her wild again. A look. A touch. The two combined and she wanted to beg him to take her.

She kissed his chest and when his fingers gently laced into her hair and he said, softly and with apology, "Ariel," she bit him again, making him jump.

"Be quiet, Sam."

He half laughed, half moaned. "You're stealing my thunder, babe."

"I want you, enough for the two of us." She tenderly licked his discolored, sore ribs while inching her way down his muscled body. His fingers tightened in her hair, holding her back for only a moment before urging her lower with sublime surrender.

"Yes," Ariel whispered and she attacked the fastenings to his pants, hurrying before he could change his mind. Every time he shifted, she kissed him through the material, stroked him beneath the zipper, did her best to keep his lust at an urgent level so he couldn't concentrate long enough to reject her.

When she finally got his fly opened she snaked her hand inside, then paused with the wonder of it, the amazing way he felt, so alive and solid and yet velvety textured, flexing and pulsing in her hand.

Staring down at him, her lips parted to accommodate her fast breathing, Ariel examined her very first up-close and personal penis. What a revelation. "Sam."

"Kiss me, Ariel." The words were so guttural, she could barely understand him but she knew what he wanted.

Holding him now in both hands, she brushed a kiss up the length of him and heard his sharp intake of breath, felt the way his hands clenched in her hair, how his big body trembled.

Amazing. And exciting. She ran her tongue up to the very end, then over the glistening tip and he lurched so violently he nearly tossed her off. She quickly repositioned herself and did it again, this time lingering on the head, on that warm bead of moisture that tasted both salty and rich and not quite how she'd ever imagined.

"Oh God."

"I like this," Ariel purred, pleased with her discovery and Sam's reaction to her touch. She glanced up at him. "Do you?"

He laughed again, but it was a sound of agony, not humor.

"Will you like this?" She opened her mouth and drew him in, not real deep because he was big and she was new to this, but taking the head all the way inside to suckle at it, to roll her tongue around him. She tasted more fluid, felt him grow even more, pulse. Sam let out a growling rumble and his whole big body jerked.

Before Ariel could fully appreciate all that splendid response, she found herself on her back, Sam firmly between her thighs, his mouth covering hers. He was ferocious, breathing hard and fast, his hands everywhere, his tongue hot in her mouth, his hips stroking her.

"Protection," he groaned and, as if by a mighty effort, pushed himself up enough to fumble in the nightstand drawer until he snagged three connected condoms. He ripped one free along the perforated line, opened it with his teeth and sat back on his heels to roll it on.

"You asked for this," he told her as he shoved his pants down and kicked them off, then wedged himself back between her thighs before she could get a good look at him completely naked. "Remember that."

For an answer, Ariel twined her arms around his neck, her legs around his waist, and hugged him tight. She loved him so much that tears sprang to her eyes. "I won't ever forget it," she promised him.

He hesitated, his chest working like a bellows. Ariel was so afraid he'd just changed his mind that she tightened her hold.

"Shh." He smoothed his hand up and down her side. "Relax."

"Don't leave me, Sam." She hated pleading, but if he turned her away now . . .

"No, I won't." And then, with sober apology: "I can't." He eased his weight onto her and carefully coaxed her arms from his neck. "I don't want to hurt you, Ariel."

"You would never hurt me."

"I might if I take you like a crazed sailor on shore leave. But you set me off, honey, you really do. I need you to help me out here."

With complete and utmost sincerity, Ariel told him, "You can take me like a crazed sailor. I won't mind."

He smiled, the most tender smile she'd ever seen from him. "*I'll* mind. Now quit talking and kiss me. No, gently. Yeah, that's right."

Ariel melted. Sam's voracious, hungry kisses were incredible, but the way he kissed her now, almost as if he cared about her, maybe loved her just a little, too, was enough to fill her up for a lifetime. And he took his time, kissing her long and slow and deep until she was the one who demanded more by pressing her belly up against him.

"Sam?"

"Yeah baby?"

"I'm dying to feel you inside me."

He shuddered. "All right." After levering himself up on one elbow, Sam reached down with his other hand to guide himself in. Ariel saw that he was shaking, the high color in his face, how impossibly blue his eyes looked. The broad head of his penis nudged her soft opening, pushed marginally inside.

Sam locked his jaw. "You are so damn wet."

"I know." She flushed. "I can't help it."

"It's good. Damn good." He sank in a bit deeper with a groan. "Small and tight." His jaw worked as he forced himself into her. "And all mine."

Ariel's heart lurched at those possessive words. "Yes. Always."

But he didn't seem to know what she said, or even what he'd said. His eyes were glazed, burning as he stared down at her and she saw the acute pleasure in his face as her body accepted him. There was a stretching sensation, a little burning, but no real pain. She felt full, complete. Wonderfully alive.

Suddenly his shoulders bunched. He cursed, squeezed his eyes shut; then he snapped. He thrust into her, causing her to lose her breath in one startled gasp of mingled discomfort and joy.

"I'm sorry," he rasped, even as he slid back out, then stroked in deeper again, gaining a rhythm, harder and faster with each turn.

I love you, Sam. But the words were only in Ariel's mind. She held him, cradling his big body close to her heart while he thrust heavily into her, his arms locked tight around her, his face pressed into the side of her throat. He was sweaty, heat pouring off him, and then he arched his back, burying himself so deeply that Ariel cried out.

His face was beautiful, harshly masculine, etched with pleasure so sharp it mirrored pain. Ariel smiled at him, stroked his chest and shoulders until the tremors passed, his primal growls faded, and he slowly sank down onto her.

The carpet on her back prickled, her thighs ached, and Sam's weight pressed her down, making it difficult to breathe. But she didn't want to move. Not ever.

Without lifting his head, Sam said, his voice a sleepy rumble, "You probably have carpet burns on your ass now to add to your other injuries."

Ariel giggled.

Smiling, he forced his head up to see her. "That damn laugh," he said fondly. And he kissed her.

Ariel was so full of love, she couldn't imagine being any happier.

"You all right?"

Dreamily, she sighed. "I'm perfect."

"Yeah." He sat up beside her, his back against the side of the bed, one leg bent, and he looked at her body. He shook his head in chagrin. "That you are. But you'll be more perfect after a shower and some sleep."

Oh no. Panic twisted inside her, but she tried to hide it. "Sam, are you sending me home?"

He shrugged, scooped her up as he stood, groaned at the pain in his shoulder and ribs, and then looked at her. "Unless you want to spend the night. Up to you."

Her heart raced. "You don't mind if I stay?"

Taking that as an affirmation that she wanted to, Sam headed for the bathroom. "The damage is done—but I'm not. Be forewarned though. If you stay, I plan to take you at least a few more times." He looked down at her. "In a few more ways."

Filled with relief, Ariel put her head on his shoulder. "Maybe," she said, tugging at his crisp chest hair, "I'll just take you instead."

He stopped in midstride, groaned again, then rushed her into the bathroom and stood her in the tub. "Virgins are the very devil." He turned away as he removed the spent condom.

"Ex-virgins." When he joined her in the tub, Ariel admired his body with eyes and hands and a few well-placed kisses. She liked the way his dark chest hair tapered off into a long thin line down his body. It circled his navel, then arrowed down to his groin, surrounding and framing his heavy sex.

"Right." Sam took her mouth, smothering her screech of outrage when he turned the cold water on full blast and it hit her in the back. "An ex-pushy virgin who gloats when she gets her own way."

"Sam!" The water quickly warmed, taking away her chills.

He lathered her up, somehow always managing to keep a good hold on her soap-slick body. By the time he finished, Ariel was ready to learn about the new ways he'd mentioned. The night couldn't be long enough to suit her.

Sam awoke to a soft, damp kiss on his lower spine. His eyes snapped open but he didn't move. He was on his stomach, his legs sprawled out, his body heavy with sleep.

Deep shadows still filled the room, telling him it was early morning. His brain felt foggy, as if he'd been on a three-day drunk but with alarming clarity, he knew it was carnal gluttony that had him sluggish this morning, not booze.

Ariel was amazing. Everything he'd ever wanted in a sex partner. Everything he'd ever wanted, period.

He felt her warm fingertips tickling down his spine to the top of his ass. She hesitated, then stroked lower, until she found his testicles and could fondle him from behind. He bit back a rumbling groan.

After the excesses of the night, he should have been dead to the world, unable to rise to the occasion. But this was Ariel—and he was rising rather quickly.

"You're awake," she murmured, sounding more than a little pleased with herself.

"I am now." Sam rolled to his back and dragged her on top of him, appreciating her early morning, sleep-rumpled appeal. "Awake and ready, thanks to a certain little sexy lady who tried to molest me in my sleep."

She gave him a willing smile.

Sam sighed. "Unfortunately we're out of rubbers and I don't take chances, so quit torturing me."

Her face fell. "Bummer."

"Yeah." She sounded so forlorn, Sam almost laughed. "What time is it?"

"Six."

Aware of numerous aches and pains, he stretched beneath her. Laughing, Ariel almost slid off him. She grabbed him tight and managed to hang on.

Her giggle, which had once grated on his nerves, now seemed beyond adorable. "What time do you have to be at work?"

"Ten."

He swatted her bare behind. "Let's go get some breakfast, then. I'm famished."

He gently pushed her onto her back, gave her a smacking kiss on the mouth, and rolled out of bed. If he'd been alone, he would have limped to the dresser for his shorts because every muscle screamed in complaint as he moved. But with Ariel watching, he did his best to do the macho thing and hide his discomfort.

She came to her knees in the middle of the bed. "My dress

is ripped and I never got around to fixing it last night, so can I borrow a T-shirt?"

He cast her a quick look. "Naw, I like seeing you naked."

Her face turned bright pink. "I can't cook or eat breakfast naked."

"Sure you can." He stepped into black boxer-briefs and hiked them up. "My house, my rules."

Her back stiffened. "Sam."

"Ariel." She was so damn cute, he couldn't resist teasing her. "You're such a spoilsport."

Her disheveled blond curls trembled in her agitation, forcing Sam to swallow a laugh. "All right, all right, don't start fuming. You can have a shirt." And then, just to tweak her anger, he added, "I suppose modesty in someone as young as you is to be expected."

He tossed her a white T-shirt, but it hit her in her glowering face, then fell to her lap. She didn't even attempt to catch it.

Sam leaned on the dresser and crossed his arms over his chest, surveying her. "Changed your mind?"

Her chin lifted; she flipped the shirt to the floor. "I believe I have." In lofty disdain, she slid out of the bed and strode naked to the door. "What's a little nudity among adults?"

Oh hell. Sam went after her, his gaze glued to her bare butt swishing and swaying down the stairs. He clutched his heart, thinking he was far too old to survive so much stimulation. He grinned at the thought, remembering that Ariel was the first one to fall asleep last night—and she'd had a fat smile on her face.

He'd literally worn the little darling out, and damn, that made him proud.

His grin died a quick death when, just as they reached the landing, an outraged knock sounded on his door. Ariel jumped a foot and dashed behind him, staring at the door as if it had suddenly become transparent and whoever lurked on the other side could see her. Scowling, Sam went to the peephole to look out. Ariel clutched at him, staying so close he felt her nipples on his back.

"Shit."

"Who is it?"

Dropping back against the door, he said, "Pete. And judging by the look on his face, he's finally noticed your car."

She covered her mouth with a hand. "Oh no."

"Oh no" was right. What the hell should he do now?

The door rattled again, and Pete yelled, "Open up, Sam! I know you're in there."

Sam gave Ariel the once over, then lifted a brow. "Now might be a good time to display that innate modesty, sweetheart. I somehow doubt Pete will believe anything I try to tell him if he sees you flitting around my house in your birthday suit."

Her mouth fell open and in a flash she turned around and dashed back up the stairs. What a sight, Sam thought, watching the way she bounced and jiggled in all the right places. He shook his head. He was an idiot, letting himself be ruled by his gonads instead of common sense. He should have sent her home last night.

Hell, he should never have touched her in the first place. But he had. And he'd more than enjoyed himself.

Now he'd have to pay.

Pete had his fist raised, apparently ready to pound the damn door down, when Sam drew it open. He took his brother off guard, saying, "Hey Pete. What's up?"

Pete's look of surprise disappeared beneath censure. He shoved his way in, looking this way and that. "Where is she?"

"She who?"

Pete whirled around to face Sam. "Don't be an asshole. You know damn good and well I'm talking about Ariel. It didn't register last night, but that's her car in your driveway and now it's still there—"

"Yeah?" Sam leaned out the open door, looked at the car, and said, "Huh. So it is."

Pete's teeth clicked together. "Where—is—she?"

From the top of the stairs, Ariel said softly, "I'm here."

Both men turned to look up. Sam took a surprised step forward. Did she have to hit him with one emotional punch after another? He knew Pete gave him a startled glance, but Sam couldn't get his gaze off her, not even to reassure his brother.

Ariel had hastily dressed in one of Sam's extra large white T-shirts. It was so enormous on her, one shoulder hung down nearly to her elbow and the hem landed almost at her knees, more than adequately covering her. Still, she'd also borrowed a pair of his drawstring running shorts. She'd tied them so tight, the string hung to her ankles. She looked . . . comically precious.

It was a wretched situation for Sam to find himself in, and still he smiled.

Pete punched him in the arm, glowering and bristling and somehow looking protective. Toward Ariel? Well hell. He'd sworn he was over her, yet here he was with his shoulders hunched and his jaw jutting forward.

"You're in your damned underwear," Pete told Sam under his breath, as if Ariel might not have already known that.

"Yeah, and you know, Ariel just might be in my underwear, too. Are you, honey? Did you find the boxers, along with the shirt and shorts, in my third drawer?"

Not amused, Pete slugged him again.

In an odd way, Sam was proud of him. Pete was a man, and apparently he'd listened to at least a little of what Sam had told him about respecting women.

"This isn't funny," Pete said.

"No, I don't suppose it is." Sam wondered how the situation could get any worse. He found out when his neighbor, Hesper, and her bloated bulldog poked their heads though the open front door.

First family and now friends. You'd think he was throwing a party, rather than debauching one very sexy, too young, slightly ex-virgin.

Emotions ran through him, guilt, regret . . . and overwhelming tenderness. He would have liked more time with her, but it appeared his time had just run out.

Chapter Five

"Everything okay, Sam?"

Before turning, Sam closed his eyes and said a quick prayer that some brilliant explanation would come to him.

His mind remained blank. "Hello Hesper." She was still in her housecoat and slippers, curlers in her hair. "What has you up so early—given you were also up late?"

"I saw the young lady's car was still here and then your brother was pounding on the door and . . . Is there any way we can help?"

"No." Sam edged toward the door, trying to block the stairs with his body before Hesper noted Ariel. "Everything is fine. Pete's just visiting, that's all."

His efforts were in vain. The damn bulldog barked, Hesper looked up, and she spotted Ariel. "Oh my. Are you all right, sweetie? Sam told us what happened."

Pete stepped forward, aghast at such a possibility. "Just how much did my brother tell you?"

"Why, everything. That she's a dear family friend who he cares about and that she'd been mugged and was upset so he brought her home to make her feel safe for the night."

Ariel choked, coughing and gasping. Pete just stared at Sam.

A smile locked firmly in place, Sam took Hesper's arm and nudged her back out onto the porch. "Everything's fine here, Hesper, really. I promise it is. But thank you for your concern."

"That's what neighbors are for." Regretfully, she made her way to the steps and the bulldog lumbered along in their wake. "Oh Sam?" She turned to give him a coy smile.

"Yeah, Hesper?"

"If Booth looked as good in his drawers as you do, I believe I'd burn all his breeches."

Sam grinned. "Why thank you, Hesper."

"My pleasure," she said, and then to herself as she walked away, "Indeed it is."

Still grinning, Sam shut the door and turned to find his brother breathing fire and Ariel standing nervously beside him.

"I thought you told her I was a prostitute."

She sounded disappointed, and Sam shrugged, only to have Pete grab his arm and whip him around. "What's this about a prostitute?"

"Nothing. I was only teasing Ariel."

Pete's dark eyes, so much like their father's, narrowed with contempt. "Looks to me like you did a sight more than tease her."

"Pete!" Ariel tried to step between the two men. They didn't let her so she settled on poking Pete with her finger. "This is none of your business, Pete Watson. Now knock it off."

"I presume," Pete said, looking between the two of them, "that a wedding will be planned for the near future?"

Sam almost fell on his ass. *"A wedding?"* Good God, surely Ariel didn't expect . . . He cast an appalled glance her way.

She stared back, white-faced and mute, her mouth pinched.

"You heard me." Pete crossed his arms, every line of his body filled with unwavering resolve. "I told you last night how Ariel felt about this sort of thing."

Yeah, he'd known. And rather than dissuade him, the fact of her virginity had been an impossible lure. His basic nature was such that the idea of being the first—*the only?*—had driven him well beyond common sense, gallantry, and self-survival. He'd *had* to have her.

Sam cleared his throat. "Yeah, well maybe she's changed her mind about it. Did you think of that?"

They both turned to Ariel. At that moment, she appeared so small, so lost and alone and wounded, Sam's stomach twisted into a knot of indescribable pain. He started to reach out for her, intent only on offering comfort, but she backed away from him.

Chin lifted, she whispered, "Maybe I have."

Just a few minutes ago, she'd been playing, smiling, and prancing around naked to drive him wild. She'd looked happy, and now . . . Now she'd shut down, her eyes flat, empty. Sam could have thrown his brother out for ruining the pleasant, no-pressure mood she'd enjoyed before his arrival.

They all stood frozen, uncomfortable and unsure what to say or do next; then Gil's voice intruded. "Damn, I expected to find you in bed, Sam, not holding court in the foyer."

"Gil?" Sam turned to his brother, took in his beat-down, haggard expression and stormed forward with concern. "What's going on? I thought you were out of town."

"I just got home." He handed Sam his briefcase and dropped back against the wall. His tie hung loose around his neck and his shirtsleeves were rolled up past his forearms. He looked fatigued, both mentally and physically. "I checked my messages and then . . . I dunno. I wasn't sure what to do, so I just came here."

Pete crowded closer. "What's happened? Is something wrong with the company?"

Ariel had backed up so far, Gil didn't even notice her. "No, the company is fine. But it seems I have a problem." He paused, looking much struck, then laughed hoarsely, without any real humor. "Well, no, that's probably not the best way to put it. Perhaps a surprise is more like it. A life-altering surprise."

Sam's middle brother was by far the most staid of the three, serious where Pete was playful, calm where Sam was turbulent. He had a great head for business and he wasn't prone to melodrama.

Sam was more than mildly alarmed. "What the hell is that supposed to mean, Gil?"

Gil's brown eyes—so much like Pete's, identical to their father's—were bloodshot. He rubbed the back of his neck. "I got a call from a young lady who lives in Atlanta. You remember I handled some business there right after Dad passed away? Well, it seems . . ." He swallowed, closed his eyes and leaned his head back against the wall. "It seems I'm a father."

Sam hadn't seen her for a week, though God knew it wasn't from lack of trying.

But now, *here,* was not a good time to run into her.

He'd tried calling and repeatedly got her machine. She hadn't bothered to return any of his calls. He'd even dropped by that fancy boutique where she worked, only to be told by one of her coworkers that she'd taken an impromptu vacation.

When he couldn't find her at her apartment either, no matter how long he stood in the hallway knocking, he finally decided she really was on a vacation. Maybe she'd gone out of town. Maybe she wasn't upset. Maybe she didn't even care about how their night together had ended.

She might well be off partying it up and having a blast— while he was smothering in guilt and worry.

But that last look on her face had continued to eat at him. He wanted to talk to her, to make sure she was all right.

After Gil dropped his bomb on them, Sam had been so floored he'd almost forgotten about her. The brothers had all milled to the kitchen for seats and caffeine, which was their normal routine whenever a situation arose that had to be dealt with. Sam had assumed Ariel would follow.

Only she hadn't.

He'd turned, expecting to bump into her, and her absence struck him like a sucker punch to the gut. He'd rushed back to the front door in time to see her little yellow car disappearing past the corner stop sign. She hadn't said good-bye. She hadn't said anything after letting him off the hook with that shaky, whispered, *"Maybe I have."*

She'd just stood there, silent and hurt.

Given Gil's disclosure, Pete hadn't questioned Sam too much when he'd returned to the kitchen, fallen into a chair, and announced that Ariel had gone home. Gil had looked at him funny, but Pete had said, "We'll talk about that later."

Later hadn't arrived yet, since Sam was avoiding Pete—much like he assumed Ariel was avoiding him. Except . . . She'd just walked in, and again, she sat at the bar.

This time she wore sinfully tight dark blue jeans and a flowing white blouse with a ruffle at the neck and long sleeves. She had her curls contained in a French braid and wore white sandals.

She looked so feminine and sexy, his heart lurched at the sight of her. Other body parts followed suit.

Because she didn't so much as glance his way, Sam couldn't see her face.

"Hey, I saw you get your ass beat down at Freddie's." The laughing comment was accompanied by a gust of sour alcohol breath.

Sam looked up into the grizzled, bearded face of an older man, maybe in his fifties, reeking of booze and ready to join him at the small round table. Damn. The last thing he needed was a real drunk that he'd have to protect. Trying to sound both slurred and surly, Sam said, "Ain't been to Freddie's."

The guy laughed and flopped into the seat opposite Sam.

"Sure ya have. I seen ya. Two cops came along and saved your ass, though."

When Sam ignored him, putting all his concentration on his glass of whiskey, the man snickered.

"You were prob'ly too drunk to remember."

"Maybe." Sam kicked back the whiskey, suddenly needing it, appreciating the burn as it went down. *Please,* he thought, *please don't get involved in this, Ariel.* He had a hard enough time keeping her out of his head without having her close while he tried to work.

He glanced up, so did she, but she looked through him as if not recognizing him at all, then went back to smiling and talking to the young man beside her. Sam wasn't sure whether he should be disgruntled or relieved.

He definitely wanted to escort her out, away from the men vying for her attention and those leering at her, away from where he had a job to do. Away . . . to maybe someplace private where he could touch her again.

His hands curled into fists.

Unwilling to test her patience or his possessive nature, Sam pulled out his wallet—again well fattened with bills—and put money on the table. In the two hours he'd been sitting in the bar, he'd noted several possible suspects, but there was one man in particular he thought might bite. He'd watched Sam with a type of greedy anger that made Sam edgy. With any luck, the guy would follow Sam out, and Ariel would not.

To the drunk who'd joined him at his small table, Sam tipped a nonexistent hat. "I gotta go while I still can."

"Yeah, yeah sure. You be careful, now."

Without answering, Sam stumbled toward the door, ran himself into the doorframe with a curse, then continued bumbling on until he was across the street on the opposite walk.

Even though it was midnight, the temperature hadn't dropped much and the hot night air washed over him, making him sweat with both anticipation and disgust. Anticipation because he sensed they were close to finding an end to this particular assignment, and disgust because he was sick and tired of swilling whiskey and listening to drunken fools grouse and rumble as they wasted their money on drink.

There were plenty of things he'd rather be doing—and most of them centered around Ariel, no matter how he tried to fight his feelings.

He'd be damn glad to finish the paperwork on this one. Maybe then he could get his head clear.

He was thinking of her, not paying any real attention while making his way to the designated spot where his backup would be able to see him. His mind was filled with thoughts of her stretched out on his bed, teasing him, taunting him, pushing him past his control—and then a sudden flash of movement came into his peripheral vision and Sam's reflexes took over. He ducked and took a pace to the right.

A heavy pipe crashed into the brick wall where Sam's head would have been, chipping the wall and reverberating with a loud clang. Sam dropped and rolled, barely getting out of the way of a sharp knife blade that sliced toward him. He came up on the balls of his feet, battle ready, poised to move.

Two of them! Not just the man who'd been watching him, but also the drunk who'd joined him at his table.

Shit. A set up and he'd totally missed it.

His senses went on alert and adrenaline rushed through him. He said, "You picked the wrong guy," and he laughed just to taunt them.

Outraged, the bigger man with the pipe lunged forward. His cover was already blown, leaving no purpose to his pretense of drunkenness. Sam went on the attack.

Eyes locked on the assailant, he judged his next move, feigned right to dodge the pipe and turned with his elbow raised, delivering a solid clip to the chin that sent the man to his knees. A boot to the belly finished the job, and the pipe fell from the man's hand with a clatter.

Sam heard the swooshing sound too late. He jumped, but not fast enough to get completely out of the way. The lethal edge of a knife sliced through his shirt along his shoulder and across to his side, not going deep but making him grit his teeth with the awful burn. A warm flow of blood trickled down his back.

Sam whirled, saw the bearded man had drawn back his arm to strike again, and he kicked him hard in the knee. Something broke and the man crumbled, for the moment, immobilized.

This particular night, Fuller and Isaac were on shift with Sam again and they ran onto the scene shouting orders.

"About time," Sam complained.

Isaac cuffed the biggest of the two men. Fuller radioed for an ambulance and backup. Seeing he was no longer needed, Sam slumped forward, his hands on his knees while he sucked in air.

The exhilarating rush of adrenaline faded, along with his normal strength. Sam felt shaky and pissed off and so damn weak his knees wanted to give out. Then he saw Ariel standing across the street and he slowly straightened, revived by a new emotion. She had her arms around herself, her bottom lip in her teeth, and her face was etched with fear.

They stared at each other until Fuller said, "Jesus, Sam. We got here as quick as we could, but it wasn't quick enough, was it?"

He felt Fuller's hand on his arm, dragging him down to sit on the curb. Sam's vision swam a little, making Ariel weave in and out of his sight. "Ariel?"

Fuller looked up, saw her, and yelled, "Hey, c'mere, Miss. I need you." Then to Sam, "Just breathe, damn it. She's coming."

Though she'd looked as still and pale as a statue up to that point, the second Fuller called her name she dashed forward. Fuller took off his shirt and folded it. "Hang on, Sam. The paramedics are on their way."

"Yeah?" He didn't take his gaze off Ariel's rapid, wild-eyed approach. When she was near, he reached up a hand and she clutched it in both of hers. "What for? I didn't do any real damage to them. Just didn't want them creeping away."

Fuller snorted. "They'll both be fine, minus a working bone or two, but you're bleeding like a stuck pig. The bastard got you. Jesus man, I'm sorry." He pulled up Sam's shirt, cursed again and pressed his folded shirt against the wound.

Ariel was so silent, Sam couldn't stand it. "Sweetheart?"

Big tears swam in her eyes and she gulped. "What?"

"I'm amazed." He would have liked to have more conviction in his voice, but even to his own ears he sounded weak and raspy, damn it. "I didn't know you could show such considerable restraint."

Not quite so pale now, she dropped to her knees in front of him. "What are you talking about?"

"You didn't interfere."

"No, of course not." She tried to pull her hand free. "Let me see your back, Sam."

He held tight. "Fuller's taking care of it."

"But . . ." Her voice shook.

"You stood off to the side like a good civilian instead of playing my White Knight. I'm impressed, really I am."

She frowned at him, shook her hand free and crawled behind him. "Ohmigod."

"It looks worse than it is," Sam told her.

"You can't even see it," she snapped back.

Sam laughed.

An ambulance's siren sounded in the distance, nearly drowning out Ariel as she said, with renewed calm, "You're a condescending, patronizing bastard, Sam Watson. The way you fight . . . well, I didn't think you needed my help. You fight dirty."

"But despite all that, you love me anyway?" He waited, breath held, his heart aching much worse than his back did.

Fuller whistled low.

As if trying to offer comfort, Ariel kept smoothing his shoulder. She stayed so close to him, Sam could smell her sweet soft scent. Then she whispered, "Yeah, I love you."

Sam's eyes closed. "I suppose that's only fair."

"What does that mean?"

But Sam couldn't do anything other than concentrate on not passing out like a girl. The ambulance raced onto the scene. Paramedics swarmed around him, gently moving Ariel aside and working efficiently over both him and the man he'd struck in the knee.

Within moments, they helped Sam to his feet. He saw Ariel wringing her hands and he whispered, "Come to the hospital with me. We need to talk."

"Sam . . ."

"Fuller, make sure she—"

Ariel huffed. "I'll be there, all right?"

Both Sam and Fuller smiled at her worried, waspish tone. Then he was inside the ambulance and they shut the doors and Sam couldn't see her anymore. He let out a long shuddering groan of intense pain.

It had been a real bitch holding it in.

Ariel waited with a crowd of Sam's family in the emergency room. They'd been notified by Fuller, who'd stopped in to see that Sam would be all right before getting back to his shift. The family had shown up minutes later, rushing in like a small battalion.

The nurse had promised them all that it was a mere flesh

wound. Yes it required numerous stitches, would indeed leave a scar, but he really, truly was fine. She'd even smiled, bobbed her eyebrows, and stressed the word *fine,* when she said it, making Ariel want to smack her. They were stitching him up and he'd be ready in no time.

And then what? Ariel wondered.

Pete continually paced, but then Pete was young enough and energetic enough that he seldom managed to be still anyway, even when he wasn't worried.

Gil sprawled in a chair sipping a cup of coffee and staring blankly off into space. Ariel assumed his mind might be divided between thoughts of his brother and his new responsibilities as a parent.

Sam's mother, Belinda, sat beside Ariel, pretending to read a mystery novel while fretting nervously.

Ariel put her head in her hands.

"He really is okay," Belinda said to her. She patted Ariel's knee, and Ariel could hear the amusement in her tone—a tone so like Sam's. Apparently, it wasn't only his mother's bright blue eyes that Sam had inherited.

Ariel nodded, but didn't uncover her face. She felt exposed, sitting with all these people who now, thanks to Pete, knew she was in love with Sam.

Gil had amazed her, giving her a big hug and saying, "Fate is the damndest thing, isn't it?" Ariel wasn't certain if he meant her predicament in loving his brother, or his current state of fatherhood.

Pete kept grumbling, saying, "I hate that he's so bullheaded and aloof and damn it, he deserves to be settled."

Belinda patted Ariel again. "Are you really so worried? Sam's tough you know. This won't be the last time he gets hurt, so you ought to get used to it."

Ariel finally gave up the dubious privacy of her hands and lifted her face. "I probably shouldn't be here."

"And why not?"

Because I told Sam I loved him but he didn't tell me any-thing of the kind. Ariel shrugged. "I'm not family."

A commotion came from the room where they'd taken Sam, making Ariel's heart lurch until the nurse appeared, pushing Sam in a wheelchair.

"It's hospital rules," the nurse insisted, "so just be quiet and sit still."

"It's a stupid rule and I do not need a damn wheelchair. There's not a single thing wrong with my legs and—"

Belinda stood. "Be quiet, Sam."

He shut down in an instant, but he still looked belligerent. Until he spotted Ariel. "You waited."

Belinda didn't give her a chance to answer. "Well, of course she waited. What a stupid thing to say. Now, let's go. We'll all take you home first and make certain you're settled and then I need to get to my bed. I have church early and as it is I'm not going to get enough sleep."

Ariel would have been shocked by Belinda's tone except that she'd already seen how Belinda hid her mothering behind a gruff show that made it easier for her sons to accept.

En masse, they exited the hospital, Belinda leading the charge, followed by the nurse pushing Sam, then his two brothers talking quietly together.

Feeling like an interloper, Ariel inched along behind them.

At Belinda's minivan, Sam shoved himself awkwardly out of the chair before anyone could assist him, and stood to look around for Ariel. He looked desperate for escape. The nurse gave up and went away, grousing to herself.

Sam stared at Ariel. "Did you drive?"

She nodded, cleared her throat, and said, "Yes."

"Good." He gave his mother a fast kiss on the cheek. "I'm going with Ariel."

Pete said, full of laconic insistence, "Oh no. I'm coming with you then."

Gil shrugged. "I'll drive Mom."

Belinda wasn't having it. "I'll drive my own car, thank you, and Pete, you're coming with me." She smiled at Ariel. "We'll meet you at his house, dear, all right?"

Ariel found herself nodding before she could give good thought to other possible responses. Sam had said he wanted to talk, but whatever he had to say . . . well, she wasn't ready to hear it yet. A week of trying to prepare herself hadn't gotten her ready.

Muttering under his breath, Sam took her arm and said, "Where the hell's your car? Never mind, I see it." And then, just to be ornery, she was sure, he added, "It's kind of hard to miss."

And Pete said from behind him, evil intent lacing every word, "Yeah, ain't it, though? Even in the dark, and even when you're in a hurry with other things on your mind." With that cryptic remark, he crawled into the backseat of the mini-van and slammed the door, leaving Sam to scowl at him in confusion.

Ariel fretted and worried as Sam crossed the lot and eased himself into her car. Plenty of bandages padded his back, but he still looked mighty uncomfortable as he tried to get his seat belt fastened.

She leaned over him. "Let me."

Sam stared into her face, only inches from his, while she pulled the belt over and hooked it around him as gently as possible. She tried not to look at him, but when she started to settle back into her own seat, he caught her. They were nearly nose to nose.

Sam leaned forward and kissed her. "I missed you."

"You did?"

He searched her face and nodded. "Let's go. The sooner I deal with my family, the sooner I can have you alone."

Ariel didn't know what to make of that, but she did as he said, driving slowly and trying to avoid any bumps.

Sam watched her, his gaze unwavering, setting her on edge. "I'm sorry you had to see that," he finally said.

Ariel glanced at him, then brought her attention back to the road. "You move so fast."

"I didn't have much choice. It was move or get stabbed." She gasped and he rushed to say, "But it didn't happen because I can handle myself. And it worked out for the best. The big guy, the one with the pipe? Fuller says he started spilling his guts, looking to cut a deal, as soon as he got him alone in the cruiser. Seems the other man, the old geezer who sliced me, he's the one who ran the show. By now Isaac and Fuller should have all the info they need."

Relief washed over Ariel. "I'm glad that's done then."

Sam gave her a long look. "I'm still undercover though, babe. There'll be other jobs."

"I know."

He waited as if he expected her to say more, but what else was there to say? Sam loved his job and he excelled at it. He was a cop through and through. That wouldn't change.

When they reached his house, they found his family congregated on the front porch along with Hesper, Booth, and the elderly bulldog. Sam groaned. "Jesus, can't a man find any peace?"

"They care about you."

"Yeah, well they could care about me tomorrow instead." He gave her another searching look, and seemed annoyed when she turned away. But she just couldn't bear it.

She'd meant to leave him alone, to let him get beyond his brother's ridiculous insistence on marriage. Then she'd hoped to go to him, to see if he wanted to continue seeing her, no strings attached. Despite what she'd originally told herself, she'd rather have Sam any way she could, than not at all.

Her trip to the bar had been impromptu, one last-ditch effort to get her mind off him for a few minutes.

And fate had stuck her in the same bar where he was working.

She'd been heartsick at the first sight of him, then terrified because she knew what would happen, why he was there. In a dozen different ways, loving Sam was going to be tough.

Sam didn't say anything else as he grunted and groaned his way out of the car. His family merely stood back, watching his progress without offering help. They seemed to know how he felt about assistance—not that Ariel gave a hoot. She took his arm and led him along the walkway that had thankfully been swept clean.

After helping him up to the porch, Ariel took his keys from him and opened his front door, but Sam didn't go in. He put his arm heavily around her and turned to face his family and neighbors. To Ariel, he looked pale and pained and her worry escalated.

Until he said, "I'm fine and while I thank you all for your concern, I'd really like to speak to Ariel. Alone."

Ariel felt her face turn bright red. Now they all knew that he was going to read her the riot act for being in the wrong bar at the wrong time again. Odds were, he'd tell her she had no place in his life, too.

Pete crossed his arms. "Got wedding plans to make?"

Ariel gasped at such a ludicrous comment. "Pete Watson, that is enough."

"No, it's not," Sam told her, and his arm tightened. He looked very put out with her attitude. "I'd like to explain about the other morning . . ."

"There's nothing to explain," she assured him, unwilling to have him forced into saying things he shouldn't have to say, especially with an audience. "I told you, I'm an adult. I knew what I was doing."

"What'd she do?" Booth asked his wife in confusion, and Hesper said, "You don't remember our youth?"

"Ahh." Booth gave a toothy grin. "No wonder the boy's riled."

Belinda shook her head at Ariel. "Let him explain, dear. This might prove interesting."

Sam glared, but none of them budged. "I suppose you all want to hear it?"

Gil said, "I know I do. Hell, I need a distraction."

"Fine." He turned to Ariel and cupped her face. She couldn't look away from the earnestness in his beautiful blue eyes. "I can't bear the thought of you being hurt."

Misunderstanding his meaning, Ariel swallowed, then tried to reassure him. "I'll be fine, Sam. You don't owe me anything." And to try to prove that, she added, "I'm sorry we ended up at the same bar again, but Duluth isn't exactly a hotbed of social outlets. My choices were pretty limited and I promise it was an accident."

Very slowly, the pain seemed to leave him and he stiffened. "What were you doing there, then?"

Ariel took a step away from that gritting tone. "I wasn't trying to watch over you. I promise."

Her assurances only annoyed him more. "Then *why?*"

She glanced around at the rapt faces of their audience. No one looked ready to intervene and rescue her, so she scowled and thrust her chin up. "I was there to . . . well to be sure again."

His face went blank, then turned red and angry. "*Damn it, Ariel.* I thought you were already sure."

"Don't you dare yell at me, Sam. I've had a rough enough week as it is."

He drew a slow breath, gathering himself. "I'm sorry."

Her shoulders drooped. "It's not your fault. I was the pushy one."

"I don't mean that."

Pete laughed. "No, he definitely doesn't mean that."

"Shut up, Pete."

Still grinning, Pete said, "You should be thanking me, you know. I'm the one who got her there in the first place."

Sam and Ariel turned to stare at him. "How's that?" Sam demanded to know.

"Why, I got a new girlfriend, that's how. I finally realized she was waiting for me to do that."

Ariel's brows shot up. "You knew?"

He snorted. "Everyone saw you two ogling each other."

Gil and Belinda nodded.

"You fought it, Sam, I'll give you that. But any time I brought her around, you watched her more than I did."

"I did not."

"Yes you did, Son," Belinda told him. "The poor girl couldn't blink without you noting it."

Hesper laughed. "If it was anything like the way he looks at her now, I'm surprised she didn't go up in flames."

Exasperated, Sam rubbed his face, then suddenly stiffened. His hands dropped to his sides and he stared at Pete. "You saw her car that night. That's what you meant about it being impossible to miss, even in the dark."

"Of course I saw it." Pete snorted. "Why do you think I told you all that stuff about her? Hell, I don't gossip about women, especially women I love—as friends—so get rid of that evil look, all right? I just wanted you to know up front how she felt about you."

Humiliated beyond all reason, Ariel tried to inch away, anxious to escape. Without looking at her, Sam caught her wrist and kept her at his side. "Then you came back here the next morning and pretended outrage, reading me the riot act like . . ."

"Like a brother who loves you, yeah. I was trying to make it easy for you to give up, you know, salvage your pride and all that. I figured you could blame me or something since I pretty much figured you hadn't told her that you love her." He elbowed Gil hard. "But Gil here showed up and everything got off track."

Ariel cleared her throat. "Really, none of this is necessary. I don't expect Sam to—"

Sam cast her a look. "Get used to it, honey. They're all pushy as hell, but they're part of the package."

"They are?"

His eyes narrowed. "My house, my rules. Love me, love my family."

Her heart started a furious pounding and she couldn't get a breath. "But . . ."

Sam gave up with visible bad grace. "I didn't want to involve you in my life, all right? I didn't want you to be at risk for being around me and with me. I didn't want you always worried and afraid." He touched her cheek, and Ariel felt the gentleness, the uncertainty. "You're so soft, Ariel. And so sweet. You aren't cut out for my life."

Belinda scowled. "What am I, chopped liver? I'm your mother and I'm certainly a part of your life. You don't consider me sweet or soft?" The venomous glare she gave her son kept him silent.

Gil and Pete, however, snickered with good humor.

"And don't forget your baby brother." Pete put the back of his hand to his head in a gesture of emotional distress. "I'm traumatized nightly, thinking about all the risks you take. I believe you've stunted my growth."

Since Pete was six-two, his claims were deliberately absurd.

Booth nodded vigorously in agreement. "Poor Hesper here can't sleep at night, listening for young Sam, wanting to make sure he gets home safe and sound." He harrumphed. "Don't see him concerning himself with the likes of us though."

The bulldog barked.

Sam said, "How I feel about Ariel is different, damn it."

With the concise, no-nonsense tone he was known for, Gil said, "Then will you please tell her so? She looks to be in an agony of suspense."

Sam took one look at her, nodded, then faced his family. "I need to sit down. Will you all just leave?" And then just as quickly, "Not you, Ariel."

Pete said, "He still has to propose."

Ariel fried Pete with a look. She would definitely get him later. Couldn't he see that his brother was in pain and not up to all that teasing? "Come on, Sam. I'll help you inside."

Sam allowed her to hug into his uninjured side, attempting to offer him support; then he looked back at his family and grinned. "Bye."

His mother said, "We'll leave, but I expect to hear from you in the morning."

Sam nodded. "Ariel or I, one will give you a call." And then he stepped inside and kicked the door shut. "Peace, at last."

"Are you all right?"

"Getting better by the minute." Then: "Upstairs, babe. I need to lie down."

"Oh, Sam." Her worry was a live thing, but Sam went up the steps without too much help from her and once in his room, he lowered himself painfully to sit on the edge of the bed.

"Will you help me get my clothes off?" When she stared at him, he said, "I want to lie down."

"Oh. Yes of course."

"I'm not hurt that bad, but the loss of blood . . ."

She went pale and rushed to get him out of the shirt Gil had brought up to the hospital for him. Snowy white gauze wrapped diagonally over his dark, powerful chest, from his right shoulder to beneath his left arm, covering him front and back. Ariel touched her hand to her mouth and just knew she was going to cry.

Sam kicked out of his shoes, then stood. "My pants?"

She shook herself. The last thing Sam needed now was a whining, weepy, overly emotional woman on his hands. The way he held his right arm, it had to be hurting him. "Of course."

Going to her knees, Ariel stripped off his socks and reached for the fly to his slacks. He was hard.

Her gaze snapped up to his.

He grinned. "Hey, you're on your knees in front of me, sweetheart, ready to take off my pants. What did you expect?"

She'd missed him so much, and loved him more than that. She just couldn't take his teasing right now. "You're hurt, damn it. Be serious." Shaking now, Ariel pulled his pants down over his hips and Sam stepped out of them.

His hand touched the top of her head. "You've been avoiding me for a week, Ariel. I finally have you here, alone in my bedroom. Believe me, I'm taking this very seriously." Wearing only his underwear—and that tented—he sat in the bed and leaned carefully back against a pillow on the headboard. He let out a long sigh. "Now strip off your clothes and get into bed with me."

Her stomach flip-flopped. "Sam . . ."

"My house, my rules."

His voice was gentle, but his gaze burned and Ariel felt a smile twitch on her mouth. "Your rules are ridiculous and you know it. There's no way you're up to . . . that."

"That?"

"Whatever it is you're thinking."

"I'm thinking that I need to hold you, and I'm thinking you're more inclined to say yes if you're naked in bed with me."

"Yes about what?"

He stared at her a long moment, then, in the softest, most uncertain tone she'd ever heard from him, he said, "About whether or not you'll marry me."

Her mouth fell open. "Sam?"

He scowled, rallying forth arguments. "Look at it this way, if you marry me you get to change some of the rules because it'll be your house, too."

Happiness bubbled up, swelled until Ariel felt ready to burst. Watching his face, her own wide smile in place, she stripped off her clothes and climbed in beside him. Sam urged her close to his left side, shifted until he was comfortable, then said, "Now, tell me you love me again. It's the truth, I need to hear it."

"I love you, Sam."

He groaned, hugged her as tightly as he could, considering he was hurt, and kissed her hair. "I love you, too, Ariel. So much that I don't think I could take it if you didn't marry me. At first . . . well, I hate to admit it, but I was as fretful as an old woman."

"If you said that to your mother, she'd bop you on the head."

He smiled. "I don't like the thought of you worrying about me when I'm at work, and I absolutely can't stand the thought of you showing up where I am, maybe interfering and putting yourself at risk."

"As long as I know where you're at and what you're doing, I won't get in your way."

"And you won't worry?"

"There's absolutely nothing I can do about the worry, Sam. I love you." She gently touched the front of his bandages. "You're a good cop—"

"A great cop."

She laughed. "And you're more than capable of taking care of yourself. But I'll still worry. You'll just have to accept that."

"I'll accept it," he growled, "if you'll agree to marry me."

"I'll marry you."

"Thank God." They fell silent for a long moment, holding each other, Ariel with her hand over his heart. She thought he might have dozed, but then he said, "About those rules? There's only one you can't tamper with, okay?"

Ariel twisted to smile up at him. He looked rugged, wounded, and horny. She laughed. "And which rule is that?"

"The one about being naked at breakfast. I've decided I like that rule, and starting every day off with a view of your sweet backside . . . well, know that you're stuck with me forever, okay?"

Ariel grinned. "As long as it goes both ways. And that, Officer, is my rule."

GOING DOWN?

Donna Kauffman

Chapter One

"We'll need to have everything delivered by the tenth. No, that won't do." Callie Montgomery firmed her tone. "Doing your best isn't good enough. Weaver Enterprises is going to be your biggest client. Disappoint us, and we'll take our annual six-figure office-supply budget elsewhere." She smiled, relaxed back in her seat. "Yes, the morning of the ninth would be just fine. Thank you."

Someone cleared her throat from the doorway. As there were only two people presently occupying Crystal City, Virginia's newest office building, the twenty-five story S. E. Weaver building, Callie knew it was her boss, Stephanie Weaver. She hung up and straightened in her chair. "Yes, Ms. Weaver?"

Stephanie was a walking billboard for HOW TO BE A BUSINESS MOGUL BY YOUR FORTIETH BIRTHDAY. She was beautiful, smart, wealthy, and about to push the latest company she'd founded into the upper echelons of the Fortune 500 list. And office temp Callie Montgomery, currently Stephanie's executive assistant, secretary, receptionist, coffee maker, and all around office slave, planned to be right beside her when she did it.

"Well done," Stephanie said, nodding to the phone.

Callie swallowed hard. It was much easier to play power

junkie when her boss wasn't around. Not that she played fast and loose with the responsibilities Stephanie had laid on her since the temp agency had sent her here six weeks ago, anything but. But she did have to admit that after Peter left her for Jennifer, their twenty-two-year old bimbette dog sitter, with legs up to here, boobs out to there, and a brain—well, Peter probably didn't care much about that miniscule body part . . . as long as the clothing covering the aforementioned body parts were equally miniscule—but since he left and took a good deal of her self-confidence with him, wielding power of any sort had been a real confidence boost.

Since there was no one around who much cared about her body parts, scantily clad or otherwise, playing mogul—even if it was just grand poobah of office supplies—was the only thrill she got these days.

Callie gave her an honest smile. "I'm learning from the best."

Stephanie smiled back. "You bet you are."

Callie figured Stephanie Weaver had exited the womb with her confidence already fully developed, and it had probably never wavered once since. She, on the other hand, was not superhuman. For a while after the divorce, she was lucky to feel even subhuman.

"Listen, I know we've been pushing the limit here lately," Stephanie went on to say. "And I probably haven't said this, but I do appreciate your dedication."

Callie could have told her she was thankful for the distraction. Since the divorce papers had been signed, sealed and delivered ten months ago—actually, since she'd walked out six months before that—she'd done little but think about Peter and her previous job failure. Who knew being a wife could be such a brutal occupation? Whatever visions she'd had about being a dedicated partner, about having a family, a future, had died the minute she'd hit that dining room door. Not that things had been progressing all that well up to that point.

So, while eighteen-hour days spent setting up the Weaver empire had left her eyes crossed and her fingers numb, and cancelled whatever little social life she had managed to resurrect, it had also left her with precious little time to think about the past sixteen months . . . and the three long years that had preceded them. For that alone she could have kissed Stephanie. "I don't mind hard work."

"I can't promise things will lighten up anytime soon, but if you don't bail on me, it'll be worth your while in the long haul."

Callie grinned, even as her stomach did a nervous little flip. This was exactly what she'd been hoping for when she'd signed on with AAA Temps, wasn't it? A ground-floor position somewhere that could lead to something permanent, with potential for upward mobility. She was a decent typist, could file adequately, was competent on the phone, juggled appointment books with aplomb, and made a killer pot of coffee. Individually not the most amazing of talents, but combined, she knew she would be indispensable to the right person. After all, hadn't Peter first hired her to be secretary at his legal firm for the very same reasons? *If only I'd stopped at arranging his file drawers instead of his sock drawer.*

"I'm thankful for the opportunity," Callie told her.

"I need to go over tomorrow's list with you," Stephanie said, "but first I've got a last-minute meeting, and it might run a bit long. I hope you don't mind staying a bit later than usual."

Considering it was already after five, and that Callie was usually still at her desk until at least nine every night as it was, that was no small request. But she was in no hurry to go home to her tiny Alexandria rowhouse and nuke another Lean Cuisine, although the frozen Hostess cupcake she treated herself to afterward *was* calling her name right about now. So, she'd have two of them instead. It was the only decadent pleasure in her life these days anyway. And if she put on an extra pound or two, who was going to care? "No, that's no problem," she said, "I don't mind." It should have made her feel pathetic, that she really didn't mind spending her life behind her desk. But she readily admitted that, right now in her life, being needed was exactly what the doctor ordered. So what if it was business? She hadn't done all that well in the personal department. Maybe professional success was where she was meant to make her mark. After all, look at Stephanie. She had no life outside the job and she was single, happy, rich. *Sexy, powerful, confident.* Okay, so her boss had a few tools Callie lacked. She'd simply start with the single and dedicated part and work her way up from there.

"Do you want me to order in dinner?" Callie asked.

"Please. Have it delivered at six. Noor's will be fine. The usual for me. Order the curry, too. I'm pretty sure hot and spicy is his—" Stephanie was interrupted when the door to the office swung open.

And in walked Dominic Colbourne. The British version of Stephanie Weaver. Only Stephanie didn't make Callie's body temperature spike and the soles of her feet sweat. Dominic Colbourne did. At least the magazine articles she'd read about him had. She'd never seen him in person. Amazingly, he was even better looking in real life. The Panther, they'd called him. Because of the silent, stealthy way he'd climbed the corporate mogul ladder. One after the other, in fact.

Seeing him in person, she thought that moniker might have been earned for an entirely different reason. He was all dark, smoldering good looks, with the rangy kind of physique that made women of all ages drool. Oh, he gave off a predatory vibe all right.

He barely spared her a look before murmuring something to Stephanie about being regrettably detained, his accent as delectable as the rest of him, then quietly disappeared into Stephanie's private conference room.

An hour passed. Dinner was delivered and consumed separately. The two of them in Stephanie's boardroom, she alone at her desk, privately fantasizing about just what was going on behind that closed door. *Figures,* she thought. Not only did Stephanie have the looks and the figure, and more money and power than Midas . . . now she got to have Dominic Colbourne, too. Probably right on the conference table. *God only knows what uses they'd found for that curry.* Hot and spicy indeed.

Another hour passed. Then another. Cassie finished the filing, faxing, and typing. Recorded all the deliveries, meetings, and various and sundry other details on her appointment book, the Palm Pilot Stephanie had assigned her five minutes after she was hired, and Stephanie's personal appointment scheduler on the computer.

She might have paused to listen on occasion . . . okay, strained to hear something, anything, even a hushed murmur, or an orgasm or two, behind the closed conference room door. But had only been rewarded with total silence. "If I have to put in all these extra hours, plus torture myself with images of Dominic Colbourne naked and doing God knows what on the conference room table, the least they can do is give me a good 'Oh baby, yes, yes, yes!' every once in a while," Callie grumbled.

She supposed screaming orgasms weren't exactly Stephanie's style. And she couldn't imagine anything more than a dark, glittering smile of satisfaction on Dominic's unearthly, gorgeous face. She sighed as she dumped the coffee filter and rinsed out the glass pot. Maybe she should stop by a bookstore and pick up a hot romance or something. If she was going to live vicariously through the orgasms of others, at least that way she'd be guaranteed some satisfaction.

Another hour passed and she'd finished sharpening every pencil in the office, wiped down her computer screen and even cleaned the lunch crumbs from her keyboard. Still not a peep from the conference room. Carnal or otherwise. She debated on whether or not to simply head home. It would likely be a bit awkward for them to come stumbling out of the conference room, all flushed with postcoital glow, only to find her perched behind her desk, waiting.

But Stephanie always demanded they do a wrap up, discuss what was on the slate for the next day, go over whatever problems needed handling, and so on. The last thing Callie wanted was to be summoned back when she was halfway home. But tomorrow she was definitely bringing the Hostess cupcakes to work with her.

It was after eleven o'clock when Stephanie suddenly emerged—not from the boardroom, but from her own offices, which had their own access to the boardroom. And a wide leather couch. Her boss looked fatigued, but was smiling.

I should be so lucky, Callie thought with a sigh. She glanced behind her boss, but the office door closed again, leaving Dominic sequestered within. *Probably washing up in Stephanie's private bathroom.* Which only spurred mental images of Dominic naked, water sluicing over his hard body, soaping up his—

"I'm sorry to keep you penned up out here for so long," Stephanie said, interrupting her visual interlude. "But I'm glad you stayed. I need another favor."

Callie sort of regretted letting go of the mental montage. It had been the highlight of her day. "You do?" she asked, forcing her thoughts back to her boss.

"I have to run out of here for another meeting."

"At eleven o'clock?" Callie said, the words popping out before she could think better of it. "I'm sorry, that's none of my—"

"No, that's okay. It's cocktails with an investor who just flew in from the west coast. It's the only time I can spare." She smiled, albeit a bit tiredly. "Success doesn't work nine to five. Never say no when opportunity knocks."

Callie definitely seconded that emotion. "What do you need me to do?"

"Stay here until Dominic is done with his call to Hong Kong. He's been on for a while. I'm not sure how much longer it will be."

Stay here. With Dominic Colbourne. Alone. Gee, what a hardship.

Not that he'd notice her any more than he had when he walked in. But even if it was only a silent elevator ride down to the lobby, she'd take it. When you put in eighteen-hour days, you had to take your thrills where you could find them. Hostess cupcakes and Dominic fantasies. She could do worse.

"If you're worried about being alone in the building with him," Stephanie said, apparently misreading her pause in responding, "don't be. Trust me, Dominic is only interested in making his next million. Women are too easy to conquer apparently." Then she shocked Callie by winking at her. "I know, I tried. Nothing. Zip."

Callie blinked. As much in shock that her boss had shared something so personal, as in the fact that even the glamorous, powerful Stephanie Weaver could get rejected by a man.

Stephanie dangled a set of keys. "These lock up the front door and activate my personal elevator. The main ones shut down when the security guy heads home at midnight." She glanced at her watch. "You might not need to use it, but just in case."

Callie took the keys. "Do you want me to lock up your offices, too?" Stephanie's private elevator was only accessible through her office.

"Please. I really appreciate this. I don't know what's holding things up. He took the call thinking it would be a fast one and he's been in there for almost an hour. Probably buying and selling a small country." She laughed. "And I thought I was driven."

"You're no slouch," Callie said, then grimaced when she realized she'd spoken aloud. She really needed some sleep.

Stephanie's eyes widened momentarily; then she laughed

again. "You're right." She scooped up a stack of folders from Callie's desk and shoved them into her leather bag. "Oh, and put us down for lunch tomorrow at Basil. We never got to finish our meeting." She was backing out the door when she paused one last time. "You should speak your mind more often. It suits you."

Peter hadn't thought so. *Screw Peter,* she thought smugly. Better yet, let Jennifer screw Peter. A mindless bimbette is obviously all he can handle. She straightened, smiled. "Thanks. I will."

"In fact, if you promise not to ever bullshit me, I'm making an executive decision right here and now. I'd like to retain you on a permanent basis as my personal assistant."

Callie opened her mouth, then closed it again and tamped down the urge to pump her fists in the air. "Thank you. I accept." Her toes did tap out a little victory dance beneath her desk, however.

"We can discuss salary after I get done meeting with Dominic." Stephanie's eyes gleamed. "Then you can start hiring your own staff. And mine, too. If everything goes as planned during lunch tomorrow, four weeks from today, the S. E. Weaver building will officially open for business. And we've got a lot of work to do. Get some sleep. Be here at seven tomorrow."

Callie stared at the closed office door for a full five minutes, not moving, as Stephanie's words sunk in. Personal assistant. Permanent salary. Hiring staff. Her own staff. Four weeks to get a twenty-five story building stocked, staffed, up and running. She didn't know whether to jump up and down . . . or throw up. She wanted to do both. But as soon as the latter feeling subsided, she was eating that whole damn box of Hostess cupcakes.

She pulled out a yellow legal pad and began making notes, writing so fast her tired brain and cramped hand finally couldn't keep up the pace and she reluctantly forced herself to stop.

Sleep, that was what she needed. A full night of it. Then she could begin taking steps toward total global dominance. She grinned. Or, at least her small corner of it anyway.

From subhuman to superhuman in sixteen months, three weeks and—she glanced at her watch and groaned. It was straight up midnight. And she had to be back here in seven hours. *So much for feeling like Cinderella on a power trip.* She stood up and stretched the kinks out of her back, then walked over to the windows to shut the blinds, but found herself staring down at the lights below. *Personal assistant to Stephanie Weaver.* A vibrant little hum of energy started buzzing through her despite the late hour. And she ignored the smaller, but just as profound twinge of regret. So, she wasn't going to do the wife and mom thing as she'd always dreamed. She'd just have to be satisfied with being Callie "Mogul" Montgomery instead, she thought, her lips twitching to a grin.

"Starting on the ground floor, ha!" she murmured, looking across the Potomac, beyond the Kennedy Center, to the lighted monuments on the mall and around the tidal basin. *For once I'm starting out on top.* "And this time I'm staying there." She punched her fists in the air, just as the door behind her opened.

"I beg your pardon."

Callie spun around, yanking her arms down and folding them instinctively across her chest. Dear God, how could she have forgotten all about Dominic Colbourne? "I—I'm sorry. I was just . . . stretching." She unfolded her arms, feeling quite self-conscious as he continued to stare at her. His thoughts were probably still a million miles away in Hong Kong, but at that moment, it sure felt like they were focused right on her.

She pasted on a smile . . . and hoped like hell he couldn't tell her nipples had gotten hard. Stephanie probably hadn't been kidding when she'd said he found women too easy to conquer. Lord knows her body was all ready to wave the white flag . . . and he'd only glanced at her.

"Do you need me to call you a car?"

"No, I'm staying close by. I could use the walk."

She tried not to look surprised. Dominic Colbourne didn't strike her as the type of guy who took midnight strolls. "Fine then," she said. "I'll escort you to the lobby if you're ready to go."

He nodded. "Lead the way."

His voice was deep, a bit rough. Was it simply fatigue? Or did it always sound like sandpaper on velvet? *Don't think about that or your nipples will stay hard for a week.* Shielding that part of her anatomy from view—not that he was noticing—she flipped the blinds closed, snagged her purse and keys from the desk, did a quick run through with the locks to the hallway door, then turned and gestured to Stephanie's office. "We'll have to take her private elevator. The others are shut down for the night."

He merely nodded, then stood waiting to follow her. She held the door to Stephanie's office open for him, then tried not to swoon when he brushed past her. He smelled like aftershave, freshly laundered cotton . . . and cumin. It packed quite a wallop at the end of an eighteen-hour day. Better than a cream-filled cupcake.

She locked the door behind him, allowing herself one brief glance at the leather couch, untouched, but so . . . available, then sighed a little as she walked over to the walnut-paneled door that led to the elevator. Maybe she'd skip the cupcake and the all-night bookstore and find fresh batteries for her vibrator instead. Of course, after tonight she'd probably never be able to look at that couch without blushing. She glanced at Dominic, thought of the fantasies she could easily come up with . . . and come to . . . and decided it would be worth it.

Using the key Stephanie had given her, she opened the elevator door. It was a small car, big enough for about six people if they stood very straight. Since it was usually just Stephanie, she supposed this was one time when size really didn't matter.

Except now it was her, alone with Dominic. And suddenly the elevator felt quite . . . intimate.

He stepped in after her, his expression more distant now. *Probably wondering what to do with the country he just bought.* And not how to ravish Stephanie's executive assistant in twenty-five floors or less. Darn it. She pushed the button for the lobby. He could have done it in less than five, most likely. Ten tops.

The door silently slid shut, making Dominic's presence even more overwhelming. She spent the next five floors wondering what he'd do if she suddenly ripped her clothes off and begged him to take her. She had to fight the urge to snicker. That would give the phrase "going down?" a whole new meaning, wouldn't it?

She spent the next five floors wondering if she should say something, perhaps verify his lunch appointment with Stephanie. She knew the urge had more to do with hearing him speak again, than any professional courtesy. But before she could open her mouth, the car suddenly lurched to a stop, throwing her back against the wall . . . and Dominic up against her.

A second later, the lights went out.

Chapter Two

Hard. That was the first thing that registered in Callie's mind. And the second.

It might have been the third as well, but then his hands were on her arms and he was gently, but firmly pushing himself away. She might have whimpered. Thankfully he misunderstood.

"I'm terribly sorry. Are you okay? Did I hurt you?"

Callie wondered how a man could sound so incredibly gentlemanly . . . and sexually carnivorous at the same time. Probably the latter element was just wishful thinking on her part.

"No, no I'm fine." *My nipples are permanently rigid and my panties are damp, but otherwise, totally fine.* She let out a little sigh.

"Don't care for the dark?"

Callie hadn't even given that part a thought yet. She was still dealing with how the full length of his body had felt pressed against the full length of hers. "No," she managed. "I mean, it doesn't bother me. It just, the whole thing took me by surprise."

She felt his hand at her elbow. How he knew exactly where she was in the pitch dark she had no idea. Panther sight, most likely. She tried not to shiver at the feel of his fingers brushing her skin, but it was almost impossible. *Afraid of the dark?* Ha! Not as long as he kept touching her, she wasn't.

"Hand me your keys."

"I beg your pardon?" she said, rattled from her thoughts.

"Your elevator keys," he repeated. "I think I can get us up and running again, but I need your set of keys."

She was glad for the dark for other reasons now. He couldn't see her hot blush. Here she was fantasizing about steamy elevator sex and he was calmly trying to get the hell out of here. And away from her, no doubt.

"Here," she said, pressing them into his hand. Broad palm, warm skin. She noticed every little detail. The dark did that to a person, enhanced other senses. At least that was what she told herself.

She shifted to the opposite wall as he stepped in front of her. She could hear the sound of the panel door being opened, but that was it. Unlike other men in crisis situations, he didn't breathe more heavily or swear. In fact, she was tempted to reach out and touch him to make sure he hadn't vaporized or something.

"No luck," he said after another minute passed. "No lights, no power. I pressed the emergency button, but if the main lifts are shut down, it isn't likely there is anyone left in the building to help us out."

She heard the jangling of the keys and reached her hand out. He dropped them in her palm without otherwise touching her. "You have excellent night vision," she uttered, impressed.

"So I've been told." There might have been the smallest hint of a smile in his words. "We should make ourselves comfortable. We're likely to be in here for a passing bit."

"Comfortable?" *Like taking all our clothes off and having hot, sweaty sex?* That would definitely pass the time. She managed not to suggest that to him. She definitely needed new batteries for her vibrator. And, perhaps, a social life might not be

a bad idea either. A shame she wouldn't have time for one anytime soon.

Callie heard the rustle of expensive fabric. Funny how his
clothes rustled far more sensuously than her Dress Shack
mark-down did.

Callie tucked her dress between her knees and carefully slid
to the floor. Then rolled her eyes at her precautions. Like he
could look up her skirt in pitch blackness. Still, she crossed her
ankles.

They sat in silence for what felt like an eternity, but was
probably only a few minutes. What did a person say to a em-
barrassingly wealthy, global magnate? A drop-dead sexy, em-
barrassingly wealthy, global magnate hunk, to be more
specific.

Several more minutes elapsed and the combination of the
silence, the darkness, and knowing he was mere inches away
from her and yet she couldn't even hear him breathe, finally
undid her.

"I set up your lunch—"

"How long have you—"

Both of them spoke, then broke off at the same time. She
chuckled. He did not. Even silent and invisible the man was intense.

"You go first," she said.

"Please, you."

You most definitely could, she thought with a private smile.
Then realized he couldn't see her anyway and let the grin surface. If she had to be stuck in this airless box for who knew
how many hours, the least she could do was enjoy her fantasies. "I was just going to say that I'd made a reservation for
you tomorrow, at Basil, for lunch with Ms. Weaver."

"Ah."

His voice gave her shivers. So cultured and smooth, and yet
somehow even a simple syllable carried an innate sexual in-
flection.

When he didn't say anything else, she prodded him. "Is that what you'd been about to ask? About your lunch meeting?"

There was a pause; then she swore she heard the slightest of sighs. What did that mean? Had she bored him to tears already? She readily admitted she didn't have the dulcet tones or smooth dialect he did, but—

"I was going to inquire how long you'd been in Ms. Weaver's employ," he asked.

Now it was her turn. "Ah." Somehow she doubted her voice gave him shivers. "Six weeks. Although I've put in so many hours, I probably qualify for major medical already."

"Yes, there is much to be done, I suppose."

He'd said it more to himself than to her. Again, they drifted into silence. Unable to see his face, or anything else for that matter, Callie found she had a bit more nerve. She'd never been particularly self-conscious before her marriage and subsequent divorce. Peter had done a bigger number on her than she liked to admit, but she'd been working at regaining her former sense of self. No sense in backing away from that goal now. Megamogul or not, she wasn't going to sit here in the dark in total silence. Not when listening to him talk was so very entertaining.

"Have you known Stephanie—I mean, Ms. Weaver—a long time?"

"Our paths have crossed from time to time."

Callie stifled a sigh. What did she have to say to get more than a handful of words out of him? Several things came to mind. None of which she actually dared to utter, not if she wanted to keep her job.

The air grew as stifled as the conversation. That was when it occurred to her that the power must have gone out in the whole building, not just the elevator. "I wonder why the generator hasn't kicked on," she mused. "I know we haven't officially taken full occupancy yet, but doesn't some kind of building code require that kind of backup system be in place?"

He didn't respond right away, and Callie felt her frustration level rise. "Listen," she said, a bit more forcefully than she'd intended, belatedly realizing that she was perhaps a teensy bit more claustrophobic than she'd ever realized. But it was easier to blame the little swell of panic on Dominic's refusal to be decent and talk to her, than to another possible weakness on her part. She had a long enough list to conquer as it was. *Speak your mind,* Stephanie had told her. Well, why the hell not? Being subservient certainly wasn't getting her anywhere.

"I know I'm a nobody, and you and I have less than zero in common, but if we're going to be stuck with one another, maybe we can at least chat to pass the time. I mean, there's nothing else to do in this stifling heat, in complete and total darkness."

As soon as the words left her mouth, Callie swore she could feel a spike of tension arc between them. And it wasn't businesslike tension, either.

"It's been my experience that there are a number of things one can do in the heat . . . and in the dark."

"I bet," she muttered, then snapped her mouth shut. Speaking her mind to Stephanie was one thing. Jeopardizing her entire career by pissing off the man Stephanie was hoping to finance a good deal of her new company was another.

"So," he said into the sudden stillness.

Callie's breath caught and held as she waited for him to tell her he'd see she was out of a job by sunrise.

"The cat has claws," he finished.

"Cat?" she spluttered, too surprised by the comment to reign it in. "And the panther has teeth, I see," she shot back. *Idiot! What do you think you're doing?* But, job security notwithstanding, a part of her took pride that she'd stood up for herself. Maybe if she'd done more of that during her marriage she wouldn't be in her current situation.

"So I've been told," he said, definite amusement in his tone now. "Although not quite as colorfully as you did, I'll admit."

This time it was Callie who let the silence spin out. She should have never provoked him.

"I can see why Stephanie has placed such a high level of trust in you," he added, at length.

"She hired me from a temporary agency a little over a month ago, sight unseen," she retorted, apparently unable to regain her common sense now that she'd tossed caution to the wind. "I don't know how much trust I've earned."

"You lack confidence in your worth to the company?"

"You're putting words in my mouth." *And why don't we just stop this verbal sparring and put other, more pleasurable things in our mouths, eh?* her little voice nudged. Right. Like she still wanted him, Mr. Obviously Misogynistic.

Well, okay, she still lusted. A little. But only after his body. And his voice. But he could keep his acerbic little comments to himself. "I'm not afraid of hard work and long hours," she told him. "I expect Ms. Weaver respects that. She definitely compensates me well for my time." *Or will, now that I've been hired full time,* Callie thought. "Trust, however, is another issue entirely."

"Indeed it is. However, Stephanie doesn't do anything without a great deal of forethought. Most especially when it comes to hiring people, even temporarily. I imagine she knows a great deal more about you than you realize."

That sat her back. Both what he'd said, and that he'd actually spoken more than one complete sentence at a time. But it was what he said that stuck in her mind. She'd hoped to present herself as confident, capable, and reliable. She knew it was silly, particularly in this day and age, to feel any sense of guilt or shame over being divorced. After all, there were myriad reasons that marriages came to an end, and it certainly didn't automatically point fingers in her direction. And yet, she couldn't honestly say she didn't point a few of those fingers at herself.

Apparently she had a bit further to go with this self-reclamation thing than she'd thought. She sighed, but curiosity got the better of her. "Did she say anything? Personally, I mean, about me?" She broke off with a little laugh. "What am I saying? Like the two of you were discussing anything having to do with me."

"We discussed a great many things," he said, as enigmatically as ever. "What sort of personal information is it you don't wish Stephanie to have?"

Callie hung her head. She'd been stuck a half an hour with the guy and somehow she'd managed to wedge her foot firmly in her mouth, along with most of the rest of her anatomy. If only he'd just ravished her instead. Now there was some guilt and shame she could have lived with. "Nothing," she said. "At least, nothing that would be important to her."

"Such as?"

Callie squinted in the dark, trying unsuccessfully to see even a hint of his face. She'd asked—demanded actually—that he talk to her. And, so he was making an honest effort, actually sounding interested in her responses, if not offering much of himself to the conversation. He didn't sound angry with her . . . actually, she couldn't quite tell what he was feeling. His words were smooth, dulcet and deep, but ultimately emotionless.

"Such as?" he prodded again, surprising her.

Enough that she simply answered him.

"Such as my entire life got turned upside down about a year and a half ago when I came home and found my husband on the dining room table with our dog sitter. Needless to say that while there was much panting and drooling involved, none of it had anything to do with our dog."

"How unpleasant."

She laughed. "Unpleasant. How British of you. Yes, it was. Bloody unpleasant actually."

He didn't laugh along with her. Instead, he asked, quite seriously, "And I take it this . . . discovery, left you feeling less than confident about your value in the relationship?"

"Can you blame me?"

"I think your husband's actions speak far more to his worth in the relationship than yours."

Callie paused, thinking that was an interesting way to look at it. One she rather liked. "Have you ever been married?"

"No."

If she stopped and thought about the fact that she was asking Dominic Colbourne such personal questions, she'd have never done it. So she didn't think about it. In the dark, they were simply two strangers, passing time. "Have you ever found your significant other in bed with another man?"

There was a pause. "No."

Callie folded her arms. "Then how can you know what it would make you feel like?" She half-laughed. "Never mind. I imagine women are so available to someone like you that you exchange them like some men change ties."

"Rather harsh."

"But true?"

Another pause. "At times, perhaps."

She nodded, satisfied. "Exactly. I don't think people like you, or Stephanie, for that matter, can understand what it's like for someone who doesn't wield much power. Not just financially, but emotionally, mentally. So sure of yourself, of your abilities, that you don't know what it's like to have your confidence seriously rattled. Or if you did, it was so long ago you've forgotten."

He didn't say anything and she compulsively filled the silence. Otherwise she'd have to realize just how insane it was to be saying this stuff to him.

"It wasn't like I was some meek, mild thing, living for her husband's approval. But at some point along the way, Peter's little comment here, well-meaning criticism there, began to add up and I allowed them to slowly erode my sense of self. It wasn't until I was no longer in the relationship that I saw how neatly he'd manipulated me into questioning myself, my value, my worth as a person. But knowing that doesn't automatically bring with it an instant reversal. It takes time to rebuild the strength and integrity you let someone else so neatly tear down. And there are all sorts of nasty little emotions that go with that, number one being guilt for letting the bastard do such a number on you in the first place, and shame for being such a stupid twit that you didn't realize it sooner."

She slowed, took a breath, shook her head, laughed a little. "Obviously, I still have some issues. All I was getting at was that some of us don't rebound swiftly from being passed over for a twenty-something blond with big boobs and the sex drive of a mink. Yes, it showed Peter to be the louse he was . . . is. But then you factor in his ever-so-rational explanation of why he was forced into it—yes, forced, as if my supposed inability to fulfill all of his needs was an engraved invitation to have sex on our dining room table with someone who wasn't as . . . I think the phrase he used was 'sexually limited.' Someone who, unlike me, didn't mind swinging from chandeliers, or flaunting her body in public, or . . . or any of the other 'sexually limiting' things I refused to do."

There was a pause, just long enough for Callie to groan inwardly at her rapid-fire speech.

"Did it occur to you that he only went on the offensive as a way to deflect his guilt back onto you?" Dominic asked into the sudden quiet. "Shifting blame is a highly effective tool, but only if the opposition allows their vulnerabilities to be manipulated."

Callie's bravado left her in a silent whoosh. "Yes, well, some vulnerabilities might exist for a reason."

"But rather than deal directly with them, with you, he took the cheap tour, fixing his problem, but not caring whether he fixed yours. I'd say *he* was the limited one, unable to meet *your* needs."

She smiled. "I hadn't thought about it exactly like that, but yes, you might have a point."

Dominic fell silent again. Callie sighed and leaned back against the paneled wall, thinking about what he'd said. If only the therapist she'd sought out when she'd separated had made half as much sense, she might have continued to see her.

"I think you underestimate yourself."

Dominic's words startled her.

"I know I did," she said honestly. "Do, still, sometimes. Like I said, it takes a while to climb out of the rut you allowed someone else to dig for you. I didn't tell you the kicker. Peter didn't even want the divorce. He honestly thought I'd be understanding, happy even, that he'd found a solution for his needs and so wouldn't have to bug me about fulfilling them anymore. As if he'd banged Jennifer on our dining room table, and God knows where else, as a favor to me." She shook her head. "And I actually wasted more than five minutes wondering if he might have a point. Pretty pathetic, don't you think?"

"Pathetic would have been giving in. You didn't, I assume, since a divorce did take place." There was an urgency to his tone that startled Callie. Surely he really couldn't care less about her personal life. He had nothing invested in her beyond knowing she worked for the woman he was working a deal with.

"You don't even know me, how do you know what—"

"I know what you've done with your life since then. You're strong. Focused. Driven."

"Ah, finally an area you do know a little something about."

"Precisely."

She smiled at the hint of amusement in his tone.

"You didn't wail and thrash about after the ugliness was over, you got on with the business of living."

Yeah, Callie thought, *but not with the business of loving.* That was an obstacle she had yet to deal with. In fact, with all the time she'd spent working for Stephanie, she'd mercifully been too tired to even think about it. And now, with her promotion, she supposed she wouldn't have to worry about it for some time to come. The idea of a further reprieve should have been a relief. Instead she felt that little nick of doubt. But she hadn't given up on love, not really, she'd simply chosen not to focus on it for a while. No one could blame her for taking a path that was more imminently rewarding, could they?

And the last person she wanted to discuss any of this with was a man like Dominic Colbourne. And yet she heard the words come out of her mouth anyway.

"Being successful in business hasn't exactly been a problem, but then, it never was. My problems were of a more . . . personal nature, I guess you'd say." And why the hell had she?

The silence descended once again, like a heavy blanket, smothering the conversation. Callie sighed inwardly, wishing yet again that she'd kept her mouth shut. She smiled wearily. So she was sexually repressed and verbally overeager. At some point in her life, maybe she'd find the happy medium between those two things.

Then, slowly, the stifling air between them seemed to take on a different charge, an added element or tension. It was as if she could sense him staring at her through the dark, those panther eyes of his seeing her clearly . . . with a predator's gleam. She shivered slightly and rubbed her arms, smiling at her flight of fancy. Add an overdeveloped fantasy life to the list. If only she had the nerve to act on even one of them, maybe she'd snuff out that last twinge of doubt.

Suddenly she felt something brush against her leg. She realized it was Dominic's foot. She stiffened slightly, edged away. He found her again, touched her deliberately.

"Would you tell me?" he asked quietly, and yet there was an edge to the request.

"Wh-what? Tell you what?"

"You mentioned feeling . . . limited."

"No, my ex thought I was limited. I thought—" She broke off then, not sure how to finish that sentence. "I don't know what I thought," she said quietly.

"Then don't tell me all the things your husband wanted you to do that you wouldn't."

Her mouth dropped open, but before she could find a reply—whatever that might have been!—he went on.

"Tell me the things you've always wanted to try . . . but haven't."

"I—" She couldn't form the words, still stunned by his request. Was he . . . what? Offering to help her out? She felt an almost hysterical bubble of laughter rush up her throat. Could he have possibly guessed where her thoughts had drifted, over and over again? And if so . . . why wasn't she insulted that he was arrogant enough to think he was the answer to all her problems?

Probably, she thought, *because he just might be.* Trapped alone, in the dark, her inhibitions were definitely diminishing rapidly . . .

"You wanted conversation," he murmured. "So tell me, Callie Montgomery," he coaxed, his tone relaxed, bordering on being disinterested. Only the sizzle zinging around them was anything but. "Tell me what you want. Then I'll tell you if it's worth doing."

Chapter Three

Worth doing? Dominic swallowed a curse or two. Since when had he thought anything that felt good wasn't worth doing? The sobering answer to that was . . . not in some time. In fact, he couldn't quite put his finger on the moment when he'd lost the ability to detect pleasure. Physical or otherwise. Or worse, caring about finding a way to experience it again in some fresh way that actually excited him.

Oh, he knew all the mechanics of achieving pleasure. But finding physical satisfaction was a long way from finding emotional satisfaction. Or so he'd so recently and thoroughly been told.

Which begged the question, when was the exact moment that everything had felt so . . . done. As if he'd accomplished it all? To the point where there was nothing left to achieve? At least nothing that truly excited him. And yet, if that was truly the case, and he'd done it all, why then did he still feel so bloody incomplete?

And why in God's name was he badgering this poor woman in some buggered effort to make sense of it all?

"That's a rather provocative request," Callie responded, finally finding her voice. A voice that was bit thready now. He could blame it on the closeness of the air, but he suspected something else entirely was affecting her. Or someone. Him.

And what a novel experience it was for him that her response hadn't been the least bit suggestive and yet managed to snag his attention anyway. Callie Montgomery. Office temp, woman scorned, survivor. With her sense of humor well intact, to boot. And perhaps that was suggestion enough for him. Because she certainly provoked him, whether she intended to or not.

"I can be a very provocative man," he said. Or, at least, at one time he had been. He couldn't recall the last time his pulse had spiked at the sound of a woman's voice, the scent of her skin, the little catch in her breath when he lowered his mouth to hers. Or when he'd stopped noticing or caring.

He was certain Isabella could tell him, and probably had during their marathon discussion this evening. He should have never placed that call to Hong Kong. Now it was his turn to smile in the dark, though there was absolutely no humor in it. Not talking to her tonight would have only delayed the inevitable. He supposed he should be thankful that she'd honestly cared enough for him to sit him down, figuratively and literally, and talk to him like she had. No screaming, no vituperative poison, though he suspected he deserved both. She was better than that, the best, in fact. She was the true meaning of friend, one of the few he'd ever had. He suspected that of the two he was the more fortunate that she'd remain his friend, even after tonight. Although she probably counted herself equally blessed that she was no longer his lover. Or his fiancée.

Neither of the latter roles had suited them, not really. He should have known better than to push things that direction in the first place. It had simply made sense to him at the time. A rational approach to moving into the next phase of his career.

The fact that he'd thought of marriage in terms of his career should have been a bold warning right from the start.

And what did it say about him that the best thing he could do for a woman was to let her go? Yet, if he couldn't love a woman like Isabella, the way a man should love his life partner, then he might as well leave the rest of them alone.

Which didn't remotely explain why he wasn't going to leave Callie alone. Or maybe it did. She'd been burned, she wasn't looking for romance, much less love . . . but she was looking to prove herself sexually. He'd done his share of burning, and it was now painfully clear he wouldn't know romance, much less love, if it came up and slapped him in the face. But he did know something about proving himself sexually. A lot, in fact. So, maybe there was something he could give a woman after all. This woman, anyway. Proof.

"Maybe that's my problem," she responded, followed by a sound that was part laugh, part sigh. "I'm not provocative. Although, I suppose it's only considered provocative if someone else thinks it is. Otherwise, it's just sort of an embarrassing attempt. Isn't it?"

He found his lips curving. Something she managed to make him do with relative ease. Considering his mood when he'd left Stephanie's office earlier, that was a remarkable accomplishment. "Are you saying I'm past my prime, then?"

Her laughter came then, and he felt something inside him begin to unwind. This wasn't the well-rehearsed cocktail banter he'd partaken in a thousand times over. In fact, he had no idea what she'd say, or how she'd react to things he might say. Which made him want to say all sorts of things to her. Provocative indeed.

"I'm fairly certain you'll be ninety and using a walker, and women will still swoon when you glance their way," she said.

His eyes widened at the flattery . . . and the dry tone in which it was delivered. Meaning she understood his appeal . . . but wasn't personally affected by it?

"I was referring to me anyway," she clarified. "As the embarrassing attempter."

"Meaning you don't think yourself capable of saying provocative things, committing provocative acts?"

"Oh, I might be able to suggest them, even do them. I'm just not certain of the reaction I'd get."

"So you'd rather go on not knowing."

Her tone was wry. "It's rather a moot point since it's not like I've been faced with much of a choice lately."

"Some opportunities have to be made. If you wait for them to present themselves, you'll miss out on the best of the lot."

"Point taken. But I work long hours, with one other woman, after which I go home, sleep, then head back to work. Where is the opportunity?"

"Everywhere. On the street corner, picking up coffee or lunch—Stephanie does let you eat, doesn't she?"

"We order in."

"Delivered by?"

Callie laughed. "Old Mr. Peterson. If he's my only shot at being a sexual rebel, I'd just as soon remain pathetically uninformed, thanks."

Dom felt his smile spread to a grin. "Fine then, we'll discuss it hypothetically."

"Will we?" she said, imitating his sardonic tone.

Oh yes, she was quite refreshing. And incredibly provocative, without even trying. Not that she'd believe him if he told her that. No, she'd require proof positive. There was that word again. Proof.

"Yes, we will," he decided, unsure exactly what it was they'd do. At the moment, he refused to put boundaries on it. "Hypothetical situation number one. Say you whistle for a taxi at the same time as another bloke, a man who catches your eye. What do you do so that you catch his?"

She didn't answer right away. Dom relaxed further, folding his arms, finding himself quite interested in her response.

"Well, if he takes the cab without even glancing my way, nothing. I don't want or need the attentions of a jerk."

"True. And if he pauses? Allows you a moment to plead your case, as it were?"

Callie sighed on another half laugh. "Well, I'm no good on the eyelash batting, hip wiggle, hair-flip thing."

"To the utter and complete disappointment of the entire male population, I'm sure."

She laughed outright. "Thanks, but even if I were foolish enough to buy that, which I'm not, I wouldn't go that route anyway. If he's responsive to the whole giggly bimbette routine, that's another guy I'd just as soon not have paying me any attention."

"First off, I must clarify that, as part of said male population, there will always be some element of the 'bimbette routine' as you put it, that we'll respond to. It's in our DNA. However, responding to it and acting on it are two entirely different things. And I respect your decision. Well done. So, how would you get his attention?"

"I don't suppose just smiling and asking him if he'd like to share the cab would be considered a provocative thing."

"Not initially. But never underestimate the impact of a fresh smile and a sincere tone." He grinned. "Of course, if you're wearing something deliciously seductive, that won't really matter."

Callie sighed. "The Woof Factor?"

He chuckled. "Absolutely."

"And here I thought British men were more staid than their beer guzzling, monster truck–loving, American counterparts."

"We're all mongrels at heart."

"So then what's the point of my trying to be provocative? Basically all I need is white teeth and a short skirt, according to you."

"And what's not provocative about short skirts, I ask you?"

She laughed. "I thought we were discussing this on a more, I don't know, intellectual level. You don't strike me as a man who drools, at least not visibly, over everything in a tight skirt."

Actually, if she wanted to know the honest truth, he hadn't drooled over much of anything of late, tight-skirted or not. And as much as he'd like to claim it was because he'd been affianced for the past several months, he knew it went farther back than that. Had he honestly become such a driven, single-minded cad that even the simple pleasures of girl watching had become lost on him? He was the pathetic one, after all. "How do I strike you, then?"

Again she lapsed into silence. His pulse accelerated slightly, and the longer the silence stretched, the more he anticipated her response. As if the opinion of a woman he'd known all of an hour or so could matter all that much? Perhaps it should. Perhaps had he cared more about the thoughts and opinions of others, he wouldn't feel so emotionally adrift. Isabella claimed that if he'd let someone inside his head, rather than simply his body or his wallet, he'd feel more whole, more complete.

And a whole lot less lonely.

He didn't want to think that of himself, that he was that closed off. Since when was being driven, focused, successful, something to be ashamed of? He didn't want for wealth or power. And if what he'd put Isabella through was any indication, love was a complication he was better off without anyway.

Callie's quiet response mercifully broke his uncharacteristic reflective train of thought. "You strike me as a dominant male. Very alpha. Yet also very controlled. I'd think you'd have little patience for game playing or vapid conversation. With either sex."

Dominic thought she'd pegged him pretty well. Domineering and impatient. Oh yes, quite the catch he was.

"I also think you appreciate finer things, including women."

"You think I value form over substance?"

"I've seen the photos in the various magazines and newspapers. You might not squire the implant-enhanced Bambi's or Bunny's of the world around town, but I haven't seen too many Enid's or Esther's either."

Dominic never paid attention to the media. Not where his personal life was concerned. He had so little of one, whatever they wrote about him couldn't be of much consequence. Though some of those women he'd squired about had felt otherwise. Isabella had chosen to remain out of the spotlight altogether, preferring to keep their private life very private. Of course that was relatively easy to do when they only saw each other once or twice a month. "I suppose you have a point there. I have no defense."

She laughed. "None needed. Honestly, if you have your pick of the litter, why go with the runt, right? But that was the point I was making earlier."

"That you consider yourself the runt of the litter? That's quite harsh and entirely un—"

"No, I have more self-esteem than that. But it's sort of the men-don't-make-passes-at-girls-who-wear-glasses defense. I'm in that group. The kind of woman who's not drop dead, not fringe weird . . . but firmly part of the invisible middle. I could probably fling myself at a guy and he wouldn't even notice."

"I doubt that."

"You know what I mean. Dog DNA or not, it only pays to be provocative when you can put some punch behind your pucker."

"And you think you lack . . . punch?"

She didn't respond. All he heard in the darkness was a little sigh. Wistful. Or perhaps simply resigned.

"So, you believe if you smiled and asked to share a cab, the gentlemen in question wouldn't accept?" he pressed.

"He might be gallant and allow me to have the cab, which is charming, but gets me nowhere since he'll be left behind on the sidewalk. Or he might accept the compromise and climb in with me." She sighed again. "Then smile blankly and spend the entire ride staring out the window."

Definitely resigned, he thought. "Which is precisely the point *I* was making earlier. That is your opportunity. Right there, in the cab. He's basically a captive audience to your charms."

Callie snorted.

"You seriously underestimate yourself."

"Do I? You walked into Stephanie's office and didn't even glance in my direction. I'm sure if someone asked you, five minutes later, to describe me, you'd have come up blank."

"Don't judge other men's reactions by mine. I'm the last person who'd fit the present scenario."

There was a pause and Dominic wished he had directed the conversation away from himself. But she'd surprised him with her comment. And he'd been less than happy to realize she was right.

"Why do you say that? Because we're from different class levels, or whatever the American equivalent is to that?"

"I can be accused of many things, but snobbery isn't one of them." He managed a smile. "Like most men, I'm an equal opportunity ogler."

"Then I was dismissed because . . ."

"You weren't dismissed, because you were never considered." He swore when she made a little insulted noise. "That came out entirely wrong."

"But does prove my point pretty darn well."

He sighed. "What I meant to say was, I haven't noticed any woman in quite some time. My attentions have been somewhat diverted from that pleasure of late."

"Well, I hate to make you drag your head out of the sand,

but you're not alone. And observant, ogling, or just plain making it through the day, men don't typically notice women like me."

"I have."

There was instant silence and another little spike of tension arced about the small interior.

"You could hardly avoid it," she said after a moment, her tone dry, dismissive. Though he'd bet a small fortune she'd felt it, too. "You were pretty much trapped into noticing me." She laughed a little then, but all the lovely warmth had left it. "Maybe that's the ticket. Get a guy trapped in total darkness so he has to overlook the form to get to the substance."

"I found nothing lacking in your form," he said quite seriously, then tried to picture her and realized, to his shame, just how right she'd been. He remembered soft brown hair, an expressive face, and a figure that was rather . . .

Invisible. Not overtly . . . anything.

The skin at the back of his neck heated and for once he was thankful for the darkness. Surely it was just him, though. Any other man, any man who was less distracted, would certainly have noticed her warm smile, her lively tone, her acerbic wit. Along with the package it came in.

"Thank you," she said at length, but didn't add anything else.

The flush on his skin deepened. He cleared his throat. "So, you're in the cab, he's staring out the window . . . and you say?"

She didn't respond right away. "I say nothing. I know I could mention the weather. Sports. Comment on the latest editorial in the *Post,* or whatever the current scandal is on the Hill. All of which might get me a nod, a grunt, or even an intelligent response. But none of which I assume is what you meant by provocative."

"Depends on the comment you make."

That got a slight laugh out of her, which in turn made him

feel like he'd won the lottery or something. Since when had making small talk, putting a woman at ease, been such a challenge for him?

Never. But that was likely due to the fact that the substance of the small talk . . . or the woman . . . rarely mattered to him. This conversation had ceased to fit that profile the moment she'd uttered her first word.

"So you say nothing rather than take the risk," he went on. "Rather than make an opportunity."

"For what? Rejection? The best I could hope for would be a nonplussed expression, followed by a very uncomfortable cab ride."

"I could toss out the trifle expression that you'd never know until you tried, but you—"

"Would toss right back that I've been faced with enough humiliation, thanks. I wasn't cut out to be provocative. Some of us aren't. So I'll have to find my future romances the old-fashioned way."

"Which is?"

"Letting well meaning friends fix me up with the remaining single relatives they have left in their families. Agonizing over what to wear, how far you'll go on your first date, then going out to dinner, smiling, nodding at appropriate moments during what turns out to be interminably boring small talk, discovering there's a really good reason why he's the last single man in your best friend's family tree, no longer worrying if you have spinach stuck in your teeth because you're not going to kiss this guy good night anyway."

He couldn't help it, he laughed. "Sounds quite horrific."

"It is, trust me. But what's a single girl to do? Bar crawling lost its appeal during my college years. Singles groups and spa memberships fell by the wayside shortly after that. I don't have time for civic or charitable organizations, being my own charitable organization of late, and the only unmarried guy in my neighborhood under the age of seventy-five, while gorgeous, spends the occasional few minutes we spend picking out fruit at the corner stand, commiserating with me over the lack of single men. So blind dates are pretty much all that are left."

"I still say you're limiting your scope. Surely there are other men at that fruit stand . . . thumping their melons, as it were."

She snickered. "Not that I've noticed. And I realize just how whiny I sound, here. Honestly, finding a man isn't something I spend an overt amount of time thinking about, nor do I think that a woman necessarily needs a man in her life to be happy or fulfilled."

The reverse being true as well, he thought. Or at least he had.

"I'm very happily focused on rebuilding a career," she went on determinedly, sounding almost too determined, if there was such a thing. "And despite the long hours and hard work, I very much enjoy working for Stephanie. In fact, just before she left tonight, she offered to hire me full time. So, it's not like I'm going to have a lot of time for romance in my life anytime soon, anyway."

He spoke without questioning the wisdom of revealing the troubling direction his thoughts had taken. "A few hours ago I would have heartily agreed with that assessment," he said quietly. "Applauded it even."

"But not now?"

"I'm not sure." He rubbed at the spot in the center of his chest, as if he could assuage the odd ache that lay somewhere below it, then realized what he was doing and pulled his hand away. "Maybe it's simply a matter of flowing toward what comes more easily to us, whether it's business, sex, love. Not to say we don't risk rejection anyway, just that, as you mentioned before, we're confident enough in our skills in whatever area we've chosen, not to allow it to affect us too deeply, or ultimately sway us away from it."

"And you're telling me you lack confidence in yourself in one of those areas?"

"Don't sound so surprised."

"You don't strike me as someone who is unsure of anything."

"Appearances are deceiving." Hers certainly were. Dutiful and loyal assistant, willingly subordinate to her boss in order to get ahead . . . and yet, on the inside, maybe still yearning to be a provocateur, the dominant one, a sexual aggressor. His body hardened at the thought of being the man who guided her down that particular carnal path. She was sharp, focused, and in tune enough with her body's needs to know she wanted things beyond what she'd experienced thus far.

"It's well documented that you made your first million when most guys were still in college," she said. "You have women throwing themselves at you right and left, and considering you didn't refute my opinion of you as an alpha male, I'm guessing the women you catch aren't complaining later."

"Which rules out business and sex, but not—"

"Love?"

Dominic fell silent.

"Is it that you don't believe in it?" she asked, when the silence dragged on. "Or are you simply too jaded to fall prey to it?"

"Jaded. I suppose I would qualify there." But he knew that was the easy out. She'd confessed her weaknesses, her vulnerabilities . . . so it was only fair that he respond in kind. Despite the fact that he'd never once thought of doing so with anyone else. But why shouldn't he? After all, this was one midnight confession that wouldn't likely come back to haunt him. Callie Montgomery was not a gameplayer or a gold digger with an agenda. He had every expectation that they'd exit this elevator come morning and go on their merry ways, back to their busy lives, never to give this conversation another thought. So there was no real risk.

And yet he hesitated even after he'd opened his mouth. *Let someone inside your head, instead of just your body or your wallet.* Isabella's words echoed through his mind. Risk indeed. "I'm not sure what I believe," he said quietly, as much to himself as to her. "I've never given it much thought, really." He let out a short laugh. "Which I suppose is worse, really, than actually having an opinion on the matter, isn't it?"

"So, you're saying you've never been in love? Not ever?"

"Boyhood crushes, perhaps. But I was focused on other achievements at a fairly early age. Didn't leave much room for anything else. I suppose, after a time, it became habit, patterned behavior."

"Well then, it's more a matter of making room in your life to allow it to happen then, isn't it? Or meeting the person who makes you want to make room." She made a little sound of amusement. "Sounds like you're the one missing out on opportunities."

He thought about that. Isabella had said much the same thing to him, that if she'd been the right one, he'd have wanted to make time for her. Would have instinctively done the right thing. He doubted her then, but now . . . ? "I'd like to believe that," he said, realizing as he said it how much he meant it. "But there have been some very wonderful women in my life, deserving women, and I haven't felt that . . . whatever it is one feels to justify the truth in all that romance mumbo jumbo."

"Jaded indeed," she said. "But just because a person is wonderful doesn't mean she's the right person. You know, *the one.* Or maybe it means you're not giving her the chance. Have you allowed yourself to be swayed by that romance mumbo jumbo? Give in to that first rush of emotion? Beyond the sexual rush, I mean," she added pointedly.

"I'm not sure I'd have the first clue how. Or that I've felt that specific, nonsexually oriented rush you talk about."

"Oh, I find that very hard to believe."

He wished he felt otherwise. "I understand the grand gesture as well as the smaller, meaningful one. But romance, so I've been told, is more than flowers or a weekend in Paris."

Callie laughed. "It's a damn good place to start while you're looking for it though."

He smiled, but it faded quickly. "Romance, the kind you're speaking of at any rate, is more than that. What you mean is the whole of the emotional involvement between two people. The longing to please one another, the need to fulfill your partner in some way beyond the material gesture, a way that brings pleasure and satisfaction to both of you on some deep, intimate level that goes far beyond the physical."

Callie sighed. "I don't know. I think that was the best description of how romance should be that I've ever heard. You're more in touch than you think. And maybe it's a matter of being more distracted than jaded."

"Well, I can describe it." Thanks to Isabella anyway. "But I haven't the first bloody idea how to experience it."

"So, you're saying we're both emotionally stunted, then." She'd said it in a clearly amused, self-deprecating way. But he responded dead seriously.

"No, what I was saying was that you could be intensely sexually provocative but you'll never find out because you don't dare to."

"Then it follows that you could be the most romantic, emotionally in tune man on the planet. But you'll never know either because you write yourself off without even trying. We are stunted."

Again, silence descended between them and Dominic found himself swearing silently. What in the hell had gotten into him? Isabella's rejection shouldn't have sent him into this kind of ridiculous tailspin. It was probably just the prolonged isolation, sitting here in the dark, with nothing better to do than dwell on the supposed weaknesses of his, which she'd so carefully itemized and detailed for him.

He'd thought he was merely provoking Callie because she was so ripe for the provocation. How he'd allowed himself to become the subject of this conversation he had no idea. Worse yet, Callie hadn't started it, he had. What he could do, however, was shut the hell up. He was facing the largest merger he'd ever put together, which meant the next ten days were likely to be the most frenetic and most important of his entire life. He had no time for this . . . this . . .

"So," Callie said softly, easily breaking his train of thought, "if we wanted to change that . . . it means we have to be willing to risk it, right? That I'd have to be willing to . . ."

She paused for so long, he didn't think she was going to finish. Only he wasn't relieved at the thought, wasn't hoping she'd give up and let it drop so he could spend his time thinking about more important things, the so very important things he spent every waking second of every day thinking about. Not one of which he could force to mind at that very moment.

Because his entire attention had been neatly captured by this one purportedly invisible brunette. And he was dying, sitting so still he wasn't even drawing breath as he literally strained to hear her next words.

"Just how would a person go about finding her inner sexually provocative self?" she queried, more to herself than to him. "Where do I begin?"

His body tightened, surprising him with the ferocity of his sudden reaction.

"I mean," she went on, her tone a bit less confident now, but nonetheless determined. "I've had romance, I've had intimacy. I know what love is, and I don't want it in my life right now. I don't have time for it anyway. But I do miss the other parts. The zing of awareness, the rush you get when you look at someone and want him. Instantly, immediately, totally. So, maybe it's time I figured out how to go after those parts, just reach out and take what I want. Maybe it's a self-fulfilling prophecy that works both ways. If I don't believe it will happen, it won't. But if I just believe, then . . ."

Dominic could have told her she was doing a damn fine job of it without even trying. He had to curl his hands inward to keep from reaching for her right then and there. It was insane, this sudden need he had to yank her against him, where he could prove to her quite easily that she was a bloody lot closer to achieving her goal than she knew.

She laughed, but this time it was tinged with a bit of resignation. "A shame we can't compare notes when the opportunity arises. I could tutor you on the finer points of emotional entanglements. At least the 'what not to do' parts anyway, and maybe a few of the 'to do' parts," she added a bit wistfully. "And you could mentor me in—"

"Name one thing you would do in this elevator with a man you want," he said abruptly and somewhat heatedly. But he was only human damn it and she'd pushed him far enough. "If you knew he'd respond positively to anything you requested, name the first thing you'd tell him to do."

He tried to slow his heart rate down, so he could hear her slightest intake of breath, but it was impossible. Bugger if she didn't have him riled up in a way he couldn't remember being riled in a very long time. Ever, perhaps. He knew it was strictly the situation they'd found themselves in, that neither of them would perhaps react like this in any other place or time. But they weren't in any other place or time. They were here. Alone. Together. And while he didn't want any of her instructional tutoring on the finer points of romance and love . . . he was pretty damn sure he could take care of one or two of her concerns.

He might not have experienced that exquisite torture of prolonged sexual tension in some time, but he bloody well hadn't forgotten what it felt like. And the tension singing between them at the moment was thick enough he was surprised it hadn't fogged the air.

"Tell me," he repeated. "We'll consider it lesson number one."

"In?" She breathed the word, her voice hardly more than a hoarse whisper.

He leaned forward, knocked off one of her high heels and drew a slow line with his finger up the center of the sole of her foot. She shuddered, then gasped when he closed his hand around her ankle.

"In how to provoke a man into giving you whatever you want."

Chapter Four

Callie swore she'd swallowed her tongue the instant he'd touched her. Either that or her libido was so firmly lodged in her throat she was going to choke on it instead. Either way she couldn't answer him.

Dear God, had he really just said what she thought he'd said? And did he mean to be that man?

His hand on her ankle said yes.

She rubbed her arms . . . and pressed her thighs together. Surely she was misunderstanding—

"Tell me what you want done to you, Callie," Dominic said, his voice dark and rough, his accent making the words even more commanding.

She opened her mouth, but surely she couldn't just say it. Hell, she didn't even know what *to* say. *Isn't this about taking risks?* her little voice nudged. Well, hypothetical risk-taking was one thing. Leaping head first into the fire for real was quite another.

"Is it the idea of doing something sexual in an elevator that's so distasteful," he asked, his fingers lightly stroking the inside of her ankle. "Or that you'd be putting yourself in an explicit situation in public?"

She started to speak, but was forced to clear her throat—

twice—before she could finally answer. "Exhibitionism isn't a big turn on to me."

"Because it was to your ex."

He'd made it a statement. And based on what she'd said earlier, she could see why he thought he was right. "I don't think I'd consider it anyway. The thrill of being caught, literally, with my pants down, instills panic, not lust."

"So, the idea of a man having his way with you in the backseat of a taxi—"

"Isn't one of my fantasies, no."

"Well then, what is?"

She'd walked right into that one. "I—" She broke off, suddenly aware of just how unreal it was that she was actually sitting in the dark, even contemplating revealing her most basic desires to Dominic Colbourne.

"Just one," he commanded softly.

"I—I don't have specific . . . scenarios."

"So, it never once crossed your mind, when you stepped into this elevator, what it would be like if I caught your eye, noticed a flicker of interest, and . . . pursued it." His hand tightened ever so imperceptibly.

She tried not to squirm, certain he would know then just how much his words, the images they painted, were affecting her. This was a lesson . . . a discussion . . . not reality. No matter how badly she wanted it to be. "But you didn't," she managed. "And anything I did wouldn't have changed that. Only made you uncomfortable."

"I'm not uncomfortable now."

"But you're also not—"

"Oh. But I am."

There was no questioning what he'd meant. Just as there was no stifling the tiny gasp that slid out between her lips when he drew his fingers along her calf. "So, you're . . . we're . . . what, role playing?" she asked, tentatively, not sure what answer she wanted him to give.

"Hardly."

Her remaining breath left her in a silent whoosh.

"Now I've made you uncomfortable," he said.

"Hardly," she said, before she could stop herself. "I—I mean—"

His fingers skated back to her foot and he began to knead her arch. The shock of pleasure that brought made her moan before she could stifle it.

"You mean the kind of discomfort this brings you . . ." He once again stroked a finger down the center of the sole of her foot. Her shuddering reaction to even that minimal stimulation was palpably intense, "isn't all that uncomfortable?"

She said nothing.

"Say it, Callie."

Dear God, his voice was downright hypnotic. Did she dare let him pull her under the spell he was rapidly weaving? Here in the dark? Away from everything that was real?

"No," she breathed, then held her breath while she waited to see what he'd do next.

"You like my hands on you."

She nodded, trying not to whimper when he took his hand away. She should have known this was too good to be true.

"You like my hands on you," he repeated.

She hadn't realized he expected an answer. "Yes."

"Then tell me where you want me to put them. And I will."

She heard the rustle of fabric, then detected the scent of his cologne as the air shifted when he moved closer to her. When he spoke, his voice was intensely close, almost touching her ear.

"You've provoked me, Callie," he said, making her skin prickle in awareness and her heart begin a rapid tango inside her chest. "With your words, your thoughts, your laughter."

"I—I didn't mean to. Not . . . like this."

Now he chuckled, and it made her squirm. Pleasurably so.

"So, you'd rather I retreat to my corner?"

She shifted slightly, knowing, even though she couldn't see him, that his mouth was a mere breath away from hers.

"Tell me to go away," he said softly, his voice vibrating in the dark. "Tell me not to touch you, not to do whatever you command me to do . . . and I'll stop this."

She felt his mouth brush against hers. Not quite a kiss, more a fleeting impression of warmth, of softness.

"Tell me," he commanded, his lips by her ear. "Tell me you don't want me to want you."

She shivered. "I—" Dear Lord, what was she about to do?

His teeth briefly pinched her earlobe. How did he know right where she was? He didn't fumble, didn't touch any part of her other than the part he meant to touch. In the dark, knowing he was so close, yet totally unaware of his intentions, of where he'd touch her next, had her fighting to sit still.

He brushed her lips with his fingertips. She quivered. "Can you see me?" The darkness was complete, and her eyes weren't ever going to adjust enough to be able to see him. How had his?

"I can scent you."

Dear God. The shiver became a shudder. The muscles between her legs tightened almost painfully. "The Panther," she breathed, not meaning to say it out loud. But it simply slipped out.

That chuckle again, only this time his breath moved her hair so it tickled against her neck, so sensitized now even that brief caress made her pulse leap. "When it suits me."

Then his fingers were on her face. Not holding her, framing her face, but tracing the contours. So lightly it was almost as if it was air brushing her skin.

"Tell me to stop soon, Callie." He reached in and nipped at her bottom lip, releasing it before his teeth could leave a mark.

She moaned.

"Or tell me to keep touching you." He pressed a long, firm finger across her lips. "But be warned . . . I'll expect to be told where to touch you . . . and how . . . and for how long." He slowly drew his finger from her mouth, making her breath hitch at the protracted contact. Then his lips were touching hers, a breath separating them from an actual kiss. "Tell me, Callie. Provoke me."

Her pulse drummed so hard it thundered inside her ears. Her throat tightened until she could barely breathe, much less swallow . . . or speak. She willed him to simply take over, take the responsibility away from her, to allow her to sink under and give in to the wicked spell of seduction he'd so expertly weaved.

Then she felt the air shift as he moved away, surprised at how swiftly she'd become in tune to his presence. "No," she blurted, instinctively reaching for him.

She'd barely brushed her hands against him when her wrists were taken hostage in his grip. Not harshly, but definitively. "I'll be the one doing the touching," he said. And for the first time, she heard a thread of hoarseness in his voice.

The sense of empowerment that roared through her was swift and certain. She wasn't the only one being affected by this. She really had provoked him.

"Yes, Callie," he said, as if he could read her mind. And maybe he could.

She was rapidly beginning to believe anything was possible. "I want to be touched by you." She swore she felt him shudder, felt the air between them tremble.

"But then we've only begun, haven't we?"

She nodded, then realized she needed to speak, said, "Yes."

"This is about you, about what you want to feel, want to be made to feel."

She pressed her thighs tight and fought against the urge to squirm.

"So there will be no touching. Only directing me where you want to be touched." He took her hands and slid one behind the small of her back. "So we can leave them here." He lifted the other one, pressing it to the wall above her head. "Or here."

Her breath locked in her throat. Trembling harder now, she tugged one hand free . . . and tucked it behind her back with the other one. Shocked at how badly she'd wanted to keep it above her head.

"Fine," he told her, then leaned in and ran the tip of his tongue along the side of her neck. "We'll leave them here." He crossed her wrists, pinning them with one hand, his grip tightening briefly, enough to let her know he wanted her to keep them that way, before withdrawing his hands all together. "For now," he added, the words barely audible above her ragged breathing.

She turned her head as she felt him move away, straining to see him, wishing she had the same sense of his body's position as he did of hers.

When he spoke again, it was clear he was back in the opposite corner. "You are completely in charge of what happens next."

I don't think so, she thought.

"Why the impatient sound? Tell me what just went through your mind."

She hadn't realized she'd made a noise. Did the man have total jungle sensory perception? The very idea made her body tighten. As it was, she was so highly sensitized she could already feel every inch of the fabric of her dress against her skin. Her nipples had tightened almost to the point of pain. And there wasn't enough pressure in the world to assuage the ache that had become an almost constant throb between her legs.

"I don't feel like I'm in control," she said, striving to sound like she was. "You understand the seduction game far better than I do."

"This is no game," he said, sounding almost insulted at the very notion.

She laughed shortly. "It's all a game."

"Now who's the jaded one?" he responded, obviously amused.

"What if I say that I trust you to take things from here?"

"Then you won't have learned anything."

Oh, I'm already on information overload, she wanted to tell him. "You'll teach me," she said, damning the quiver that threaded through her words. But the very idea of him "tutoring" her in the finer points of seduction . . . and all the pleasurable things it might lead them to do, was almost enough to make her climax just thinking about it. And though he'd moved out of her immediate personal space, that hadn't remotely lessoned the tension screaming between them. In fact, it seemed to increase it somehow. Her crossed wrists even more so, along with the slight arch to her back the position forced her into. Supplicant, she thought. And felt her panties soak at the very idea.

"No," he said, then flicked his fingers lightly against the sole of her foot making her flinch—and moan softly. "You'll teach yourself."

Callie was overwhelmed with conflicting sensations, emotions, but was afraid if she let herself analyze them in any depth, she'd lose whatever nerve she had to see this through. And after long months of celibacy, she was *not* going to jeopardize what was looking to be the highlight of her entire year. Hell, maybe her whole life.

She heard the rustle of fabric as he shifted away from her again . . . and made her decision. "Take off your jacket."

There was a sudden stillness and she held her breath. Then there was another rustle of fabric, followed by the twin sensations of linen and silk lining as he drew his suit jacket across her legs as proof that he'd done as she'd asked.

It was immensely heady, the duality of her position here. She commanded him, and yet it was she who willingly kept her wrists pinned behind her back.

"Now your tie."

"Do you plan to undress me entirely?"

"Isn't that my prerogative?" She grinned when he paused. "You set up the rules."

"That I did," he said quietly.

She said nothing, merely waited. She was rewarded shortly with the sounds of silk sliding on silk. Never had her sense of hearing been so acute. Then she swiftly drew in her breath as her hypersensitivity to touch was also tested. He drew the length of silk tie along the inside of her ankle . . . then higher.

"What—are you doing?"

"Offering proof."

She struggled to keep from moaning when he continued the soft torture up past her knee. She could easily flick away the tie, but that would mean ending the invisible bond on her wrists . . . and possibly the end of their agreement. No, he'd set it up so that she'd have to tell him, clearly, what she wanted. And what she didn't want.

"I didn't ask you to do that," she said, not in as commanding a tone as she'd have liked. The silk was doing incredible things to her senses. But she instinctively knew she shouldn't let him have the upper hand, no matter that she'd been ready to beg him to have just that.

You won't learn anything that way.

She wasn't entirely sure she believed that, but he was right in that she wouldn't necessarily learn the things she'd been most curious about. One of which was finding out what she could get . . . just by asking for it. But doing that was a lot harder than she'd expected.

The tie stopped moving, but remained just brushing at her leg. "You don't like the feel of this on your skin?"

"I didn't say that," she managed, working hard not to tremble as the tip of the tie continued to tickle her senses.

"Ah," he said. And the tie disappeared.

She stifled a sigh. If she was going to keep the upper hand, push her own boundaries, she had to be decisive . . . and direct him before he directed her. "Take off my other shoe."

Her heel was popped off almost instantly.

"I—I liked it when you began to massage my foot."

His hands skimmed over her feet. "You want me to continue."

It seemed about the safest way to start. If there was such a thing with him. "Yes."

But the instant his thumbs pressed directly into the arch of her feet, she moaned . . . and realized nothing about this interlude would fall under that heading.

He kept the pressure up. Kneading, stroking, then concentrating both hands on one foot . . . then the other, until she thought she'd simply slide down the wall completely onto her back. And here she'd been upset when she hadn't been able to find a pair of panty hose with no runs in them this morning. She decided right then and there she might never wear panty hose again.

She also knew she couldn't have him massage her feet forever.

As if sensing this, his hands slowed, then finally rested on her ankles. He said nothing, letting the silence—and the tension—build between them.

"I—you—would you—" She broke off, disgusted with her inability to be simply bold, daring.

"Would I what?"

For God's sake, just say it. She swallowed, hard. "Your mouth." She paused, licking suddenly dry lips.

"What about my mouth," he asked quietly.

"Your hands feel wonderful," she said. "So did—" Her heart was pounding almost uncontrollably. It was only partly terror . . . the rest was an almost unbearable spike of anticipation. "So did your mouth."

A shocking moment later, she felt the tip of his tongue trace a circle around her ankle bone. She hadn't meant him to replace his hands with his tongue, but as he began to work his way up the curve of her calf, she didn't stop him.

"Your skin is soft," he murmured. "Sweet."

She sighed as he shifted his body around, so he could continue the torture. Her legs were only an inch apart. She silently begged him to push them wider, wishing she had the nerve to do it herself. Or tell him to.

He hovered just above her knee, pressing hot kisses on the tender skin just inside. She trembled, she shuddered . . . but when he started to move higher, she lost her nerve. "Don't."

"Don't what?"

She could feel his warm breath, caressing the skin on her inner thighs. "Come—come here. Up here."

She'd meant for him to sit beside her, bring his mouth to hers, or even to her neck, or her ear, as he had before. To her continued shock, he straddled her legs, keeping his weight on his knees as he braced his hands on either side of her head . . . and leaned down until he was so close she swore she could hear his heart beat.

"I'm here," he said softly. "What do you want me to do to you, Callie?" He moved in until his lips barely touched hers. "Kiss you?" He moved slowly, his lips almost but not quite brushing her chin. "Lick you?" He moved along the curve of her neck until he was beside her ear. "Taste you?"

Her control snapped and she slid her hands out from behind her back. She ran her fingers over the hard contours of his face and told him exactly what she wanted. "Take me." She ran a shaking finger over his lips and felt his swift intake of breath. *Yes.* That was all the provocation she needed.

"I want you, Dominic Colbourne, to take me." He groaned, somewhere deep in his throat. She slid her fingers into his hair, and stepped off the highest of cliffs. "All of me."

Chapter Five

He took her hands from his face, rocked by the power of her words. Of the trust she'd placed in him. He pinned them to wall well above her head, swallowed the little gasp with his mouth.

"I've been dying to taste this mouth," he said, kissing the corners, nipping at her slightly fuller lower lip. "I could spend hours making love to your mouth."

"Dear God," she whispered.

"He can't help you now. Don't you know you've just signed yourself over to the devil himself?"

It was his turn to be surprised when she laughed and said, "Then my prayers *have* been answered."

And that was when he felt the first real tug at his heart. The first sense of what she'd meant . . . about those other emotions that weren't entirely sexual.

She was teetering on the edge, an edge he'd purposely pushed her toward . . . and yet despite the power he knew he wielded over her, she continued to tease him, spark him, nudge him toward his own edge. Defense mechanism . . . or natural instinct, he didn't know. Didn't care. What mattered was that it wasn't a calculated response, it was simply Callie. And he intended to take her. Couldn't imagine not taking her now. She'd all but demanded it of him.

He'd intended to go slow. Take them both to the very ragged edge of control. But when he finally took those lips, parted them with his tongue and barely dipped himself into her . . . he lost his focus. And when she whimpered, opened herself to him, arched toward him in an effort to feel more of him than his lips on hers, he ceased to care how they got there. Fast and furious this first time, he thought, racing past that edge. Slow and languorously the next. Because, oh, there was going to be a next time. He'd led her into this exploration as a guide, but had somehow become the adventurer himself. And it had been a long time since he'd discovered a new treasure. He planned to savor every last bit of it.

As he sunk more deeply into her mouth, tangling his tongue with hers, coaxing her into a duel, he was tempted to drag her the rest of the way to the floor and strip them both just enough that he could truly sink into her. He'd felt her quiver with every touch of his lips and tongue along the delectable skin of her legs, had scented her readiness, which had made his body harden to the point of pain. He could take her right now, fast, deep, and rip them both over the edge in no time at all.

But he couldn't seem to let go of her hands, or take his mouth from hers long enough to accomplish the task.

"I ache to feel you wrapped around me," he said against her lips, shocked at the desperate need he heard in his own voice. "Every inch of you." He speared his tongue back into her mouth, then withdrew it just as quickly. "Every." He dipped his tongue again. "Inch." Again. "Of me." This time she took him tightly into her mouth and didn't let him go, moaning deeply when he met her silent demand, thrust after thrust.

She tried to slide down, all but growling at the limitations their current positions had put them in. He understood the frustration. Agreed wholeheartedly with her notion. Which did nothing to explain what he did next.

He left her mouth, rocked back onto his feet, and dragged them both upright, walking her up against the wall, hands still pinned above her head. It took every last scrap of his control to keep from shoving his hips into hers, or yanking her dress up and his pants down so he could wrap her legs around his waist and bring their bodies truly together.

He just barely brushed the contours of her body with his. A slight tease of her dress against his shirt, a brush of her skirt against his pants.

"Imagine what this would feel like if I were to undress you," he said, his own voice sinking to a rough whisper. "How my shirt would feel against your bare skin. And my pants shifting across the damp skin of your thighs."

She quivered hard beneath his grip. "Yes."

He shifted forward, fabric rustling against fabric, making her moan. But she didn't arch her back, or buck her hips in a blind search for his. Which told him she wanted to extend this exquisite torture, too.

"So do it," she said, a bit of a growl in her words.

He thought his heart would claw right out of his chest. That he wouldn't need to take off his trousers as he'd simply bust through the zipper. He pressed her wrists to the wall, then slid his hands slowly down her arms, around the outer edges of the swell of her breasts, bringing his hands to rest on the span of her waist, trembling himself as he felt her quiver beneath his touch. He couldn't remember the first detail of what she'd had on, not even the color of her dress. He really was as blind as Isabella claimed, as Callie had so adroitly noticed only seconds after meeting him.

No more. And never with her. It would be impossible now. In fact, at that exact moment, he couldn't imagine not being consumed by the burning need to know every last thing about her. Her taste, her thoughts, her scent, her laughter. Her dreams, her desires. He could tell himself it was lust driving those thoughts . . . but he'd lusted before. And it didn't come close to feeling anything like this. To consuming him the way this did. The way she did.

He flattened his palms on her stomach and pushed upward with his thumbs, moving his hands slowly up the center of her torso. He stopped just shy of cupping her breasts. Her chest was moving in and out as she took rapid, shallow breaths. No buttons. No zipper. He slid his hands back to her waist. She whimpered. His pulse thundered in his ears.

Then he spun her around, pushed her up firmly against the wall. She moaned at the contact the hard wood made against her hypersensitized body. He groaned just thinking about it. He traced his thumbs up her back, walked just close enough that every aching inch of him brushed against the insanely sweet curve of her buttocks. He thought he'd lose it then, would have for certain if she'd moved even a fraction of an inch back against him.

But she stilled instead. Completely. "Yes," she breathed.

And he realized, with stunning clarity, just what it was his Callie wanted now. She'd made her demands, gotten him to do what she wanted. At least as much as she knew what she wanted. Because she'd never been shown the actual breadth of what she could have. Never truly seduced to the depths and sparkling heights he now knew she could be taken to.

Her former husband had been a complete idiot. If he'd only taken the time to show her, to teach her body the wide range of pleasure it could feel . . . he'd have never let her go. But Dominic knew without a doubt that even if her ex had been clued in enough to know that . . . he'd have been far too selfish and insecure to do anything about it. Hence his harsh criticism. Much easier to make Callie out to be the one with the problem.

Dominic's mouth curved wickedly in the dark as a certain

kind of peace settled over him, despite his highly aroused state. Because he knew, with absolute certainty that he did possess the patience and the skill to take her to whatever limits she was willing to allow him to take her. Yes, she'd wanted—needed—to know she could drive someone mad with desire. And Lord knows he thought they would both easily agree she'd done that in spades.

But that was only the beginning. Now it was time for someone else to step in, take her. Drive her. Remove responsibility for all the decision making so she could simply feel, absorb . . . react.

And though he was fully aware how limited he was in terms of emotional connections . . . he could bloody well push this physical connection to whatever extreme she desired. And he planned to.

Did that mean he intended to pursue this beyond a stolen couple of hours in a broken lift? He refused to think about it . . . or put limitations on it. He also refused to think about what she'd do with this new knowledge he'd bestow on her . . . and with whom. Another tug at his heart, this one surprisingly painful. He forced his thoughts away from that path, knowing now he was out of his mind. He'd only just met her, surely there was no connection between them but physical. His body certainly agreed. His head . . . and heart . . . weren't part of that equation.

He didn't know what in the bloody hell he was doing. He was operating on instinct. And he didn't question his instincts . . . even when they drove him into new territory . . . drove him to take risks others would deem insane. So what if this new territory was personal, not professional like the others had been? So what if he learned something new about himself in the mix of things. Would that be so bad?

But if it wasn't so bad . . . then why was he so terrified?

Because he had no clue where it would lead him. And yet he'd be damned if he was going to stop. So they'd proceed.

One step at a time. One breath. He very deliberately drew one finger down her spine, stopping just above the curve of her sweet derriere. One shudder.

He took her hands and placed them, palms flat, beside her head. "Keep them here," he commanded softly next to her ear. Then traced his tongue around the delicate shell.

She said nothing. Her breath, coming in short, shuddery little pants, was enough of a response for him.

He shifted his body so that he was close, so very close, to hers . . . but no longer touching. If he'd continued pressing his aching length into that sweet backside of hers, all the patience in the world wouldn't keep him from a rather abrupt end to their little interlude.

Her cheek was pressed to the wall, so he drew his attentions to the side of her neck, nudging her hair aside and dropping hot kisses around to her nape.

"You taste like sin," he told her, feeling a bit seduced himself. Just the taste of her tested his control. "Hot, sweet, wicked." He pressed his lips to the base of her neck, darting the tip of his tongue so that it pushed against the heavy pulse there. She gasped. His body throbbed.

Just who was pushing whom to new depths, he began to wonder.

"You want my hands on you," he told her, grasping for control.

"Yes," she breathed.

He drew his finger from the base of her spine up the length of zipper that held her light cotton dress together. Then pulled the tab back down. Slowly exposing her damp skin to his lips, his tongue. He followed the zipper with his mouth, all the way to the end, dropping to a crouching position behind her. With his lips pressed to the small twin dimples just above her panties, he let his hands drop to her ankles. She sucked in a small breath as he circled them with his fingers.

"Part them for me," he told her, nudging her feet apart a

few inches. Then a few inches more. "Wider." He loosened his grip, allowing her to move them herself. She did. "More," he commanded. She slid them again, until they were about a foot apart. He squeezed them. "Lovely," he breathed, as he began skimming his hands upward, over her calves. "Strong," he murmured, feeling the flex of her muscle.

"Horses," she rasped.

He glanced up, though in the darkness he couldn't see her. "You ride?"

"Yes," she said, panting as his hands paused to draw little circles at the backs of her knees.

He grinned. "How . . . handy."

She moaned, and his grin turned almost feral. Damn but she made him feel downright primal. It was daft, really.

He continued his path, smoothing his palms up the outside of her thighs, beneath the dress that now hung limply from her shoulders. He slowly stretched to a stand behind her, continuing to skate his hands up to her hips, taking her dress with him. He paused, his own breath hitching slightly when his fingers encountered the slender strap that held the front and rear silk panel of her panties together.

He slid one finger, then another beneath the straps on either hip. "How . . . naughty of you," he murmured against the side of her neck. "You're barely covered." He crowded his body close to her again. "How incredible that silk would feel against me. Hot . . . wet."

She shuddered hard, a small moan escaping her lips when he brushed against her. Or maybe it had been him. He was so wild for the feel of her now, he wasn't sure who was more in danger of losing control.

He tugged at the slender bands. "Or I could just rip them off of you."

She moaned again . . . and he tugged, making her gasp, her body tense beneath his hands. "Oh."

"Oh yes. You'd have to walk home in the morning, with nothing on beneath this tidy little business dress of yours."

Another moan. His, hers, it no longer mattered.

"Only you would know, every time your thighs brushed, about your naughty little secret."

"Ahhh," she gasped, her damp palms squeaking as they tried to grip the wooden paneling as he brushed against her again.

"Only you would know, as people pushed and rushed past you, what you'd been doing all night. Here. In the dark. With me."

"Jesus," she swore heatedly, her hips bucking back ever so slightly.

He immediately pulled back. Though he wasn't sure whom he was torturing at this point.

She groaned in frustration.

"Keep still," he admonished, then pushed up behind her again. He put his lips next to her ear. "Don't move." He pushed his hips tighter into hers, so close to where he wanted to be, and yet far too many layers of clothing restricting them both from having what they so badly wanted. He rocked his hips, pushing his aching length against her soft buttocks. "I want to rip these off," he murmured against the skin of her neck, tugging at the thin bikini straps. "I want to bury myself in you." He twitched. Hard.

She groaned as her body jerked in response.

"Keep your hands on that wall," he instructed, then tugged her hips back into him as he stepped back. He reluctantly released her panties and wrapped one arm around her waist, palm flat against the bare skin of her stomach, tugging her fully against him, running his free hand up the bare expanse of her back. His hard bulge was snugged up tight between her legs and he thought he would howl with the ravaging need demanding he take her fully, completely.

He slipped his hand into her hair, stroked his fingers across her scalp, making her arch her neck and moan. Then he slid his fingers down her spine, flicking open her bra as he skimmed over it, then slipping that hand around her waist, inside her loosely gaping dress.

With both palms flat on her abdomen, he moved her so her back arched, pushing her more fully onto his erection. He groaned, a deep guttural sound that felt like it went on for ages. It took considerable will not to climax right then.

"Do . . . not . . . move," he told her, his voice shaking with need.

He released her, making them both groan at the absence of touch.

He stepped back, just enough to unhook his trousers. He had to feel that hot wet silk directly on his skin or he'd surely go mad. She moaned softly at the sound of his zipper opening, continued to moan as he kicked free of his clothes.

When he put his hands back on her waist, finding her with unerring precision despite the darkness, she jumped at his touch. His fingers sunk into her soft flesh as he fought for the last bit of control that was so rapidly deserting him. He stood just behind her, struggling to even out his breathing, not daring to brush against any part of her until he did.

"Dominic," she whispered. "Please."

"Dear sweet God," he swore, and yanked her back onto him. The long hard length of him pushed between her thighs, gliding along the slick, damp panel of her panties. He slid his hands inside the back of her dress and molded her to him. One hand slid down to the elastic edge of her panties, the other up to shift her brassiere out of the way so her breasts were free to his touch.

He stopped then, breathing heavily, groaning as she twitched on him. "You feel what you do to me," he all but growled. "As God is my witness, I have never ached for anyone the way I ache for you." The confession was torn from him before he could think better of it, or be stunned at the depth of sincerity in which he'd said it.

"Then do it," she all but begged. "It's torture. Sweet, but incredible torture."

And it struck him then, the real danger of the dance they'd entered into. He had no way to protect her. And doubted seriously she did either. He could have roared with the rage of sexual frustration that realization sent thundering through him. His hips flexed, pushed in instinctive rebellion, urging him to ignore the fear, take what he wanted and damn the consequences.

He bent over her, pressing his cheek to the bare skin of her back, squeezing his eyes tightly shut as her thighs squeezed just as tightly around him.

"Dominic," she whimpered.

Hearing her all but moaning his name, knowing the depths to which they'd driven each other, almost undid his resolve. He held on to her, fought to steady himself, his breathing, his raging, intense, aching need. And only when he thought he could move any inch of himself without ripping her panties off and shoving himself deep inside of her, did he dare continue the dance.

He slid his fingers along the swell of her breast as he slid his other fingers beneath the elastic of her panties.

She moaned and squeezed him between her thighs. He all but bit his tongue off, but managed not to pump himself along that wet stretch of silk until he came. He smoothed his hand over one bare breast, rubbed one delightfully hard nipple along the width of his palm, making her shudder hard. He rolled her nipple between his fingers, squeezing it slightly, earning another rippling shudder and a long, shuddering moan. He slid his hand to her other breast, and continued to wring pleasure from her as he rubbed her nipple between the length of his fingers.

And when she began to twitch against him . . . he slid his other hand lower, praying he could do to her what he wanted, give her what she so badly needed at this point, without coming all over her in the process.

"You are ready. For me," he said, struggling mightily to return to the role he'd so swiftly abandoned.

"Yes," she groaned. "Very."

He slid his fingers lower, and his own breath caught tight in his chest. "Slick, so needy."

"Yes," she growled.

He pushed one finger along the slippery crease. "What will it take, sweet Callie, to make you come for me?"

"Not much," she managed, somewhat dryly, which surprised a tortured little laugh from him. But also gave him the shred of an edge he so badly needed to see this through.

"One finger?" he queried, sliding the tip of his finger into her, while at the same time squeezing her nipple between his other fingers.

She gasped and jerked hard against him.

"Or two?" He gave her no warning, but slid two fingers deeply into her.

She convulsed immediately into a shuddering, gripping orgasm.

He continued to move his fingers inside her, holding her tightly to him as she twitched and groaned. Continued, even as the muscles ceased to constrict around him.

She squirmed against him, trying to move away as her climax subsided. He slid his free hand back to her waist and held her tight against him . . . but kept his fingers inside her. "One more," he told her.

Her head thrashed against him. "Can't," was all she managed.

He slid out of her and spun her back to the wall. "Can," he told her, pinning her wrists to the wall and himself to her as he took her mouth in a deep, soul-thrusting kiss.

He pushed between her legs as he thrust his tongue into her mouth. Her soaked panties clung to the length of him, the scent of her filled the air, driving him mad.

"Can," he said raggedly, when he forced his mouth from hers. He left her wrists pinned beside her head and drew his hands down her body, shoving her dress up and pinning it behind her back, before sinking to his knees. "Will," he told her, then yanked her panties down and drove his tongue into her.

She screamed then in wild, convulsing pleasure. Her knees buckled and he thought she was going to take them both crashing to the floor. He no longer cared. As badly as he wanted to be inside her, as painfully as his tortured body needed release, he wanted to do this more, to drive her someplace she'd never been, show her the heights of pleasure her body could ascend to . . . and take her screaming all the way there.

He braced her waist to the wall with his hands when she could no longer bear her own weight, and never once let up in his assault. She quivered, grunted, growled, then shouted when he ripped her over the edge again.

And then he pulled her down on top of him, falling to his back as he took her full weight on top of him. Shuddering, panting, gasping for breath. Himself, as well as her.

His body quivered like a bow strung too tightly and he was forced to roll them to their sides, willing his aching erection to subside. He stroked her damp curls, fighting for rational thought. It was beyond him. How could bringing someone else pleasure leave him feeling so incredibly satiated? His body still raged, demanding its own release, and yet there was this intensely . . . settled feeling, somewhere deep inside his chest. He'd gone raving starkers, it was the only explanation.

Sweat streamed down his face, sliding beneath his eyelids, stinging his eyes. He shifted to rub his sleeve over his face and she slowly shifted her weight away from his. He pulled her close, instinctively unwilling to allow her to leave him, tangling her legs and arms with his. She murmured something he couldn't understand, then slid her hand across his chest, wanting to keep him close, too. He turned his head then, seeking her, blindly now, with his mouth. He found her forehead, then her cheek, kissing both, before finally nudging her mouth to his.

He didn't want to think about the emotion that soared through him as their mouths met, mated anew. The kiss drew out, slowed . . . deepened, changed into something that wasn't completely carnal. Evolved into something else entirely. Something far more intimate. Far more powerful. Far more dangerous.

He told himself it was the heightened awareness from the intense sexual interlude they'd shared. And yet, somewhere deep inside, he knew it was a whole hell of a lot more than that.

He stroked her hair, broke the kiss, but continued touching her with his lips as their breathing gradually slowed. He couldn't shake the feeling that she was his now, in some unnamed, intangible way that defied explanation. As if he were somehow responsible for her now . . . her pleasures, her needs. Maybe more. And even stranger still, he yearned to fulfill them. That was the only word he could come up with for the deep ache settling inside his chest. Coupled quite alarmingly with fear. He wasn't a man who feared anything.

And yet as her fingers curled over his chest—over his heart—he knew true terror. Terror that he wouldn't be able to do for her all the things he wanted to do . . . be the man she'd need him to be.

And as the air ceased to be filled with their panting gasps, the silence grew. And so did that terror. For the first time in his life, Dominic had no idea what to say. Much less what the next step should be. Surely she'd think him just as starkers if he so much as uttered one word of the wildly fantastic thoughts and feelings careening about inside his head.

The wise thing to do was say something urbane or witty, that would put them both at ease and allow them to view their coupling in some abstract, serendipitous way. They'd make a few gentle jokes, rearrange their clothes, comment on what a fantastic memory this would be and—

Bugger it.

He didn't want to say any of those things to her. Didn't want to reduce what they'd shared to some superficial sex act between two consenting adults. Because it hadn't been. Never would be.

Which meant he wanted . . . what?

That train of thought was almost instantly derailed when she began unbuttoning his shirt.

"What are you doing?" he asked, not particularly minding. In fact, her questing fingers, tickling between the ridge of muscle leading from his chest to his navel, was actually quite delectable. His body, still half hard, stirred anew. He wasn't sure he could withstand any more, though, and with a sigh of great regret, took hold of her clever fingers and stopped her.

"Fair is only fair," she said, not remotely put off.

He found himself grinning, wondering why he was always surprised by her direct, wry little comments. Perhaps it was the duality of her somewhat untried sexuality, and her almost jaded sensibilities. The possibilities were so tantalizing he—

She slid her hand free and shifted her body down, pressing warm, damp lips along the center line of his abdomen. "I've had two, it's only fair you have at least one," she was saying.

And then her hand was around him and he lost all rational thought.

"I trust you'll tell me what to do?"

He could only nod, forgetting she couldn't see him in the dark.

"I've never been very . . . encouraged in this area," she said, sounding anything but discouraged at the moment.

"Mmmph," he managed, then groaned when her tongue darted out. "Dear God in heaven."

She laughed, then sighed a little as he grew rigid in her hand. "Imagine that. I guess it helps when you actually want to try."

"Yeah," he grunted. "No problems with your punch, or your pucker."

She stroked him once and his hips bucked wildly, as if he'd never had a woman touch him this way before.

"Had I only known it was this easy," she murmured.

He started to tell her there was nothing easy about any of this, but then she was sliding her mouth over him. And rational speech deserted him.

Chapter Six

Callie could hardly believe what she was doing. So she didn't think about it. She simply let herself feel it, experience it. And when she made him shout, buck, and growl his way through a control-ripping climax, she felt like she'd hit the peak of Everest.

He was still shuddering when he dragged her up next to him and wrapped himself fully around her, burying his face into her neck. It was pure fantasy, but as he tucked her almost fiercely against his chest, she swore she felt like she'd found the one spot in the universe created exclusively for her.

Amazing the havoc multiple orgasms could wreak on a person's rationale, she thought, but couldn't wipe the accompanying smile from her face. She did wipe the approaching stampede of questions, concerns, and what-next worries from her mind. He was holding her so tightly it was doubtful he was letting go anytime soon. That was all she needed to know. For now.

The silence this time was easy, contented. She stroked lazy patterns on his back and kept conscious thought at bay by letting herself float on lingering sensations and a wondrous replay of what they'd just done together. Never had she known, suspected even, that her body was capable of hitting that kind of peak. Once, much less twice. Never had she known she could make a man scream when he climaxed. Her smile grew. All she needed now was the cape and leather thigh-high boots to complete the superpower image she had of herself at that very moment.

Knowing Dominic, he might enjoy a little dress-up sex.

"What was that little amused noise all about?" he asked, his deep voice delightfully drowsy.

Sexually sated, she thought. All because of her. She reveled in the thrill that thought sent through her. Her superpowers emboldened her. "I was debating the merits of dress-up as part of foreplay."

She felt him lift his head, suspected he was looking down at her despite the dark. "Were you now?

She shivered at the predatory tone.

"And who would you be wanting to dress up as?" he asked.

"I'm torn," she said, quite seriously.

"Between?" he asked, equally deadpan.

Had she known postcoital banter could be so tantalizing she might have tried it sooner. Thinking back on Peter's ability to go from climax to snore faster than most sport cars go from zero to fifty . . . she knew it wouldn't have mattered. Funny just how clearly a good orgasm could make you see where the flaws truly lay in previous attempts. And with whom. "Catwoman," she said, decisively. "Or Barbarella."

He laughed then. "I would definitely enjoy either."

She should be so lucky. "What about you?" she asked instead.

"Me?" he asked, obviously surprised.

"You don't think I'm going to be the only one risking mortification, do you?" As soon as she spoke, she bit her tongue. She sounded like she assumed they'd be doing this again sometime. And though she realized the chances of that were about nil, she wasn't quite ready to hear him put it into words. She spoke quickly, before he could say anything. "I was thinking something suave and debonair."

"Cary Grant?"

"Mmm. More like James Bond." She grinned when he snorted. "You definitely left me shaken . . . and stirred."

He pinched her bottom lightly, making her squeal even as she laughed. "Quite the cheeky one," he said devilishly.

"Apparently. Who knew I had such an adventurous soul, hmm?"

His hand stroked up her back and sunk into her hair, tilting her head as he rolled her to her back and lowered his mouth expertly to hers. Rather than ravenous or playful, his kiss surprised her by being slow, drugging, touching down somewhere so far inside her, she couldn't give it a name.

"I knew," he said quietly, when he finally pulled his lips from hers.

At that moment she would have given anything she owned to see his face, see what was in his eyes, because she was very much afraid she was reading far too much into his words, or the oh-so-intent tone threading through them.

He stroked her face, and she sighed, wondering if it was possible to fall in love with someone in a matter of hours. *Of course not,* her logical mind interjected. *That's the climaxes talking.* After a prolonged abstinence, it wasn't surprising she was going emotionally overboard for the first man to take the time to attend to her needs.

Only she didn't quite buy that either. Dominic, for all his intensity, his focus on business, and his professed inability to connect emotionally, was connecting pretty damn well with her. And with far more than the location of her G spot.

"What are you thinking?" he asked, skimming his hand down her arm.

She couldn't dare tell him the truth. She didn't know the whole truth herself. Wasn't ready to dare find out what was real about this interlude they'd shared, and what was fantasy.

She should just accept the joy of discovery, and be satisfied with that. Now if only she had a clue how to do that.

He drew her hand up over her head, then wove his fingers through hers. That simple twining, such a natural joining, so intimate in ways joining bodies could never match, unhitched something inside her, and she sighed wistfully without meaning to.

"Callie—"

This time she turned to him, taking his mouth with unerring aim, not wanting to hear his next words. Words of appreciation, perhaps, but words of good-bye. Not yet.

His fingers squeezed hers as they took the kiss deeper. He sunk into her mouth, slowly, surely, and drew her into his the same way, until they were mating with their tongues in the one way they hadn't yet mated with their bodies.

"I have an almost desperate need for you," he said, his breath warm against the damp skin of her cheek. "It's insanity really."

"I know," she said, thinking that was exactly what this was. And she was insane for thinking it could ever be more than a fast, hot coupling between two people caught in a place out of time. Where it didn't matter who he was, what he did, what they did together. Once they stepped out of this airless box, back into the real world, this time spent together, what they'd done, would shift to a memory. Replayed endlessly, in her case, she was certain. But a memory was all she'd have to hold on to. Better to understand that right now.

She shifted next to him, her body twitching with renewed hunger. He pulled her more tightly against him and she gasped at the velvety, rigid feel of him brushing against her. Apparently she wasn't the only one who wasn't finished yet. She'd felt him, tasted him, ran her fingers and tongue down the glorious length of him. And now she had an almost screaming need to feel him in the one place he belonged, and had yet to be.

No, that was crazy. The one place she wanted to feel him, certainly. But . . . belonged?

"Callie," he whispered next to her ear.

She rolled her head so their lips brushed. "Mmm. I love the way you say my name, so elegant, so—"

"Desperate," he repeated, his voice somewhere between amused and strained beyond control.

She laughed and pulled him on top of her as she rolled to her back. "Never let it be said I left a desperate man in need."

He settled so easily on top of her, she almost swooned at the sweet perfection of it. "As long as that desperate man is me," he murmured, as he settled between her legs.

Her heart paused for a split second as his words filtered past the pulse drumming in her ears. But her body was already moving to accommodate the insistent nudge, pressing so close . . . so close.

"Bloody hell," he swore, shifting away slightly, but enough to make her moan in dismay. "Callie, we can't—I don't have—"

"Oh," she said, relaxing, tugging him back. "That." She shifted her hips and he slipped easily between her legs again, making her clench tightly in anticipation. It dragged a deep moan out of her when he pushed his hips. "Don't need it," was all she could manage as he began to nudge inside her. She was never so thankful in all her life that she'd continued taking the pill after she'd left Peter. She'd done it to keep her period in check, and she supposed in the blind hope that someday she'd meet someone and would have one less thing to worry about if it turned serious. Never had she thought it might come in handy because of hot elevator sex with a gorgeous British magnate.

The thought made her grin, even as her body strained up against him, searching, wanting, so close to having what it now desperately needed. "I'm—" She gasped as he teased that tiny little part of her that was so enormously sensitized. "On the pill—please—Dominic—for God's sake, just—"

With a growl that was somewhere between feral and primal, he pushed deep inside her in a single thrust, driving them both across the slick marble floor. His hand was still joined with hers, and even as they bucked, clawed, and pumped wildly against each other, he never let her go. He rolled to his back and pulled her astride him . . . another first for her.

She'd always been too self-conscious to display herself so overtly. But there in the complete darkness, she let herself go, moving on him any way her body demanded she move. He met her rhythm, matched it, drove her farther, higher . . . And their fingers stayed joined as she arched her back, sinking fully down onto him, feeling more in tune with her body, freer, heart and soul, than ever before. So much so, she didn't stop him when he moved their joined fingers to where their bodies joined . . . letting him guide them both into teasing her into a thrashing, screaming climax, the intensity of which was far beyond anything she thought possible.

She was still shuddering, convulsing almost, when he rolled her to her back, then slid her hips high as he pushed to his knees and took her with him. Back arched way up, he wrapped his free arm around her waist, tugged her snug down onto him, again and again, as he thrust into her. Small screams pushed past her lips with each thrust, her climax literally vibrating with the steady friction he'd created, paired with grunts and growls as she tightened around him each time. Faster, deeper, with a fury that took her somewhere beyond all thought, into some primal place where she was reduced to her most basic self.

How long they went on she had no idea, it seemed like an endless mating, that they'd stayed joined like this for all eternity, were maybe meant to. Then it was his turn to shout as the last of his control was ripped away and he went over the edge.

And when they collapsed into a coiled mass of tangled limbs and sweat-soaked flesh . . . their fingers remained twined.

"And here I thought women were the only ones who could

be multiorgasmic," she murmured drowsily, unable to wipe the smug smile off her face.

He only managed to grunt in response, which made her laugh.

Then he pulled their joined fingers to his mouth, where he dropped a warm kiss on each knuckle, then tucked their hands over his heart.

Callie's breath left her in a long, shuddery sigh. Oh boy, she was in serious trouble here. But she couldn't manage to make herself worry about it at that particular moment.

She didn't realize she'd drifted to sleep until Dominic kissed her awake. "How long have I—"

"Shh, we have to get dressed. It's almost six."

No, her heart screamed. She wasn't ready for it to be over.

"I imagine if the building crew works till midnight, they come in early as well," he told her.

She tried to pull away, at least mentally. It would take more strength than she presently had to make herself pull away from him physically. One step at a time, she told herself. Only she couldn't even make the mental step.

It didn't help when Dominic lowered his mouth to hers and kissed her, slowly, so assuredly. Like she was his. Or something.

She sighed, feeling tears burn behind her eyes, thanking God it was dark so he wouldn't see, would never know. "Thank you," she whispered, unable not to say that much. It sounded lame, inadequate, especially after what they'd shared, but she meant it. More than he could possibly know. Or maybe he did. And that was what made this so damn hard.

He said nothing, just kissed her again. And even though she knew it would only make it harder on her, she sunk into the kiss, reveled in how well their mouths were mated, how easily they'd learned each others' bodies.

When he finally pulled away, she wished desperately that

she could make some witty comment, something dry and humorous, that would allow her to—

A sudden clanking noise somewhere below them in the elevator shaft, had her leaping off of him as if scalded.

"Wait, wait—" Dominic started to say, reaching to keep her from slipping on their clothes.

"Mr. Colbourne? Ms. Montgomery?"

Someone was shouting their names.

"Yes," Dominic called out, smooth and unruffled. "We're in here. Unharmed."

There were sounds of arguing, some muffled swearing; then the voice returned. "We'll have you out shortly, sir. Ma'am."

"Well done," Dominic called, sounding every bit as urbane and witty as she'd wished she could be.

She started casting about for her underwear. Her bra had come off at some point as well. Dominic helped her, and in a silence punctuated only by their breathing, they quickly, if awkwardly, pulled everything back to rights. Callie had no idea what her hair looked like, but she supposed no matter how bad it was, it would be chalked up to a night spent in an airless elevator. Now if she could only manage not to flush hotly the minute the doors opened. It wasn't even that she was worried about herself, her reputation, even her job. But she didn't want to jeopardize anything with Dominic and his deal with Stephanie.

She groped around for her shoes, then felt Dominic's hand beneath her elbow, helping her to a stand. Her knees were wobbly and he caught her against him.

"Callie—"

Just then the lights flickered once, twice, then burned steadily, making them both squint and look away from each other.

"Hold on in there!" the voice shouted.

Dominic shifted his weight into the corner, and when Callie would have groped for her own space on the wall, still blinking furiously against the sudden return of light after so much time spent in complete darkness, Dominic pulled her against him instead.

She instinctively braced her hands on his chest. "We can't," she whispered.

The car jerked once, then smoothly began the remainder of its descent as if nothing was wrong.

"The doors are going to open any second," she said.

Dominic merely lowered his mouth to hers and kissed her hard, fast, making her sigh before she could catch herself. At the last possible moment, he broke the kiss and stood her away from him, his hands at her elbows until she steadied herself. It was then that their eyes locked on one another for the first time. Ever.

Her breath caught in her throat at the intensity of his gaze, the directness. The naked hunger.

She swallowed convulsively. "Dominic," she managed, but had no idea what she would have said next as the car jerked slightly as it came to a halt on the ground floor.

He reached out and smoothed her curls from her face, his fingers brushing her cheek, making her entire body vibrate with the same need she saw in his eyes. Then he turned her toward the door and pushed away from the wall, his hand at her elbow, keeping her steady, maybe keeping himself steady as well.

When the doors slid open, revealing three men in blue work garb, the two morning security guys, and Stephanie, they stood as impersonally as they'd begun, with the exception of his hand still on her elbow. However the gesture probably looked gallant, rather than intimate. It felt both to Callie. He was both things to her. Always would be.

"Are you okay?" Stephanie asked, looking more frazzled than Callie could ever remember.

In fact, she'd never seen her boss look anything other than

completely put together. But right now her hair was mussed, and she wore no makeup. If Callie hadn't been so worried about her own appearance, she would also have immediately noted that Stephanie was wearing the same thing she'd left the office in last night.

West coast investor, late night meeting, hmm? Callie thought, barely suppressing a smile. But she could hardly fault her boss for mixing business with pleasure, now could she?

"Building security paged me the minute they came on duty this morning and realized the power had shut off."

"It probably went down with a number of others during the storm we had last night," one of the serviceman said. "Generator didn't kick on and it knocked the whole system out of whack."

There had been a storm last night? Callie worked hard not to shoot a glance toward Dominic. They'd shared their own storm, hadn't they?

"I buzzed you at home," Stephanie said, pulling Callie's gaze back to her. "And I realized this might have happened. I am so sorry." She turned to Dominic. "Please accept my apologies. We've never experienced any malfunctions before, but—"

"With new buildings, things such as this are bound to arise," Dominic said easily, guiding Callie out of the elevator.

Stephanie moved in, placing one hand on Callie's arm, the other on Dominic's, unintentionally forcing his hand to drop away. Callie managed not to sigh. Or cry, for that matter.

"Are you two okay?" Stephanie asked, sincerely concerned, despite the fact that she must also be nervous about what this might do to her negotiations with Dominic.

"We're fine," Callie said, as her boss came between them, literally, separating them even farther as she turned to Dominic once again.

Best to let the distance grow wider and wider, she thought,

working hard to shore up her defenses. Before she caved and launched herself into his arms and begged him not to walk away from what they'd begun last night.

But what had they begun, really? The sex was phenomenal, but surely all the rest, all the deep emotions, the soul connection she felt, was simply a manifestation of their predicament. She was going to be adult about this, mature, just as she'd been after discovering Peter in flagrante delicto with Dog Girl. She hadn't made a scene then, she wasn't about to make one now. Better to just hold the memories close and appreciate what their interlude had shown her, taught her, about herself. That Peter was an idiot when it came to women. And that she'd allowed the insecurities his rejections had spawned to propagate themselves way out of control. Never again. Not after this.

"I'll call and have our lunch postponed," Stephanie was saying. "Will you be able to stay in town an extra day, or do you want to meet this evening?"

Stephanie sounded like her typical direct, in-control self, but Callie detected the thread of nervousness beneath her words and found herself holding her breath, waiting for his reply. Except her trepidations weren't because a multimillion dollar deal hung in the balance. Hers were far more private, but every bit as crucial. It took all her willpower not to look at him, connect her gaze to his in any way. It was all she could do to remain standing here at all, pretending like nothing had happened, when her entire world felt like it was eroding beneath her very feet.

She might be able to pull it together, if she never had to see him again. But if he stayed, came back to the office, would she really be able to deal with him professionally, without giving any outward indication of what had happened between them? And would he?

Of course he would, she thought. That was what he did best, divorce emotion from action. Only he hadn't seemed so

divorced last night. *I've never ached for anyone the way I ache
for you.* His words echoed through her mind, sent a shiver of
sensation all the way through her. Had he meant it? Or had it
been the passion of the moment? Maybe he said that to every
woman he made love to?

The very thought of him touching anyone else made her fingernails dig into her palm. Made her want to lash out, dare
anyone to even think about coming near her man. That very
visceral reaction stunned her so thoroughly, she missed
Dominic's answer.

"Fine, fine," Stephanie was saying. "I'll have the arrangements taken care of." She turned to Callie. "Why don't you head
home, grab a few hours of sleep and freshen up. I wish I could
give you the entire day, but I can't. I'm really sorry, it's—"

Callie held up her hand. "It's okay." And it was. She'd far
rather be kept too busy to think right now. The idea of being
all by herself, with nothing better to do than think about
Dominic, held all the appeal of a multiple root canal. "I'll be
back by one at the latest."

"I called a cab for you, if you don't feel up to driving yourself home."

"No, that won't be necessary." In fact, had it not been so
far away, she'd have walked. She needed, desperately, to clear
her head. She thought about the horse ranch out in Upperville
where a friend of hers worked, who used to let her come out
and exercise some of the horses on her days off. She hadn't
had a day off in so long, she wondered if she'd still remember
how to ride. And out of nowhere, a rather wicked grin curved
her lips before she could stop it. No, she hadn't forgotten how
to ride, she thought, remembering how she'd sat astride
Dominic.

"Listen," Stephanie said, concern clear in her voice. "I'm
packing you into that cab right now. You look like you're
going to pass out on me here. Make sure you get something to
eat, too, okay?"

Not the most maternal of women, Stephanie's concern touched Callie, but then she was being steered out the lobby doors to a waiting cab before she'd gotten a chance to say anything to Dominic, to even send a silent good-bye. Not that she'd have known what to say, silently or otherwise.

"But, Do—Mr. Colbourne," Callie stuttered. "What did—"

"We're meeting at his hotel this evening. He has a flight out to Denmark tonight that can't be changed, so we'll just have to wrap this up quickly." She stuffed Callie in the back of the cab. "Listen, I don't know what you said or did to keep things on level ground, but thank you for not letting him blow this deal off. I appreciate it." She grinned. "And I'll make sure that shows up when we discuss salary later." The door was closed before Callie could reply. Stephanie slapped the roof twice and the cabbie pulled away from the curb.

"Where to?" he asked.

Callie looked back at her office building in time to see Stephanie and Dominic in conversation as a sleek black limo pulled up to the curb. Her heart stuttered, then dropped. And cracked a little on impact.

"Good-bye, Dominic," she said, thankful at least that she wouldn't have to see him again. At least not so soon. Surely if the deal went through, their paths would cross in the future. But just as surely by then she'd have been able to put this all in perspective. "Yeah," she muttered, "if it's about a hundred years from now."

"I beg your pardon, Miss?"

Callie turned back to the driver and gave him directions to her apartment.

And missed the searing look that Dominic sent at her retreating cab when Stephanie finally turned away.

Chapter Seven

Dominic hadn't heard a single word Stephanie had said to him in the lobby earlier. His mind had been clouded with Callie. Thoughts of Callie, the scent of Callie . . . her vulnerabilities, her laughter . . . her whispers in the dark, her humor. Her innate strength. How had he stood there and just let her walk away?

He paced the floor of his penthouse hotel suite, ignoring the riveting view of the nation's capital, sprawled below him, just across the river. He'd repeatedly told himself since he'd gotten back here, that the whole thing was simply a result of that call from Isabella. But it wasn't news to him that he wasn't, what had Callie called it? "The most emotionally in tune man on earth." And yet, he'd been quite easily and thoroughly in tune with her. Still was. For Christ sake, he had millions of dollars and over a thousand jobs on the line with this merger with Stephanie, and what was he doing? Wondering what in the hell he could say to Callie to get her to give him a chance?

Yes, Dominic Colbourne was afraid he wasn't going to get the girl.

The only one he'd ever wanted.

But there were complications. His business deal, the fact that she worked for Stephanie. The fact that she was rebounding from a bad marriage, and he was rebounding from yet another failed romance. "Romance," he snorted. "Like you know the meaning of the bloody word."

He understood corporate strategy, but he'd never developed a strategy for relationships. Which might well be his problem, that he thought of it as some sort of campaign to be waged. He didn't want to "win" Callie. She wasn't some trophy to be collected. He wanted to—

He stopped dead in his tracks. "What in the hell do you want?" And the truth was, he didn't know. Beyond seeing her again, he had no idea what he wanted. To see her again after that, he supposed. And again. And again. Not just sexually. She said she rode horses. He'd never had the pleasure, but perhaps he could learn. That was something they could do together. Travel. He suspected she hadn't seen much of the world. He could show her that. The idea of seeing it through her eyes excited him in ways he hadn't felt in some time. And then it had been about some acquisition. Except she wasn't an acquisition.

He slumped down on the coffee table and raked his fingers through his hair. "Dear Christ, I'm lost." He propped his elbows on his knees and rubbed at the dull ache forming behind his forehead. An ache, he suspected, that had its roots not in fatigue, or even frustration. But something that felt a lot like fear. An emotion as foreign to him as love.

Love.

He straightened. Could it be this was his heart finally stirring to action? "Either that, or I've got an ulcer," he said, rubbing at the queer clench in his belly. He stood again, suddenly restless, unable to sit still, as the ramifications of this amazing discovery attacked all his senses. It was ludicrous, obviously, to fancy oneself infatuated with someone they'd only just met. Despite the wild night spent together, despite the screams of passion they'd shared, despite the fact that— "I can't get her out of my bloody lunatic mind."

He yanked at the tie that was suddenly too tight, clawed off his jacket and flung it on the couch, pacing more like the panther he'd been compared to, than the financial bigwig he'd become. What was he going to do about this? He had his meeting with Stephanie in—he glanced at his watch—three hours. A flight to catch a mere three hours after that. The clock was ticking and he felt perilously close to losing control. "What to do, what to do," he murmured, pacing to the bar and pouring himself a stiff two fingers of Scotch, then ignoring it to pace back to the thick sheet of glass that made up most of one wall.

He should let it go, he told himself, not seeing any of the lighted monuments below. Get on with what he did well and stop trying to become something he wasn't. Let Callie get on with the new life she was building, finish healing the wounds that bastard had inflicted on her. He'd be a bastard to try to forge some kind of relationship with her as he'd likely only be the next in line to hurt her when he royally screwed up. Which he would. Bloody hell. Since he knew not the first thing about pleasing a woman, not the way this demanded of him anyway. Keeping her satisfied required some kind of commitment on his part, and not just of time or money. Of himself. His heart, his head, his thoughts, even his dreams. He'd never shared that part of himself with anyone. In fact, what little he'd told Callie in the elevator was more than he'd told Isabella during their entire relationship.

And that had come easily enough, hadn't it? a little voice nudged. He wanted to ignore it, because the fledgling little thread of hope attached to it was too risky to even contemplate. He laughed, but there was no humor in it. Risk. Since when had he run from that?

Since this morning, when he'd watched that taxi pull away from the curb. When he'd tried to tell himself he was doing her a favor by letting her go. That the pain in his chest had nothing to do with his heart, was merely a signal he'd gone too long without a meal.

Which merely triggered another round of images from their encounter in that elevator. When the only thing he'd wanted to consume had been her. Would he ever stop thinking about it, stop imagining what it would be like to spend endless hours with her, days, months. Years.

"Sod it," he growled, his control finally snapping. He stalked over to his private elevator, stabbing at the button. He stepped in, punched the button for the garage level, then squeezed his eyes shut as the doors silently closed, and the images assaulted him again. He needed to see her. Talk to her. That was all. One last time. So they'd both be able to walk away for good, get on with their lives, settle things between them. Because, bottom line, nothing felt settled right now. He was beginning to wonder if anything ever would again.

Callie sat at her small breakfast counter and stared at the phone in her hand. "You're overreacting." Saying it out loud didn't help. She still wanted to call Stephanie and tell her she wasn't coming in today. Or maybe any day. Not that it mattered. Stephanie would fire her for sure.

And it wasn't that she didn't want to risk seeing Dominic. She didn't, not yet, anyway. But if she had to face him, she would. No, this was bigger than that. Deeper than that. This went all the way to the core of what she really wanted. Who did she want to be? Where did she want to end up? Did she really want to end up like Stephanie, or even Dominic for that matter? Driven, focused, taking pleasure only in successes earned on the corporate playing field? Was she so willing and ready to give up her dreams of home and family?

The sad truth was yes, she had. Not because they weren't worthy goals, but because she honestly didn't want to risk reaching for them again, and losing. Because it meant too much to her. Climbing the corporate ladder was easier. She only had herself to deal with, only had her own limitations to overcome. Only had professional failure to risk.

She laid the phone down, but continued to stare at it. "What *do* you want?" She'd been so excited—had it only been last night? When Stephanie had offered her everything she thought she wanted. It was the answer to her dreams. Or was it? Certainly it was the answer to financial security. Was that enough? Was that really all she wanted?

All. It had seemed like so much when she'd taken the temporary job. So huge, so all-encompassing. But had it really just been a refuge?

"And if you don't figure this out in the next fifteen minutes, you're going to be late for work," she muttered.

Work. That was what had started this whole train of thought. Okay, so that was a lie. Dominic, and what they'd shared in that elevator last night was where the whole thing had really begun to unravel. But it wasn't until she was pulling on yet another "tidy little business dress," sliding her feet into her sensible pumps, brushing her hair into a corporate-acceptable style, that her unrest had truly begun to surface.

She'd wanted nothing more than to pull on her oldest jeans and get in her car—which she didn't even have as it was still in the underground parking lot at work—and drive west toward the Blue Ridge mountains, head to her pal Sally's farm and beg her for a mount for the afternoon. And when she realized that not only was she not going to go riding today, but not tomorrow, or the next day, or the next week, or probably the next six months, she began to wonder why she'd so quickly traded her entire life for corporate success.

"Because it was the only kind of success I could actually measure," she said quietly. And this time, saying it out loud did help. She did enjoy her job, but not at the expense of her entire life. Yes, a paycheck brought stability, security, confidence, along with the gratitude and sense of worthiness she'd been in search of. And she'd proven she could have all of those things. Did have them.

And now that she did? "I want my life back," she said on a laugh. "Christ, you're a basket case." Or worse. Because she wanted more than her life back. She wanted Dominic Colbourne in it.

She stared at the phone. Did she really dare? Was she fighting for her life, or making the biggest idiotic decision of her life? Stephanie's offer gave her the validation she'd thought she needed. So, why was it that validation no longer seemed all that important? Maybe the fact that she'd earned it was enough. She could go back to temping, moving around to different companies, helping them out when they needed it, making some friends along the way, then moving on. She'd truly enjoyed that, but had never considered the benefits. It wouldn't make her rich, but it paid the bills. And, more important, she had the personal time to spend with those friends. At least, she would know that she realized she needed them more than she needed a new title or a fancy retirement plan.

And it had only taken six hours in an elevator with one man to figure all that out. Okay, that, a half a box of Hostess cupcakes and a great deal of soul-searching.

She picked up the phone and stared at it. Maybe the true meaning of success was knowing what made you happy, and going after it. Being willing to work hard at it, being confident enough not to be swayed by anyone else's definition of happiness or success, and being determined enough to fight for it. *And,* her little voice nudged, *if that's good enough for your professional goals . . . shouldn't the same apply to your personal ones?*

Dominic's image punched through her thoughts, and her newfound confidence flagged momentarily. She did want him. Wanted to know him better, spend more time with him, find out what *he* wanted and what would make him happy. From what he'd said last night, she suspected it wasn't absorbing yet another corporation, or moving up another notch on the *Forbes* list.

But could it be something as elemental as being with her? She laughed. Okay, so she wasn't *that* sure of herself yet. And, even if she was, how would she go about letting the man know she wanted him? *Maybe you could start by telling him.*

Her heart began to pound. Could she really do that? "Will you ever forgive yourself if you don't?" The worst he could do was blow her off. Sure, her heart would shatter into a million pieces, but hell, she'd recovered from some major body blows in the past, right? She blew out a shaky breath. "Yeah. Right."

She tapped her fingers against the number buttons, her pulse continuing to accelerate as she allowed herself to truly consider going after everything she wanted. Everything.

Risk.

What the hell. It was only her whole life, right?

"I *am* nuts," she said, feeling a distinct craving for cream-filled chocolate coming on. "Certi-freaking-fiable." And yet, when she glanced up at the tiny mirror hanging over the counter, she saw she was grinning. Realized that, if she did this, for the first time in what felt like forever, and maybe it was, she would truly be the one driving the train.

She stabbed the speed dial for Stephanie's private line before she lost her nerve. When her boss answered, she took a deep breath . . . and turned down the job offer.

She hung up minutes later, feeling slightly nauseous, but that was more because of the phone call she'd yet to make. She punched in information and asked for the number of Dominic's hotel. Then decided this was something better done in person and dialed a taxi service and ordered a cab instead. A quick run to the bedroom to change back into jeans and a T-shirt—after all, if things were going to go anywhere with Dominic, he might as well see her as she really was, right off the bat. She was all thumbs, shaky with nerves and anticipation at the thought of seeing him again. "Think positive, think positive," she murmured, digging under her bed for her other sneaker.

She dragged a brush through her hair, not daring to actually look in the mirror, for fear of chickening out entirely. But she'd just turned down a probable six-figure job, what the hell else did she have to lose?

Everything, her heart answered. But if she didn't try, then she'd already lost, hadn't she?

Her doorbell buzzed just as she dashed back into her living room to find her purse. "Wow, a gallant cabbie. I didn't think they even got out of the cab anymore."

"I'll be right there," she called out.

She grabbed her purse and glanced out the window on her way to the door . . . just in time to see the cab drive off.

"What the—?" She yanked open the front door, not that she could have run the guy down, but still—and froze.

"Hi."

She tried not to swallow her tongue. "Uh . . . hi."

"I hope you don't mind. I sent your cab away."

"Yeah. I mean no. I mean, I was just coming to—" She stopped and shook her head, then reached out to touch his arm. Just to make sure she wasn't on some sort of sugar-induced fantasy trip. She laughed a bit nervously. It was that or just yank him full body into her arms. "Just want to make sure I'm not hallucinating."

Dominic grinned. And it was so far beyond what she'd imagined in the dark, she felt her whole body grow damp. "Good hallucinating or bad hallucinating?"

She pressed a hand to her chest, willing her heart to settle into a speed her body could accommodate without exploding. She didn't think that was going to happen anytime soon. "Good," she said, then let out a whooshing breath as she laughed again. "I can't believe you're here."

"I'm afraid I took another liberty."

"I believe you've pretty much taken as much liberty with me as humanly possible," she said dryly.

He grinned again, but there was still something almost twitchy about his demeanor. If she didn't know better, she'd say he seemed almost nervous. Dominic?

"What liberty did you take?" she asked, curiosity vying with an aching need to just blurt out everything she'd been thinking since she'd left him this morning.

"I called Stephanie and told her you wouldn't be in today. At the same time I cancelled our meeting, and my—"

"Tell me you didn't let what happened between us screw up your business de—"

He shook his head. "In fact, I told her to draw up the papers, that I'd sign anything she wanted."

Callie's mouth dropped open, then snapped shut. "She's a total shark, Dominic, and elevator stall or not, she'll take full advantage—"

"I know," he said, obviously unconcerned. "In her position, I'd do the same thing."

"Then why—" She stopped, realizing they were still standing in her doorway. She stepped back. "Do you want to come in?"

"Actually, I'd love to, but I sort of had other plans."

For the first time since she'd flung open the door, Callie's heart clenched painfully. "Oh," she said, not urbane enough to hide her crushing disappointment. "Then why did you send my cab—"

He stepped back and waved toward her driveway. She leaned past him, and gasped. "Is that a real—"

"Aston Martin. Yeah, it is."

Then she looked at him. Really looked at him. And for the first time, realized he was wearing a full dress tuxedo. "Why are you dressed like that?"

He nodded toward her. "I might ask the same thing. Something tells me you weren't planning on heading to the office in that taxi."

"No, I wasn't. It's a long story."

"I'd like to hear it."

"But you have plans. And you still haven't told me what you're doing in that tux."

He smiled a bit sheepishly, something she wouldn't have thought possible for Dominic Colbourne. And absolutely endeared himself to her for life because he could. "I guess I don't do a very good James Bond impression."

"James Bo—" She stopped, covered her mouth.

"Go ahead, laugh," he said. "It was probably a loony idea in the first place. But my ability to reason has been a bit dodgy since you climbed in that cab this morning and left with without so much as a farewell."

"I really didn't have much of an option. Stephanie was there and—" She broke off. "You didn't exactly make an effort either."

"I didn't want to embarrass you in front of your boss. And I wasn't sure you wanted me to."

She propped her hands on her hips. "Since when do you care what others think about what you do? I thought you went for what you wanted and damn the consequences."

"I did." He stepped closer to her. "Until I met you. Now I find myself questioning every last thing and second-guessing the rest."

She opened her mouth, but no sound came out.

He pulled a box out from behind his back. She hadn't even been aware enough to notice he'd had his arm tucked back there. "I'm guessing this will go over about as well as the Bond idea. It's not exactly what you wanted, but it was the best I could do on short notice."

She looked at the box he was holding out to her, then up at him. She couldn't tell what was going on behind those enigmatic dark eyes of his, other than to note that he looked even less sure of himself than he did five minutes ago. Interesting. And incredibly appealing.

She took the box. "What's in it?"

He sighed.

She smiled. "What?"

"I might be a complete cad when it comes to relationships, but I have given my share of tokens in the past. It's been my experience that women generally enjoy getting gifts. You're looking at me like—"

"Like what?"

He shrugged then, and it was as endearing as the sheepish grin.

She shook the box, which was the size of a sweater box. Something rustled within. She looked back at him. "So this is just another one of your tokens? Because, frankly, I'd rather have that lunch in Paris."

His mouth dropped open at her deadpan tone.

"I was kidding." She touched his arm. "You're really worried I won't like this, aren't you?"

"Terrified. In fact, give it back to me. It was a stupid idea. I was just trying to think of something that had meaning, just between you and me, and—"

"And I'm sure I'll love it. For exactly those reasons." He was so flustered she wanted to do anything to reassure him. But she couldn't seem to stop smiling. She, Callie Montgomery, had flustered Dominic Colbourne. Apparently there was no limit to her powers. She wanted to laugh herself silly at the mere thought, but the box and Dominic, beckoned.

And then she put it together. Tuxedo. James Bond. "Wait a minute, this isn't—" She laughed as she tore open the box. "Are you here because you want to have costume sex?" Then she gasped as a familiar looking blue, red, and gold cape and body suit fell out into her arms. A pair of stretchy blue boots lay beneath.

"I had to guess your size."

She shook out the Wonder Woman cape. "They come in sizes?"

He sort of shrugged. "Catwoman was sold out. And I couldn't find a seamstress on short notice to do justice to a Barbarella outfit."

She clutched the box and its contents to her chest. "So, did you really did come here for—"

He shook his head. "No, no. I'm really making a royal muck of this, aren't I?" He motioned past her. "Maybe it's better if I come in after all. I'd thought to take you for a drive. Out to the country. Maybe take a look at a horse or something."

"Horse?"

He actually shifted from one foot to another, looking entirely nervous. "You said you rode. For pleasure. I thought maybe that was something I could stand learning a bit more about. I thought, I guess, that maybe you would be the one to show me."

Now her heart started up again, back in its rightful place. And the grin came quite naturally to her face. "After we have the costume sex, you mean, " she deadpanned. "Or were we supposed to go all gussied up like this?" She gestured at his suit. When he looked almost desperate, she dropped her hand. "I'm kidding, Dominic."

He let out his own whooshing breath. "I really should have—"

"You did, and I love it. As for the horse lessons . . . well, I suppose it's only fair, seeing as you gave me a lesson in what you excel in."

He actually blushed. Blushed!

"Callie, listen, I didn't mean any disrespect with the costumes. I was simply trying to do something, I don't know, original. It was meant in fun. I don't care if we ever have sex, in or out of costume—wait, that didn't come out right. I do want to have sex with you. A lot of it. It's just not what I was thinking about when I—what I mean to say is—oh bloody, buggering hell."

Callie tossed the box to floor and simply yanked him inside. "So just tell me," she said, quite seriously. "Why did you come here?"

He looked down at her, then let out a deep, somewhat shaky sigh. "Because I can't stop thinking about you. And I don't want to stop thinking about you. Because I don't need another corporation. But I do need you. I need your laughter. I need your frank responses. I need your smiles, your pithy little comments, your directness, and most of all, I need you to be willing to share them all with me."

"Oh," she said on a sigh, totally unprepared for the emotions his words unleashed inside her. "Oh, Dominic. I shouldn't have teased you. I want the same—"

"Wait, let me finish. I know I've admitted I don't have a clue about handling relationships, and I'm sure I'm a bad bet in just about every area but bed." A hint of his grin surfaced. "Though, if you're willing to start there and let me work my way up—"

Somehow she managed the comeback, despite the fact that her heart had started up its staccato beat once again. "And here I thought you were more interested in working your way down."

His smile flickered to a grin, then faded again. "I want you, Callie Montgomery. However you'll have me."

Now it was her turn to tremble. "I want you, too, Dominic Colbourne. In fact, I—"

"If you're worried about this deal with Stephanie, I—"

"No. No, that's not a problem. I quit about an hour ago."

"You—you what? Because of what happened between us?"

"Yes, but not for the reason you think. I just realized that a high-powered career didn't equal success. Not the kind I want. I realized that having a life, forging my own path, deciding for myself what success means, and what it doesn't—for me—is what's important." She fingered the lapel of his tux. "So I decided to stick with my temping job. At least for now. I enjoy the variety of it, now that I've let myself sit back and realize it. And I enjoy the time it gives me to explore all those . . . possibilities I guess I was letting pass me by." She stopped then, knowing what was left to say, but finding this part a bit harder, despite all he'd said. "And . . . and—"

He tugged her arms. "Callie—"

"No, now you have to let me finish." She took a breath and leaped. "I also decided I wasn't ready to walk away from you. That I thought there was something there, something more than, than—"

"Screaming orgasms?" he said, his lips twitching.

"Yeah. Something like that."

"And so, where were you headed when I got here, if not to work?"

"I was coming to find you." She looked down at her clothes and laughed. "I know we took the opposite approach in terms of apparel, but I figured that if we were going to take any step beyond the ones that had us walking away from each other this morning, then I wanted to take mine as the real me." She swept one hand downward. "This is pretty much who I am. I'm not glamorous, I'm not sophisticated. And I wouldn't know an escargot fork from a butter knife."

"The fork is the one with the prongs," he said, the amusement and the excitement, twinkling in his eyes now.

"Ah."

Dominic reached out, touched her chin, turned her face to his. His finger was quivering. Or maybe it was just her.

"I know who you are," he said quietly. "At least all I needed to know to want to learn about the rest of it. I want you. All of you." He glanced down. "But, unfortunately, this is who I am. Or who I've been. I know all about silverware placement and how to make reservations anywhere in the world. But I'll tell you, glamour and power isn't all it's cracked up to be. And none of it is any real fun if you don't have anyone to share it with, to make it real. To give it value." He looked back into her eyes. "I don't know where I want to go, or how good I'm going to be about getting there. But I do know I want you with me while I bumble my way along."

"You? Bumble?" She was grinning, but her eyes were swimming with tears.

"Yeah," he murmured. "And I'm afraid I'll do a fair lot of it. Will you help me, Callie?"

She wiped at her eyes, laughing, feeling so giddy she was faint with it. "Do I have to wear the Wonder Woman suit?"

He shook his head, tugging her closer, so his body, so perfectly lean and hard and, well, perfect, was up against hers. Then nuzzled her ears and said, "Maybe just the boots?"

She laughed.

And his control finally snapped. "Can I kiss you now? I'm dying here."

"Yeah," she said, weaving her arms around his neck. "I was wondering what was taking you so long."

He groaned and yanked her tight up against him, surprising a little squeal of delight out of her. What little part of her heart she still controlled, was lost the moment his mouth joined with hers.

She groaned, or maybe it was him, when he expertly shifted them around, so he could push her up against the wall.

"Something about this position works for you, doesn't it?" she murmured against his lips.

"It did have its merits," he said, running the tip of his tongue down the side of her neck. "But I'll admit to being more partial to a nice down mattress."

She leaned over and bit the lobe of his ear.

He sucked in a breath and reflexively pushed his hips into hers. "Of course, any—any flat surface will do."

"There's a bed about twenty yards behind you, through that door."

He didn't take his mouth off of her, even as he bent to scoop her into his arms.

"Dominic!"

"Just call me Bond," he said, with a sly wink. Then rolled his eyes even as his cheeks flushed, which made the whole thing too perfect.

"Okay, James," she said, looping her arms around his neck. "Stir me." She grinned. "But first, why don't you let me get those boots."

"But of course." He let her feet drop and bent for the box. She beat him to it and snagged the latex boots, and the cape while she was at it. "I'm thinking I might need this."

He snatched the cape and the boots from her hand and tossed them over his head. "You don't need anything."

"Just you."

He tugged her close. "Yes, thank God. Just me." He scooped her up again and carried her to bed.

"And maybe one other thing," she murmured into his ear. "Seeing as you have all that power and all . . ."

"What were you thinking," he said, nibbling at her chin, the corner of her mouth.

"Oh, nothing fancy, just a small, tasteful—"

"Diamond?"

She just gave him a look.

"What?"

"Elevator. For when we get nostalgic."

"Our own little lift," he said, then tossed her on the bed, just before dropping onto it himself. "Hmm."

"Hmm, yourself." She traced a hand along his body. "Ah, going up?" she teased, as he grew beneath her touch.

He nipped her earlobe. "Cheeky." Then he began to trail kisses down her body, leaving damp marks all the way down her T-shirt.

"Oh," she said, on a groan, as he unzipped her jeans and tugged them down over her hips. "Much better."

"This way you get both," he said, grinning up at her.

"Uh-uh," she gasped, letting her neck arch, her eyes might have rolled back in her head a little. "With you I get it all."

A Fast Ride

Nancy Warren

Chapter One

The low rattling hum, like a hornet refusing to retreat, had Gertie's head jerking up from the middle row of the vegetable garden, where she'd been staking peas. Those dratted motorcycles were as bad as hornets, too, she thought as she wiped perspiration from under her straw hat. There was never just one. They came in swarms, causing nothing but trouble.

Pests.

And like pests, the motorcycle gang should be fumigated, swatted, and otherwise encouraged to leave.

Gertie'd lived in Harleyville all her life. The town was named for Dr. Ernest Harley, one of the town's founding fathers, and not Harley *Gee Dee* Davidson. Gertie's swift movements belied the bent crow angles of her aged body as she scuttled to the two-lane road that bordered her property.

Well, if those motorcycles couldn't respect speed limits, or the peace of the Lord's day, she'd remind them with her own homemade speed bump.

With jerky movements she dragged out the felled poplar branch she'd placed at the roadside for just such an occasion and swiveled it across the road, huffing a little with the effort and the heat.

The buzzing grew louder and she did an arthritic sprint

back to the pea patch before the sight she'd begun to loathe came around the bend in the road faster than the wrath of God Almighty.

She caught a glimpse of leather vest, too-long tangled brown hair blowing in the wind, sunglasses—the kind that looked like twin mirrors so you couldn't see the eyes behind them—and the nasty, low motorcycle.

Then everything happened at once.

She heard a curse that made her clutch her arms around herself in horror and duck her head. Then the sound of the motor changed. Good. The crazy devil must have seen the speed bump and was slowing down.

But the driver slowed too late. The front wheel hit the branch, and the next thing she knew the motorcycle lifted right off the ground.

Gertie's jaw dropped until her upper teeth threatened to slip off her gums. She shut her mouth with a clicking snap.

Up they went into the air, motorcycle and rider. They seemed to hang airborne for a long timeless moment; then the bike dropped while its occupant kept flying—head first into the string beans.

Gertie took one trembling step toward the silent lump of leather and denim in the middle of her vegetable garden, then another. Before she could take a third, her great-niece, Nell, came tearing out the front door and raced to the man's side.

Gertie'd never been so glad to see anyone.

She watched Nell drop to her knees in the dirt, bend over the motorcycle man, and press her ear to his massive chest. After a long moment Nell raised her head and their gazes met.

"Damn it, Gertie! You've killed him."

Nell pushed her fingers harder into the man's neck. She was pretty sure that was his carotid artery she was pressing on. He had a muscular neck, so it was difficult to be certain, but there was still no pulse. She bit her lower lip trying to dredge up everything she'd learned in that CPR course she'd taken a couple of years ago.

Heat prickled the back of her neck and pure blind fear prickled every other part of her body. He *couldn't* be dead. That would make Gertie, whom she loved more than anyone in the world, a murderer.

He sure looked dead, though.

He was utterly still, wild strands of dark toffee-colored hair trailing in the dirt behind him. He wore the colors of the Hog Squad, the motorcycle gang that had turned quiet Harleyville, Kansas, into Trouble, USA, in the last few months, but in death his face didn't look mean.

It appeared strong and sensuous. Dark lashes lay in innocent silky crescents under his eyes. His nose was a bit on the big side, but straight. His lips were full and firm, but parted as though in sleep.

She wished she could shake him awake and send him on his way. He was warm, which gave her hope, until she recalled the sun could be heating his body.

She heard Gertie grunting and muttering and turned her head in time to see the older woman drag the branch out of the road. She didn't have time to help her. How many minutes was it before brain damage set in? She couldn't remember.

Gingerly she placed her hand beneath the man's neck.

Taking a deep breath, she slowly tilted his head back. Not hearing any gross crunching bone noises gave her the courage to pinch his nostrils shut and put her lips over his.

His lips were warm, too. She forced her own breath into him, trying not to think about how different it was blowing into a man's mouth than practicing on a plastic dummy.

She pulled back, breaking the warm connection, and watched his chest begin to deflate. That was good.

She placed her palm in the middle of his chest, fisted the other hand on top of it and started pushing, counting to five.

Back to his mouth. She breathed out, forcing her breath into his body.

Back to his chest.

"Come on!" she wailed as he continued to lie there.

His mouth, his chest, again, and again. How much time had lapsed? Would he be brain damaged? Was she even doing this right?

She shoved harder against his ribs, trying to get through all that muscle and bone to massage his stubborn heart.

"Beat, you bastard!" She yelled, scuffling on her knees in the dirt as she bent forward to force more air into his lungs.

A fly hovered over his face and she brushed it away. Her hands were trembling from her efforts and from fear. He was probably brain dead anyway from all the drugs and booze. "If you'd worn a helmet maybe this wouldn't have happened," she told him sternly, then clapped her lips against his once more.

She pushed her breath out and it caught on an obstacle. A big, wet obstacle. With a strangled shriek, she tried to pull back.

The corpse had stuck his tongue in her mouth.

But, as she moved back, she felt his hand on the back of her neck, pulling her in closer while his tongue made a slow but very deliberate tour of her mouth.

She should be glad he was alive, but mostly she wanted him dead again.

She squirmed, trying to get away, but he misread her intentions and yanked her flush on top of him where she discovered another part of his body was also alive and well and functioning just fine. Trust a man to come back from the grave horny.

At last the pressure eased on the back of her neck and she was able to yank her head out of tongue range and stare down into hazel eyes that gleamed with carnal intentions, the corners crinkled against the sun.

She felt the surprising pull of answering arousal deep in her belly before common sense returned. Her breath was coming hard and fast. After first breathing for two people, then having the breath kissed out of her, she felt lightheaded.

"Hey baby," he said in a deep, gravelly voice. "You were great. Fuckin' A!" He rocked his pelvis against hers and winked.

"Thanks," she replied. "You should see me splint a fracture."

He glanced around, puzzled. "Why'd we do it in the bushes?" Then his eyes roved slowly over her face and dropped to her heaving chest. "What the hell. Let's do it again."

Oh, oh. It looked like she was too late to prevent brain damage. She tried to figure out what to say to him, wondering how his eyes could look so intelligent when his brain was obviously nonfunctional. Then his lids closed and he was gone.

"Whew," she let out her breath on a shudder.

"Thought you said he was dead," said Gertie.

She glanced up to see the old woman tugging a bean plant from under the man's booted foot. She always had bits of twine in her pocket, and she tied the plant up against a still-standing stake with fingers gnarled by age and hard work.

"He *was* dead. I brought him back to life," she said not without pride

"Hmm. What are you going to do with him?"

Harleyville didn't have an emergency room. Not even a hospital. Its three thousand souls were still serviced by one country doctor. The closest hospital was fifty miles away.

"There must be some kind of ambulance."

"He got medical insurance?"

"I don't know." She had to tug and pull at his hip to get to his back pocket, where she assumed his wallet would be, but the way he groaned when she moved him had her dropping him back in place. "I'm not sure how badly he's hurt."

"I'll call Dr. Greenfield," said Gertie, rising and dusting off her hands. "He'll know what to do."

Nell stayed where she was, moving her body so the sun didn't beat in the injured man's face, and watched his large chest rise and fall. She'd retrieved his sunglasses, amazingly unbroken, but didn't slip them back on. If he opened his eyes again, she wanted to know about it.

Shit. What had he been doing? Everything hurt. His head ached, his leg burned. He tried to move his hand to rub the leg and a sharp pain shot through his wrist.

He opened his eyes and frowned. Three faces loomed over him. An old crone who looked like Granny on *The Beverly Hillbillies* grimaced at him, making him feel like a kid who'd peed on her rosebushes. An old guy in a suit was taking something off his arm, and, finally, he saw a face he recognized.

His vision was blurry and her image shimmered for a minute. He squinted harder, trying to bring her face into focus. She was a stunner with gold-blond hair, big sexy green eyes and a mouth that looked as if it could do things that would make a grown man cry.

She had a jaw with attitude, he noted hazily. Looked the kind of woman who'd enjoy making a man beg. A challenge. His favorite kind of woman. He winked at her.

"Well, he's awake."

Her voice was flat Midwest with a hint of California. She made him think of prairies and surfing. "Corn and sushi," he mumbled, his voice emerging hoarse and unfamiliar. "Hard wheat and soft scallops."

"See what I mean? I think he was deprived of oxygen too long," the hottie said to the suit, who nodded gravely.

Her voice was as intriguing as the rest of her. Like thick luscious honey over something hard. Which brought on an image so intense that he instantly had something hard for her to pour honey on.

He quickly shifted his gaze to the old crone, which solved his temporary problem. But not the bigger problem of where he was and why they were staring down at him. "What's going on?"

"You were in an accident," the old guy said in a matter-of-fact tone. "Can you tell me what day it is?"

He rolled his eyes. "It's . . ." He frowned. Turned his gaze back to the babe, as though her familiarity might remind him what infernal day it was. "It's . . ." He was a big believer in bluffing his way out of sticky situations. "It's Tuesday," he said firmly.

Those beautiful green eyes fluttered in distress. Damn. "I mean, Wednesday." Another flutter. Hell, he couldn't play Russian roulette with the calendar. "I can't remember," he finally admitted with a scowl.

The old guy nodded.

He was tired of staring up at these people. He'd managed to figure out he was in a bed. A single brass bed with a crisp cotton bedspread covered in faded roses that couldn't possibly be his.

"What's your name?"

He beat back panic as he tried to focus. *What the hell was his name?* "What's yours?"

"I'm Dr. Greenfield."

There was a pause while he breathed slowly, noting this room smelled musty, like nobody'd been in it for a while.

"And this is Gertrude Hopkins and her great-niece, Nell Tennant."

"Hey, babe," he said to Nell. Did he call her Nell? He doubted it. He probably had a pet name for her, but his aching head couldn't dredge it up.

By gritting his teeth hard he made it to one elbow. He

panted with the effort and felt sweat break out on his fore-head.

"What's your name?" His sexy angel asked him, dropping to her haunches so her eyes were level with his.

"Hell if I know," he admitted.

This time, distress didn't flicker in her eyes, it darkened them and a worried frown puckered the creamy skin of her forehead. "Can you remember anything?"

He smiled at her. "I remember how you taste," he said softly, hoping only she could hear. "And the way you feel against me." He let his gaze roam her body. He might not know his own name or what day of the week it was, but at least he had great taste in women.

Her cheeks pinkened at his low words, but he had the satisfaction of seeing the worry disappear as her gaze heated beneath his.

"Are you my wife?" he asked her, a momentary shaft of alarm poking him at the thought. He didn't feel married.

Her eyes widened and in them he read an answering panic. "No. I'm not your wife."

He was feeling better by the minute. All that sexy sweetness and no shackles. He nodded sleepily. "Girlfriend."

Much better. Her lips opened and he wondered if she was thinking about kissing his hurts better, hoped she was, and then darkness claimed him.

Chapter Two

"I am not your girlfriend!" Nell snapped in a voice much too loud for a sick room, but it was clear she could bellow into his ear and she wouldn't get a response. The injured gang member had passed out again.

"What are we going to do with him?" she asked the doctor whose somber expression didn't bode well.

"I could send for an ambulance to transport him to the hospital, but he's got no identification on him. You'd be responsible."

The sick feeling in her stomach came from knowing they were completely responsible for him lying here in the first place. They couldn't afford costly medical treatments, but on the other hand, she couldn't let him remain here if he was seriously hurt.

"He doesn't look like he's carrying Blue Cross, but we'd better make certain." Between the three of them, they managed to get the man's jeans unzipped and carefully removed them.

He had muscular legs, tawny skin and dark hair that thickened as it approached his groin. The fact that he was wearing underpants was an unexpected bonus. They were plain white briefs and even though she tried not to peek, she noticed that he filled them nicely.

She hated to touch the filthy jeans, but forced herself to search the pockets while Gertie and the doctor watched.

"No wallet," she said as she pulled out a money clip, in the shape of a dollar sign, untidily stuffed with bills. She counted quickly. "Around three hundred dollars."

"Not even enough for one night in the hospital," Doc Greenfield said as she dug through the rest of his pockets.

The final pocket yielded a crumpled piece of paper. She opened it, glancing at the unconscious man. *Wes,* the note said, *Market day, Thursday.* In place of a signature was a single scrawled initial. It looked like a *D* or maybe a *P.* Not much to go on.

Gertie and the doctor were staring at her curiously. She shook her head. "His name's probably Wes, but he doesn't have a single piece of identification on him."

"I can tell you where he belongs. Down at that noisy clubhouse with all the other hooligans, destroying our peace, leaving their beer cans all over. Causing trouble," Gertie glared at the comatose man.

"He won't be causing anyone trouble for a while yet," soothed the doctor. "Come on downstairs and we'll work out what to do with him."

With no better ideas, and happy to escape the disturbing presence in the spare bedroom, Nell followed the other two into the hallway and downstairs.

As she was leaving she heard the man mutter, "girlfriend." She turned back in surprise and, even though his eyes remained closed, she could have sworn his lips twitched.

"In my opinion, he's better off here than in a hospital," Dr. Greenfield said over coffee in the big old kitchen.

Gertie harrumphed but didn't argue. Maybe they weren't

begging for Dr. Greenfield's services at the Mayo Clinic, but here in Harleyville he was well respected. He'd attended more births than deaths, since most of his patients recovered from the various ailments and accidents he treated them for. Nell supposed that counted for something. And besides, Gertie thought the doctor was infallible. Nell, however, had to seriously question his latest plan.

"Stay here?" she all but shrieked.

The old doctor shrugged and sipped his coffee. "He's got no broken bones, just some bumps and bruises. His . . . forgetfulness will likely pass in a day or two."

She tapped her fingernails against the pale green Formica table top. "Have you ever had an amnesia patient?"

"Oh, sure," the doctor replied with a casualness that had her widening her eyes. "I had a few after the war. Then there was old George Hayden," he chuckled. "Remember him, Gertie?"

She nodded her head and chuckled right along with the doc.

"He fell head first out of a tractor and woke up thinking he was a bronco rider. But he got his memory back after a few weeks. Most of them do."

"But not all?"

"Don't fuss, honey." Dr. Greenfield patted her hand. "Time is the best healer. Time, bed rest, good food, and fresh air. He can't do better than stay right here."

"But he's part of that motorcycle gang. Shouldn't they be looking after him?"

"Are you going to waltz on down there and return him? Explain how he fell on the straight road outside your property and now he doesn't know who he is?" The doctor's faded blue eyes shifted from her to Gertie and back again. He hadn't asked for the particulars of the accident, but it was obvious he had some suspicions.

Nell chewed her lip, knowing she couldn't send the injured man to a bunch of bikers for TLC. Not when she knew how he'd been hurt. She shook her head.

"My guess is, he'll be up and around in a few days and anxious to be on his way."

There was one item that rankled. "But he thinks I'm his girlfriend."

The old man nodded, a twinkle lurking. "Best to let him go on thinking it. Like we did with old George and the rodeo. For some reason, you're familiar to him. It's something for his mind to hang on to while it's healing."

"But . . . but . . ." She was familiar to the biker because he'd woken with the assumption they were getting their rocks off out among the string beans when all she'd been doing was saving his miserable life.

"You don't have to worry about somebody else getting jealous do you?"

"That's not the point." But it was. In fact, that was why she was here in the first place. After breaking up with Peter, she'd pulled the plug on her old lifestyle, quitting her job and getting right out of Los Angeles. She'd run home to Gertie to lick her wounds and plan her future. She needed a calm, quiet routine. A chance to think about her life and what she wanted to do next. Having an amnesiac criminal in the house didn't seem all that conducive to peace and quiet.

She sighed and sipped coffee. But what, really, were her options? She and Gertie couldn't afford hospital treatment and the doctor was right. They couldn't simply dump the guy back in the arms of his gang members without an explanation.

A dull headache throbbed behind her eyeballs. "All right," she said. "But if he starts pawing me he'll be dead again, real quick."

He woke with a groan, certain the jackhammer in his head had hauled him from sleep. Instinctively, he tried to put a hand to his head and then winced again at the pain in his arm. What the hell?

Slowly it came back to him. Not that there was a lot of it to come back. He recalled this room, the green-eyed hottie, and that he'd been tormented by nightmares, none of which made a damn bit of sense. The part that he hadn't dreamt was the fact that he didn't know who, what, or where he was, which frustrated him as much as his pounding head and aching body.

Then his sexy angel entered the room carrying a tray of things that smelled good and his day perked up. At least she was real, a connection to the identity and past that eluded him.

"Good morning," she said with a searching look.

He answered the unspoken question at once. "I can't even remember my own name."

She smiled lightly, but the furrow didn't disappear from between her eyes. "It's Wes."

"Wes." He digested that, rolled it around and decided it felt right. "And you're . . . ?"

For some reason she looked as though she didn't want to tell him. Since his only memories were of the feel of her body pressed intimately against his and the taste of her on his tongue, he found her hesitation amusing. "Did we have a fight or something?"

"No. We didn't fight. My name's Nell. I was hoping you'd have your memory back this morning."

"You and me both." He couldn't rid himself of the notion that there was something important he needed to do. Something urgent, but what it was, he hadn't a clue.

He hauled himself up to sitting, trying not to cry like a baby as aches and pains stabbed him, and she settled the fragrant tray over his lap. Steaming coffee, a pitcher of cream, a sugar pot, a glass of orange juice so pulpy it had to be fresh squeezed, and a bowl of oatmeal.

Oatmeal? Beside that was a small plate with a couple of

white pills. He took a life-restoring slug of coffee and picked up the pills, raising his brows as he did so.

"Painkillers. Doc left them for you."

With a silent thanks to the doc he popped them in his mouth and washed them down with hot coffee. Then he glanced at the rest of the tray and back at her. "What are you trying to pull?"

"Me?" She started and looked guilty as hell.

"I may not know my name, but I know for damn sure that I hate oatmeal."

"Eat it. It's good for you," she said and started backing out of the room.

"I'll eat it on one condition."

She narrowed her eyes at him. "What?"

"Stay and talk to me."

She didn't move for a second, then eyed the tray. "You have to drink the orange juice, too."

"Every drop," he promised. She headed for the wicker chair in the corner but he wasn't having that. "Uh-uh. Sit on the bed."

It seemed she struggled with herself, then came and perched down by the foot rail. They must have had a humdinger of a fight, he decided. "Did I drive off mad at you? Is that how I got in the accident?"

She blushed and wouldn't meet his eye. "Not exactly. You were driving too fast, that's all."

"I looked out the window. That road's straighter than the path to hell. Doesn't look like it's rained or snowed recently either," he said, thinking that was the only possible way he could have lost control unless he'd been driving stupid because he'd had a fight with his girl.

Still, she didn't say a word, simply plucked at the bedspread with delicate, manicured fingers.

Time ticked by and he felt as though he'd gone back in time

watching her, so prim in the old-fashioned surroundings. "I'm sorry," he said gruffly.

Her head shot up at that. "What for?"

"For whatever we fought about." He stared at her lush pink lips until she blushed deeper and ran her tongue over them. "I'm sorry for something else, too."

"What?" Her lips were wet and luscious where she'd licked them.

"You're so mad at me, I didn't even get a good morning kiss."

"Oh, well . . . you're not really well enough . . ." She ran a hand through her hair making a mess of it. He bet she looked exactly like that when they made love. Damn, he was a lucky man.

He spooned into the oatmeal, so she'd stay, trying not to gag. He gulped orange juice to help it down. "Talk to me," he said. "Take my mind off this stuff."

"Talk to you . . ."

"What do I do? What do you do? How did we meet? Basic stuff. I'm trying to figure out who I am."

"Oh. I keep forgetting I know more about you than you know about yourself. Well, let's see. You're a member of the Hog Squad."

The spoon hit the oatmeal with a wet slap. "The what?"

"It's a motorcycle, um, club."

He was getting a bad feeling in his gut. "You mean a gang?"

She nodded.

"I'm a gang member?"

"Yes."

It didn't sit well, but he'd think about that later. "What do you do?"

"I'm unemployed. I'm spending the summer with my great-aunt until I decide what I want to do. I was working as a publicist in LA but I . . . got tired of it."

There was a story there, but he'd pursue that later as well. Right now he wanted to know what a woman like her was doing with a loser like him, though he was pretty certain it was the animal attraction thrumming between them that was responsible. He didn't care who or what she was. He wanted her. No wonder images of their love life were the single thing his mind had brought with him from the accident.

Having scraped his bowl clean and swallowed the last of the juice, he pushed the tray away and grinned at her. "Doesn't sound like we have a thing in common."

She rose and came toward him, presumably for the tray. "Not really."

"The sex must sure be hot, then."

She looked at him and her mouth opened and closed once, then twice. "You'd be better off using your energy getting your health back." She reached for the tray, then paused, head lifted, and turned to the window. He heard it too. The ominous sound of a herd of small engines getting louder by the second.

Motorcycles.

A gang of them.

He kept his ears cocked. Nell had her face pressed to the window. As he'd feared and dreaded, the engines changed timbre and one by one fell quiet outside. Nell glanced at him, a worried frown in her eyes. "I don't want your . . . associates here bothering Gertie."

He nodded, thinking he didn't want them here either. "They know about us?"

"No."

In spite of the knot in his stomach, he forced himself to remain calm. A fist banged on the front door and Nell flinched then moved toward the bedroom door.

"Let Gertie answer it," he ordered. "You stay here."

She seemed about to argue, but he knew his instincts were right. "Trust me," he said.

After a strained moment, she nodded and moved back to the bedside. He had an odd feeling she was standing between him and the door in a bid to protect him, which made him smile and reach out to pull her close.

They heard Gertie's voice, and it was none too polite, then the thud of boots coming up the stairs. Nell shuddered and, without thinking why, he pulled her off balance so she sprawled on the bed beside him.

"What are you—" Her furious words were cut off by a louder voice.

"Wes, buddy. What's happening, dude?"

A massive bald man in a leather vest, chaps, and boots clomped into the room. With him were three others. They shuffled in and said, "Hey, man," then left the talking to baldy, who was clearly the leader.

"Hey," said Wes, his arm tightening around Nell as she tried to wriggle out of his grasp.

"You didn't call home," Baldy said with a grin that did nothing to hide the cold anger in his pale blue eyes.

"He's got amnesia. He doesn't know who he is," Nell explained in a firm tone at odds with the trembling he felt running through her.

"Looks like he knows who you are fine," the massive man ran his eyes up and down Nell's body as though they were his filthy hands.

Anger simmered in the pit of Wes's belly. "Nell's my lady," he said, putting a slight emphasis on "my" just to make his position clear.

"Thought you had amnesia."

"Some things you don't forget."

After a tense moment, Baldy laughed. "Gals down at the roadhouse are going to be disappointed to hear you got a regular squeeze. Kept her real quiet, didn't you?"

"That's right. I don't like sharing." To make his proprietary claim clear, he slipped a hand under her shirt, holding her so his thumb rubbed the underside of her breast. Warm and firm, her flesh delighted him. He caressed her both to reassure Nell and to place a KEEP OFF sign on her body, just so his buddies didn't get any ideas.

She stiffened for a moment, then relaxed, snuggling up against him. He stared into her green eyes and felt the warmth build. "I was just reminding Nell she forgot to give me a good morning kiss," he said, then dipped his head and took her mouth.

His hair fell forward to provide a scanty privacy screen while his lips played over hers. Desire punched through his system as he tasted her, his arms tightening to bring her in closer. He wanted to delve in and continue the love play, but he never forgot his audience. He intended to stake his claim, not get them so turned on they gave these losers a peep show, so he dragged his mouth away from hers, winking down into her desire-clouded gaze then turning back to his visitors.

"Haven't forgotten old Louie, have you?" the bald man asked.

"Who's Louie?"

There was a short burst of laughter, quickly stifled, from the henchmen. "I'm Louie. I need to talk to you. Alone."

He didn't like the way Nell was being eyed by the other bikers so he shook his head. "She stays."

Louie came forward. "You have something that's mine. You better get your memory back, fast. I'll be watching you."

He strode for the door and Wes stopped him. "How did you know I was here?"

Louie snorted. "It's a small town. News travels fast. I'll be back in a week. You better have my stuff."

Chapter Three

Nell scooted out of his arms and off the bed the second the front door slammed. She went to the window and he watched her watch their unwelcome visitors leave in a roar of engines.

"Do you have any idea what stuff Louie was talking about?" he asked her.

She shook her head.

So far the knowledge he had about himself wasn't immensely reassuring. He was a biker in a gang and he didn't think the "stuff" Louie referred to was cotton candy.

Damn. How did a guy like him ever get an uptown girl like Nell to look at him twice? "How did we meet?" he asked her.

She smiled faintly. "You dropped by one day while I was in the garden and . . . one thing led to another."

He let his gaze roam her body, wishing his memory would give him a picture of her naked. What color were her nipples? Did they crinkle when she was aroused? The milky skin of her throat and collarbone had intrigued him while he was kissing her. Was her skin as pale all over?

He wanted to remember with a fierceness that made him flinch.

"What's the matter?"

"I'm trying to remember how you look naked."

She rolled her eyes but her pebbling nipples gave her away. "You must be feeling better."

"Well enough to get out of bed," he insisted even as she protested. He couldn't laze around while big guys in leather were threatening him and eyeing his girl.

He made it to his feet and swayed. She rushed forward and, even though his head had cleared, he let throw her arms around him and prop him up. He was naked but for cotton briefs so he felt the rub of her silky shirt against his naked torso. Her hands were small but strong as she clutched at his back. Her breath stirred the hair on his chest and where her legs were bare below her shorts, they rubbed against his own.

He rested his chin on her head, wondering if an artistic tumble back into the bed, taking Nell with him, wouldn't be a better start to the day. Except he had a feeling he was going to have to find out what he had that belonged to Louie and where the hell it was.

Still, he indulged in another moment snuggled up to Nell enjoying the contact and the almond smell of her shampoo. It reminded him that he didn't smell nearly as good. "I need a shower."

"You could hurt yourself."

"Not if you come in with me."

She glared up at him and he grinned down into her gorgeous face. "Just to hold me up."

"Gertie doesn't have a shower. You can take a bath. I went out this morning and got you a few things."

"Thanks. I still probably need you in there with me."

She tried to look stern but he saw her lips twitch. "To hold you upright?"

"No. To wash my back." He did his best to look innocent but he had a sneaking feeling it had been a lot of years since he'd pulled that off. "Very hard to reach back there because of my injuries."

* * *

"You're just in time for lunch," Gertie remarked as Wes came through the door, hair still damp from the bath. Now that his hair was clean it hung thick and dark, forming loose waves as it dried.

Nell couldn't say anything at all. She felt as though her darkest fantasy had come to life before her eyes.

Without the stubble and grime, his face was lean and hard, all angles and planes except where his chin was softened by a dimple. His eyes were the hazel of a forest at sunset, full of secrets and mystery. His body was solid, long limbed, and muscular beneath the soft gray T-shirt she'd bought this morning and his own freshly washed jeans.

His gaze caught hers and she recalled how he felt when she grabbed him that morning, strong and hard, every inch of him potent, sexual male. She felt as though he saw right through to her secret self, the part of her no one knew existed. The part that was lured helplessly. For the first time she understood the term "animal magnetism." In his presence she became the zoological equivalent to an iron filing.

"You shaved," she finally managed to blurt.

His hand rubbed his strong jaw line. "Yeah. I found a pink plastic razor on the side of the tub."

"I'm sorry, I forgot to buy you a razor." Her pulse was leaping about shamelessly, which annoyed Nell, but how could she have known a member of the Hog Squad would clean up so well or gaze at her in that devastatingly intimate way? As though he planned to devote himself to discovering all her secrets.

The way he gazed at her, so still and serious, had her heart hammering in her chest and her mind flooding with memories of how she'd felt tucked against his body, his thumb teasing her breast, his lips taunting her, while his buddies had stared at them.

She should have been outraged, but she hadn't been. She'd liked being kissed by Wes. She'd liked it the way she liked a drink before dinner to whet her appetite for a gourmet meal. Except she had a strong feeling she ought to be resisting this particular meal. Still, she could look couldn't she?

He surprised her by showing perfectly good table manners while they ate lunch, and then she was ashamed of herself for assuming that a motorcycle gang member must be an uncouth thug. Thug he most certainly was, though, and she had to remember that. She'd found a knife tucked into his boot.

His gaze strayed to hers while they ate, and each time she recalled his words about seeing her naked.

The man was a stranger with no memory who appeared to be a criminal. And she'd never, ever been so hot for any man in her entire life.

Maybe that was why she'd driven an extra ten minutes to a drugstore she never frequented to buy condoms. Even knowing they were tucked into her bedside table underneath the novel she was reading, she grew warm every time she thought of what she was contemplating.

But why shouldn't she, for once in her life, throw caution to the wind? She'd lived with caution too long and it had turned out to be a lousy roommate. With her long-term relationship over and a break from her workaholic ways, she felt as alive as a young tree in springtime. Damn it, her sap was rising.

In fact, her sap wasn't just rising, it was heating, simmering, settling in her breasts and her womb, hot and heavy. She felt bold and alive and more womanly than ever before.

For some reason, this rough, scary stranger made her feel things she'd never felt in five years with Peter, who scheduled sex into his Palm Pilot along with all the other obligations of his busy life.

"Nell, go get mystery boy here his pills," Gertie said, breaking into her reverie. "Then he ought to take a nap."

"His name's Wes," she replied, knowing her aunt hadn't yet recovered from having four gang members tramp through her house without a single one of them removing his boots.

She fetched the pills and without much protest they did get him up for a nap.

Nell glanced at her bedside clock as she leaned over to turn out the light. It was after eleven.

She was physically tired, but mentally jittery. Her book hadn't been able to hold her attention, and as she settled under the covers she found herself practically vibrating with tension.

Downstairs, in her own room, Gertie, whose farmer's genes had her rising with the crows and bedding down by nine, slept like the dead, but Nell hadn't yet reverted from an LA night owl to a Kansas early bird.

As she turned grumpily in bed, she accepted it wasn't simply the early hours she was keeping that were affecting her like this. It was the thinly veiled threat of the gang member, Louie.

She thumped her pillow, knowing she was still lying to herself. She felt as though her body were crying out for fulfillment. Out here, in the middle of Hicksville, where she'd come to get away from all the pressures and demands of her former life, her body suddenly craved sex.

She throbbed with unfulfilled needs, right to the end of her fingertips.

She flipped to her side facing the window, trying to find a comfortable spot. Moonlight filtered between a gap in the curtains upping her irritation a notch. Moonlight meant romance and romance made her starved body think of sex and sex made her think of . . .

The man in bed across the hall. Oh, how she wished she'd bought him a pair of pajamas. He hadn't struck her as the pajama type, but at least she could have imagined him in them. As it was, she pictured him naked.

Naked and fully aroused.

She tossed and turned some more, cursing her vivid imagination, wondering if she should go downstairs for a glass of milk. Or an ice pack for certain overheated body parts.

A board creaked in the hallway and she held her breath, listening. She'd left her bedroom door ajar, refusing to think about why, and she heard the quiet *shush* as it opened into the room.

She didn't turn her head, or make a sound, simply waited, her body all but wriggling with anticipation while her conscious mind was appalled at what she was contemplating.

Even though she'd expected it, her body quivered with shock when he touched her. It was only a hand on her shoulder, but she felt it, warm and tingling, all the way to her toes.

The leathery pads of his fingertips traced the scoop neck of the stretchy cotton designer nightshirt that clung to her curves. She hadn't let herself ponder why she'd slipped it on earlier, or the number of times she'd run the brush through her hair, or the tiny dab of perfume she'd touched behind her ears and between her breasts.

A woman was allowed to look nice and smell nice simply for her own company wasn't she? She was certain she'd read that in a magazine article. Making herself pretty and scented for bed wasn't about a man. It was about self-love.

Except it wasn't self-love she craved tonight.

It wasn't even love she wanted, it was pure, uncomplicated down and dirty sex, and she had her sights on a prime specimen. He might be a thug, but he was sexy and earthy and everything her previous men were not. Besides, whatever her mind thought, her body was in charge tonight. Perhaps if they didn't speak she could pass it off as a dream.

Dreamlike was exactly how it felt when his fingers reached the vee between her breasts. She trembled at their slight roughness against the sensitive spot, and the way he took brazen ownership of her body.

There was no conversation, no "do you feel like it tonight," no hurrying because of an early morning meeting. There were just the two of them, two bodies as highly tuned to each other as the people inhabiting them were worlds apart.

He turned her so she was flat on her back and she gazed up at him, so very foreign and yet somehow so familiar. He wore nothing but the new white briefs she'd bought him, and in the near dark he seemed both sinister and exciting. His hair hung free to just past his shoulders, shadowing his face so all she could see was the predatory gleam of his eyes.

She looked into them and began to tremble.

With one knee on the bed, he knelt over her and, when his mouth was only a breath away, whispered, "I forgot to kiss you good night."

A tiny sound broke from her throat, part acceptance, part plea as her lips opened in anticipation. The second their mouths met she felt his passion and hunger. This was no gentle caress but a fierce and hungry possession of her mouth. She tasted frustration and felt his desire keen and barely restrained as his tongue delved into her mouth as though ready to drag forth a response. He'd been thinking about this all day, she realized with a dash of smug vanity, holding himself in check until nighttime.

Then all thoughts, smug and otherwise, flew out of her head as he shucked his briefs and climbed into bed.

He went back to her mouth, but with the impatience of a man who wants everything at once, broke off to trail kisses down her throat. He traced the edge of her nightshirt with his tongue, then breathed warm, moist air through the cotton onto her nipples. She gasped at the sensation, feeling the tingle as her nipples tightened beneath the now damp cotton. His palms followed his mouth to brush over the sensitive peaks until she was squirming.

Where moments before he'd seemed almost beyond control, he'd now reined himself in, although the tension in every line of his moonlit body told her how tenuous that control was. She wanted to cry out to him to let himself go and at the same time wanted this slow caress to go on forever. Her breathing was nothing more than choppy sighs when he slipped his hands down the sides of her breasts and molded the curves of her ribs, waist and hip as intimately as the clinging cotton.

He got to the midthigh hem and paused to trace the edge of the fabric, just as he'd done with the neckline. She tried not to moan or beg, when he got to the seam of her thighs, but eased them apart for him in a silent plea. Either he didn't notice, or chose to ignore her body's invitation; instead he raised his gaze until it locked with hers.

Then he grasped the hem of her nightshirt and slowly drew it up over her body. His gaze followed the same path and she thought no one had ever looked at her with such focused passion. "How could I forget?" he whispered in amazement.

She sighed, and raised her arms so he could pull the garment over her head until she lay before him, stretched out, naked.

"Don't move," he ordered, and, striding to the window, he pulled the curtains wide so her body was bathed in moonlight.

Was he trying to kill her?

She fought the urge to cover herself with her hands. He'd think she was nuts. He didn't know this was the first time they'd made love, that they were strangers and that she was shy with him, so she tried to pretend it was fine, even though nerves skittered in her stomach and her heart pounded.

She only hoped the moonlight was pale enough to disguise the head-to-toe blush that suffused her. Her whole body wanted to roll into itself and hide from this inquisitive predator, but once more she called on her self-control. She couldn't seem to control her toes, however. They curled tightly, preserving the modesty of all ten toe pads.

He was a dark silhouette as he moved with easy grace toward her, but that silhouette was tall, broad shouldered, and narrow hipped. And when he turned to face her, and the moonlight gilded him, she forgot about herself and sucked in a breath at the sheer beauty of his body.

She'd never thought a lot about the penis. It was an appendage with a job to do and frankly she thought men spent far too much time and energy obsessing over what was, proportionately, a pretty small piece of their anatomy. But Wes's penis, all silvery gold in the moonlight seemed both mysterious and imbued with energy. She couldn't resist the impulse to reach out and touch it.

It was warm and hard, heavy in her hand as she wrapped her fingers around the shaft and squeezed. Now it was his turn to suck in a breath as she explored him, tormented him a little, and then slid her hand beneath him to cup the heavy sac, already tight against his body.

Aching with the need to feel him inside her, she released him and reached for her bedside table, pulling out a couple of the condoms she just happened to have handy. He took one and sheathed himself before covering her body with his own.

Oh, the slide of warm flesh against warm flesh, the feel of his lips against hers and his hands on her body, exploring and exciting. While he kissed and licked her breasts he trailed a hand down her belly and between her thighs.

She swallowed her cry when he touched her.

"You're so wet," he whispered hoarsely. "Are you wet for me?"

She might be ready to weep with wanting, but such arrogance could not go unpunished. She wrapped her hand around his erection. "You're so hard," she taunted him right back. "Are you hard for me?"

"Oh, yeah," he said through his teeth.

She thought he'd take her then. Pound into her with all the suppressed tension she felt vibrating beneath his flesh. Again he surprised her. He parted her folds, baring her clitoris, and stroked it with a light touch that kept her on simmer without letting her boil over. As her excitement built she hardly realized her hand was tightening on his shaft until he gave a harsh groan and pulled her away.

"Oh, I'm so—" Then she cried out as he pushed her knees up to her belly and thrust inside in one long, smooth stroke.

Her cry ended on a gasp as he filled her, more than filled her, so she felt the delicious stretch and tug of her inner muscles accommodating his length and thickness. Hell, they weren't just accommodating him. They were hugging and kissing him in gratitude for the pleasure that was already zinging through her system.

She clutched at Wes's sweat-slick shoulders, fisted her hands in his thick silky hair, grasped his straining biceps as he thrust, deep and hard and steady, while she wrapped her legs around his waist and rose to meet each thrust.

"I can't—" She gasped, twisting against him. "I need . . ."

He lifted her hips and changed the angle slightly so he was hitting her hot spot and then there was no stopping the wave that built, crested, and crashed. Her body spasmed and her throat clutched, strangling her own cries as he dropped his head, biting softly into her shoulder as he groaned his own release.

He collapsed at her side, one arm thrown possessively over her, his breath warm against her hair while she tried to regain her own breath. Not to mention her wits.

She'd just had the best sex of her life with a guy whose last name she didn't even know. This from a girl with two university degrees and a professional designation behind her name.

She couldn't stop the grin from stealing over her face.

"You know what's great about having amnesia?" he asked several minutes later.

"What?" She felt smug and sleepy and ridiculously happy.

"That felt like the first time with you."

She turned to kiss him softly on the lips, noting the uneven stubble where he'd had to use her razor. She'd have to remember to get him one of his own in the morning, otherwise whisker burn was going to be a big part of her immediate future.

"Is our sex always this good?" he asked, stroking her breast idly.

She nipped his jaw gently. "Every single time," she assured him.

Chapter Four

Wes woke with a jerk from another nightmare. He reached automatically for Nell's warm body and encountered the edge of his own single bed. He couldn't believe he'd let her boot him out of her room after they'd made love.

She claimed he was getting the heave-ho out of consideration for Gertie, but he was getting the uncomfortable feeling he was pussy-whipped.

In fact, the more he learned about himself, the less he approved. He was most likely some kind of petty criminal. He shoved a stray hair off his face and wondered what had possessed him to grow his hair as long as a girl's so it was always in the way or tickling his neck. How could falling on his head have made him hate his hair and his lifestyle?

He'd searched his body carefully after bathing yesterday and been relieved to find that while he had some colorful bruises, he sported no tattoos. There was an indentation in one earlobe that suggested he'd pierced his ear at one point, but luckily there were no other puncture marks. No needle marks either and he didn't crave anything but coffee and sex so presumably he wasn't a drug addict.

He did discover a couple of old wounds. A jagged curve with bumpy scar tissue in his leg that he suspected was caused by a knife and another on his shoulder that looked like a bullet wound. So, he liked to fight, did he? When he recalled the burn of possessive anger he'd experienced when the other gang members checked Nell out, he wasn't surprised.

The only thing he liked about his pre-accident choices was Nell. Of everything in his life, she was the one thing that felt right. Except that she obviously henpecked him, not letting him stay in her bed all night because of that sour old biddy downstairs.

Wes stacked his hands under his head and stared up at the white ceiling as dawn poked its head in the window. He had to face facts.

He was a putz.

He was also having some disturbing dreams. Breathing slowly, he tried to capture the images that had awakened him, sensing that his unconscious was trying to tell him what his conscious mind had forgotten.

In his mind he saw a back-country road that wound around a fenced field with a row of tall trees out front. Poplar? Birch? He heard the hum of his own motorcycle engine and was conscious of feelings of dread and excitement in his gut. There was a farmhouse ahead of him, but that was not where the wavy dream road took him. Behind the farmhouse, at least he thought it was behind, hard to tell with a dream, he noted a derelict barn. His heart rate increased and his hands clenched, though he had no idea why.

That was it. As hard as he tried, he couldn't raise any more images from his dream.

It looked like a perfectly normal, everyday farmhouse with a derelict barn. Not exactly an uncommon sight in this part of the world. So why did it wake him every night? What was his subconscious trying to tell him?

Then a slow grin lit his face. Maybe he woke with a pounding heart not because he associated that barn with something bad, but something good. Maybe he and Nell had found a place where they could be alone, away from the prying eyes of her aunt and his associates.

He shifted, realizing how helpless he felt without any memories. Did he have parents? A job? He'd gauged his age to be midthirties when he looked in the mirror, but the guy with the long hair and no tattoos was a stranger.

The only person he trusted was Nell. He was disappointed that making love with her last night hadn't brought his memory back. How could a man forget being with a woman like her?

He felt as though he'd stumbled into the wrong body. He was definitely a putz.

For some reason, when she saw him at breakfast, Nell blushed.

He was wrong, he realized. Knowing what she looked like naked hadn't eased his mind, it merely increased the urge to get her naked again.

He shot her a wolfish grin that made her blush even deeper.

He waved away the painkillers, feeling better than he'd ever felt. Of course, given that his memory only stretched back two days, that wasn't saying much. Still, he felt damn good. They'd loved far into the night and still he wanted her again with a fierceness that surprised him.

"If you're feeling so good," Gertie's voice intruded on his lascivious thoughts, "there's some fencing out back needs fixing."

"Gertie!" Nell protested. "I'm sure Wes isn't well enough to—"

"Sure I am," he interrupted. "Some fresh air and exercise will be good for me." The sex had taken it out of him some, but his aches and pains were a lot milder today. He must be a fast healer.

Nell stared at him over her coffee. "Do you know how to fix a fence?"

He thought about that for a second. "No idea. I guess we'll find out."

"It's not brain surgery," Gertie reminded them both. And, as it turned out, whether or not he'd ever done it before, he found there wasn't much science in nailing up broken fence boards and replacing the rotting ones. Painting them all would be a bitch, but from his short acquaintance with Gertie, he figured that was next on his handyman agenda.

Fine with him. It kept him occupied and the task left his mind free to wander. He was hoping it would find its way home, real soon. He couldn't rid himself of the notion that there was something important he had to do.

When Nell brought out a picnic basket to where he was working, he felt like kissing her.

So he did.

"I am so happy not to have to eat lunch with that old woman glaring at me."

"She can't help it. She really has it in for that motorcycle gang."

She led him to the shade of a big old cherry tree and then laid out the blanket she'd brought, sat down and unpacked the contents. A plate of sandwiches, a jug of lemonade, some kind of cake and a couple of apples.

"I didn't think you'd want to go to the house to wash up so I brought you a wet-wipe." She passed him the square packet he'd already spied and hoped was a condom.

He slit the packaging and removed a damp white square, shaking his head. He really doubted they stocked wet-wipes down at the gang's clubhouse. "How did you and I ever end up together?"

She laughed, but didn't elaborate.

He cleaned off, tossed the used wipe in an empty corner of the picnic basket and sprawled beside Nell and closed his eyes.

"Tired?"

"No. I was hoping if I didn't look at you I wouldn't want to take you right here, right now."

"Is it working?" She asked in a voice that trembled slightly with sexual awareness.

He opened his eyes half way. "Nope."

Nell eyed him, so long and lean, relaxed as though he hadn't a care in the world, and warmth rushed through her as she remembered how he'd touched her last night. The things he'd made her feel.

He ate without hurry, but with precision as though it were a job to be done quickly and efficiently.

His gaze was directed to the new section of fence he'd repaired but when he turned to her, the heat in his eyes told her he hadn't been thinking about fencing.

Even before he spoke her heart started to pound.

"You know what I hate most?" he said.

"No, what?"

"I hate that I don't know how to please you."

Was the man blind and deaf that he hadn't noticed her response last night? "You do please me," she assured him. Knowing she owed him something for the deception she was pulling, she dragged up her courage and admitted, "More than anyone ever has."

He shook his head impatiently. "I don't mean last night. I mean all the stuff I've forgotten. The little things you learn about a person. I don't know your fantasies, or the private games we like to play."

She felt hot and stifled as though he'd literally backed her into a corner.

She dropped her gaze and fiddled with the edge of the red plaid blanket. How could she tell him that *he* was her fantasy? A stranger on a motorcycle with no past, no burning corporate ladder-climbing ambitions, a man with magic hands and a knowing mouth.

A man who put her pleasure ahead of his own.

"I . . ."

She felt his hand cup her cheek, slide through her hair. "I want to know. I want to remember," he said in a husky whisper.

She almost laughed. When he remembered, she was going to be up one very murky creek without a paddle. When his memory came back he'd know she'd been lying, using him for sex.

She ought to be appalled at herself, and yet her deception didn't seem wrong. No one was getting hurt and if Wes was anything like every other man she'd ever known, he'd be only too happy to say "thanks for the hot sex" and be on his way.

In the meantime, she was being offered her secret desires on a silver platter. She wasn't strong enough to turn them down. No man had ever wanted to know her fantasies or shown any desire to make them reality, and here was Wes, who didn't even know her, staring into her eyes as if he really wanted to know.

"We love to find new places," she whispered, mortified to hear herself saying the words aloud. She'd never done anything so bold, but always secretly wanted to. Wes was a born rule breaker. He wouldn't care about his reputation if he were caught making love under the stars, or up a tree, or any other foolish place the urge took him.

"New places, huh?" He grinned. "I'm thinking of one right now."

The hand that had been idly caressing her hair now moved, and he trailed a lazy finger down her neck to the collar of her white T-shirt.

"You are?"

"Uh-huh. I'm thinking of a place out under a big cherry tree, with a blanket spread out and—"

"And Gertie knocking herself out peering at us through the kitchen window," she finished.

He laughed. "You worry about her too much."

"I love her," she told him. "I can't hurt her."

Instead of rolling his eyes or calling her a prude, he nodded. "She loves you, too. That's why she doesn't like me. She doesn't think I'm good enough for you."

Her eyes bugged out of her head. "Gertie told you that?"

He shrugged. "She may have, before I lost my memory. But she tells me every time she catches sight of me."

Wes was more perceptive than she'd given him credit for. "Do you mind?"

"No. She's right."

A bee buzzed lazily by and she felt drowsy in the warm summer afternoon. She hadn't had much sleep, after all.

As she'd suspected—as she'd hoped—Wes hadn't seemed a bit put off by her spoken desire. She decided to push the subject, since she had no idea how long he'd be without his memory—how long he'd be here at all.

"So, I was wondering. About making love in different places. Could we—"

Suddenly his eyes widened and he grabbed her arm. "Did we make love in an old barn behind a farmhouse?"

Her mouth opened and closed a couple of times as she tried to formulate a response that was truthful but not. "I don't think so. Why?"

He shook his head impatiently, as though he could rattle his memory back into place. "I keep seeing this place in my dreams. It feels like it's important. I was just wondering if my sex memory was returning first."

She punched him playfully in his impressive bicep. "I wouldn't be a bit surprised. You seem to have a pretty strong sex drive."

"Oh, babe. You have no idea how much I want to drive it into you right now."

Heat shot through her at his crude words. "Me too."

He gazed at her, a steamy, taunting look. "What are you doing after lunch?"

She squirmed on the blanket, so hot for him she couldn't hold still. But unfortunately, fantasy fulfillment would have to wait. "I promised I'd take Gertie into town to get groceries. And you have a fence to mend."

He groaned good-naturedly, grabbed an apple and got to his feet. "Let's make a date for later. We can take my bike and—"

She shook her head and saw the moment it hit him his bike wasn't going anywhere for a while. "We'll have to take Gertie's truck."

"Right."

"And I'll drive."

As she'd suspected, he did a male-puffing-out-his-chest thing and spluttered that he knew how to drive a truck.

"You've had a head injury. Driving is off your list until you've seen Doc Greenfield again."

"Do I have an appointment?"

"Day after tomorrow."

She'd wondered if he'd be difficult about seeing the doctor, but he merely nodded. He must be as anxious to get his memory back as she was for him not to. At least for a little while.

Wes worked late into the afternoon, slaking his thirst with the pitcher of lemonade Nell had left him, wishing he felt as peaceful as the quiet afternoon warranted.

His bumps and bruises weren't more than an irritation, but there was a nagging sense of disquiet.

Again and again he revisited the image of that barn. If it hadn't been a place he and Nell had gone to play their adult games, then it must be important for some other reason.

But what?

He was feeling hot, frustrated, and tired when he felt an odd prickling sensation at the back of his neck. Someone was watching him.

He maneuvered his body around while he pounded in a nail, but he couldn't see a soul. Pretending he had to scratch his leg, he reached for the knife in his boot.

It wasn't there.

He kept a knife in his boot? He didn't like the implications of that. He didn't like even more that he no longer had it. His only weapon was the hammer he held in a vise grip.

He went back to pounding nails, but the sensation of being watched persisted.

His first instinct was to get back to the house and protect the women. But Nell had said she was taking Gertie shopping, so with luck he was alone here and just as inclined to meet whatever danger lurked at the back fence.

Even though he was expecting something, it was still a shock to see a short, weedy, furtive-looking man appear.

Wes tightened his grip on the hammer and narrowed his eyes.

The man approached stealthily, his gaze scanning the area as he came up to Wes. "Jeez you scared me. I thought you'd bought the farm."

Wes stared at him.

The nervous fellow fished out a dented pack of Marlboroughs and lit up. "Did you get it?"

"Get what?"

Wes had no idea who this man was, but he sure didn't look like he belonged to a bike gang. He looked like a down and out car salesman with too many kids. His watery blue eyes narrowed against the smoke from his cigarette. "This amnesia thing is bullshit, right?"

Wes thought about lying, but what was the point? "I wish it were."

The man shook his head as though bad news was never a surprise. "Tell me you remember where you put the stuff."

"I don't even know what stuff you're talking about. I also don't know who the hell you are or why you were spying on me before sneaking up."

The man tipped his head back and stared at the sky. His lips moved as though he were praying, which Wes doubted was his actual occupation.

"You're Wes Doman." The man cast a glance all around before leaning in and murmuring, "DEA."

"Drug enforcement? You mean I'm not in some two-bit bike gang?" No wonder he hadn't felt as though he were in the right body. It was a profound relief to discover he was one of the good guys.

"You're undercover. The gang sent you to organize a coke buy, which we were going to bust. We arrest this bunch and close down this cell; then we go back home to our lives." He waved his cigarette hopefully in the air. "Any of this sounding familiar?"

Wes shook his head.

"Great. Just great."

Wes slumped against the fence and tried to think. If he was undercover, a lot of things made sense. His hair for instance. He must be wearing this mop to blend in with the bikers. It was a relief to discover he didn't belong with guys like Louie.

And Nell. She must not know or she would have said something.

Of course, he might be an amnesiac, but he wasn't stupid. "Do you have some ID?"

With another furtive glance, and a smoky huff of irritation, his companion pulled out a wallet and flipped it open. Sure enough, there was a DEA badge. Wes waited for a flicker of recognition, but nothing came. The guy's name was Harvey Brown. Didn't mean a thing to him.

In all this mess, the only person who'd seemed even vaguely familiar was Nell.

He blew out a breath. "I take it Nell doesn't know who I really am?"

The nervous man stared at him. "Nell?"

"My girlfriend. Nell Tennant."

Harvey dragged too hard on his cigarette and exploded in a hacking cough. "Buddy, you don't have a girlfriend."

Chapter Five

Wes quelled the urge to punch the lying sonofabitch in the face, but he couldn't stop his fist tightening on the hammer. "What are you saying?"

"You'd never stopped here in your life before the accident. I had a hell of a time tracking you down. Had to hang around bars and listen to farmers' gossip. Ever since you arrived here you've been hanging around with the bikers. Why would you start seeing a girl who'd make them suspicious? Doesn't make sense."

He was right. It didn't make sense. Any more than it made sense for Nell to pretend to be his girlfriend if she wasn't. It was a puzzle that needed solving. And fast.

"This coke. How much of it was there?"

"Maybe around ten kilos. They wouldn't have trusted you with more."

"And you have no idea where it is?"

"Market day was supposed to be Thursday. My guess is you stashed the dope somewhere and then planned to set up the sting. Only you had the accident before you had a chance."

"So it could be hidden anywhere."

"Yep."

"There's a guy named Louie who's pointing a gun at my back."

"Yep."

He immediately thought about his dream. That must be what it was telling him—the hiding place of the drugs. Now all he had to do was find one particular derelict barn in an area full of them.

He also had to figure out why Nell had lied to him.

Nell stacked cans of tuna fish in Gertie's pantry, trying to keep her mind on unloading the groceries and not on the delectable possibilities she'd unleashed by telling Wes of her secret fantasy.

Making love outside wasn't all that wild, but it was her fantasy and she wanted to try it out just once. Sex in the moonlight; out in the middle of a field; heck, even in the back of a parked car at a drive-in—if there were one in Harleyville, which there wasn't. She wouldn't care. All she cared about was giving in to the urge to be wild and free with Wes, her own personal rebel without a cause, easy rider, and lone wolf all rolled into one sexually explosive package.

Since he had amnesia, he couldn't be expected to think up any good places for them to try out her whim. That would be her responsibility, and she was pretty sure she was up to the task. She'd had all her adult life to dream up exciting places to seduce a sexy stranger.

Tonight's moon would be even brighter than last night's. She couldn't think of a better time to start showing Wes exactly what she had in mind.

"What are you grinning about?" Gertie asked.

"I had an idea. If I drive Wes round some of the local scenery, it might help his memory return. Don't you think?"

Gertie slapped the lid shut on a jar she'd refilled with raisins. "You be careful around him. You know what those motorcycle fellows are like. All rough and rude with their loud music and nasty loud engines and their smoking all over town and spitting on the sidewalks. He's not your kind, Missy."

And that was exactly the attraction. Nell stuck her chin out. "Maybe I'm sick of my kind. The bloodless corporate sharks who care about profit and loss and bottom lines more than they care about people."

"He's probably a criminal."

"I don't think so," Nell said thoughtfully. "He worked all afternoon, even though we left him alone for several hours. Would a criminal be so diligent?"

"Maybe, if he was locked out of the house," Gertie said with a touch of defiance.

Nell swung round, her mouth dropping. "You locked him out of the house?"

"Course I did. It was a mistake ever letting him stay here. We should have dropped him off down at that biker clubhouse they have in town. Let the rest of the motorcycle boys look after him."

Nell swallowed her argument. Gertie knew perfectly well that it was her own sidewalk vigilanteism that had deposited Wes so colorfully in their lives. When his memory did return, he could very well press charges.

He seemed a little pale when she went to fetch him for supper and for the first time he wouldn't meet her eyes when she spoke to him. Her heart sank, realizing he'd probably overdone it and wouldn't be up to their "date." She was shocked at how disappointed she felt.

"Do you want to go straight to bed and have your supper on a tray?" she asked, lifting a hand and laying it across his forehead to check for fever.

He gripped her wrist and pulled it away, his hazel eyes burning into hers as though if he tried hard enough he could see right through to her inner thoughts.

"What is it?" she asked, feeling as though she were looking at a different person.

For the space of a couple of heartbeats he stared at her; then he grinned, that cocky grin she'd come to love in such a short time. "I hope you're not planning to chicken out on our plans for later, because I have a hankering to take you up against a barn, in a hayloft, maybe even on a boat, floating out under the stars."

A quiet hum escaped her throat as her body quivered to life at the images his words evoked. "I can't wait."

"I don't want to get boring and repeat history, though," he said, running his fingertips up her arms in a way that made her long to be already out under the stars with him. "Did we already do those things?"

"What things?" she whispered, hardly able to think for the sensations running riot in her body.

"Have I ever taken you up against a barn?" He stepped even closer, so his body was barely brushing the front of hers.

Only by squeezing her jaws together did she stop herself from whimpering with longing. "No. No barns."

"How about the hayloft?" He ran his lips up her throat and she wondered if he could feel the whimpers she was trying to suppress.

"No," she panted.

His lips traveled slowly up until he took her earlobe between his teeth and bit lightly. "How about on the water floating under the stars?" His breath against her ear sent flurries of excitement racing through her.

She shook her head.

He raised his head and his eyes were dancing with devil lights. "Well, where the hell have we been doing it?"

Maybe she should just tell him now. She'd made it up. She could explain about Doc's advice, apologize for leading him to believe things that weren't true. But then she'd never experience sex up against a barn, in a hayloft, or out on a floating boat, at least not with this man. And she wanted to do all those things and more with him.

She resolved to get Doc alone for a few minutes tomorrow and get his advice. After all, this going along with being Wes's girlfriend was *his* prescription. It wouldn't be right to end the charade without professional medical advice. Or at least, that was the excuse she gave herself.

She sucked it up and opened her eyes for her first actual lie to Wes. As she gazed into his strong, sexy face and caught his wickedly taunting gaze, she could have sworn he was teasing her.

She pulled out one of her fantasies. "Once, we were out in the middle of a wheat field. No one could see us; the wheat was so high that when we lay down we were invisible. But we could see the sky, so blue, and feel the sun shining down on our bodies." She had to stop for a breath, warmth suffused her chest as she pictured the two of them out there, hidden but exposed, imagined the sound of the wind shushing through the nearly ripe grain, the smell of the earth and the crops in the air, the feel of the crushed stalks like a coarse mat beneath them.

"Screwing in a wheat field, huh?"

She nodded, forcing herself not to blush.

"Just the two of us?"

"Yes!" What did he think they'd done before he lost his memory? Had orgies? Swapped partners? Sex outside was as wild as she got, and she was about to explain that in no uncertain terms when she saw the glint in his eyes. "You're teasing."

"Uh-uh. I'm making sure I get it right. I wouldn't want to screw up our secret games. We've obviously done a lot of this in the past. I don't want you to be disappointed."

"Oh, I won't be." After last night, she was certain he'd never disappoint her as a lover. She only hoped she could fake being confident and outrageous enough not to disappoint him.

Dinner was a simple, high-cholesterol affair. Gertie didn't believe in low-cal diets, she believed in hard work to keep her arteries clear. So far, it seemed to be working in spite of meals like tonight's: fried chicken, oven-fried potatoes, cornbread, and fresh peas from the garden.

It wasn't fears about her cholesterol level that had Nell picking at her food, but the nervous anticipation churning in her stomach.

It was one thing to imagine making love in the great outdoors. In the privacy of her head she could be as wild as she wanted—but in reality, there were all sorts of logistical details to fuss over. The first of these being the possibility that one of the good people of Harleyville might stumble onto the two of them cavorting around in the buff. Then there were bugs, dirt, poison ivy, animals to worry about. And the biggest detail of all—where the heck were they going to do it?

She should simply call it off. But every time she glanced up, there was Wes looking at her with barely banked fires in his eyes and that would spark her blood so she couldn't contemplate the possibility of not making love to him out in the wild—which, with his savage appearance and rugged body, seemed like his natural milieu.

"I'll do the dishes, Gertie." She jumped up the minute dinner was over.

"I'll help," Wes said and joined her at the sink.

"You don't have to do that."

"It goes quicker with two," he said, nudging her as he said it so it was clear he wanted to get on with the after-dinner entertainment in the great outdoors.

She shivered and squeezed dish soap under the running water.

The man used washing dishes as shameless foreplay. He stood too close, rubbed against her every chance he got, leaned across her instead of stepping around and generally teased her until she was so rattled she could barely stop herself from breaking all the china.

She tried to frown him down and encountered such smoldering heat in his gaze that she gulped and turned back to the sink.

"Hurry up and wash those dishes. I'm dying to get my hands on you," he said softly, rubbing his torso across her back as he reached to put a dried plate away.

"Gertie," she called to the woman who was in the next room with the television blaring, "I'm going to take Wes for a ride tonight. All right if I borrow the truck?"

"Drive careful. And don't wake me if you come in after nine."

"Okay."

She turned to find Wes leaning against the kitchen counter looking big and rugged and wonderfully male. "I'll just brush my teeth and freshen up," she said.

"I'll meet you out front."

She'd been racking her brain to think of a place where they'd be unlikely to be disturbed, but she was coming up blank.

With a shrug she decided to take a back road and see where it led. This was her fantasy and she was finally having a chance to fulfill it. She couldn't waste time being a wimp.

So she brushed her teeth, combed her hair, and tried to get in touch with her inner wild woman. She grabbed her purse and then as she thought ahead to possible scenarios, turned back to her bedroom and changed her jeans for a white denim skirt. She gnawed her lip for a second and then, with a spurt of bravery, slipped off her underwear.

Chapter Six

Nell felt like the bold and daring woman of her fantasies as her own naked thighs slid against each other. A breeze rode up her skirt and wafted over the heat in the center of her body as she hoisted herself in the driver's side of Gertie's truck.

The dusty red pickup rattled down the lane she'd chosen at random, leaving a plume of dust in its wake. Cornfields marched on either side of the road and she hoped this back lane led somewhere or she'd not only feel foolish—she'd lose her nerve.

Wes traced circles around her bare knee which didn't help either her nerves or her driving ability. She bounced over a pothole she'd planned to avoid and a stone hit the truck sounding like a bullet.

"I like this skirt," Wes said, as he slipped his hand beneath it.

"Thanks," she replied, hearing her own voice low and husky in reply. His hand inched higher and she tightened her hands on the wheel. Higher still, drawing idle patterns on her inner thighs that had her holding back a moan.

And finally, he worked his way up to where she was wet and hot and already open for him.

"You forgot your panties," he said in a low growl, his fingers parting her folds.

"Silly me," she gasped, sliding her legs wider apart and hitching her hips forward to give him easier access.

He eased a finger inside her, slow and deep, and she nearly ran them off the road. As they hit the gravel shoulder the truck bumped up and down, up and down, causing her body to bounce on his embedded finger. Up and down, up and down, until she thought she'd fly apart right then and there.

"I have to tell you, you are one bad driver," he said with a quiver of humor.

"If you don't take your hand away, we'll both be picking unripe corn out of our teeth."

"I knew I should have driven."

"I'm an excellent driver," she told him, groaning slightly as he pushed into her a little deeper. "Most of the time."

"What's the matter, honey? Am I making you nervous?" He pressed his palm against her pubis so she wanted to grind herself against him.

"I'm going to kill you," she whispered. "If you don't kill me first."

He chuckled softly, and she could tell he was enjoying her torment. She wanted to reach over and give him a taste of his own medicine, but she knew that if she took even one hand off the wheel she'd be in serious trouble. He seemed to sense how close she was to the edge, because, while he didn't withdraw his hand, he didn't move either so she felt like a pot about to boil over.

Would this road never end? She felt hot and quivery and she was having trouble concentrating since lust seemed to have flooded her brain, drowning out any ability to think, plan, or reason. She'd got the pair of them into this; it was her stupid fantasy; now it seemed to be turning into a nightmare before her very eyes. The road went on and on and on with nothing but dusty cornfields to the right and left.

The good news was they seemed to have the road to themselves. And she had a blanket. And a pickup truck. Well, she'd wanted to be spontaneous. She guessed it was time to accept that spontaneous didn't always work out quite the way you planned it.

At the next intersection, she turned right into a narrow rutted lane, pulled to the side and cut the engine.

He glanced around and she did the same. Through the dusty windshield she saw nothing but the big red ball of the setting sun, rows of dark green cornstalks as far as she could see, and not a hint of a building or vehicle or animal or man. Not bad, she decided smugly. Not bad at all.

He turned to her. "This is it?"

She had the advantage of being able to tell him anything she liked about their supposed relationship before his accident, and she called on the privilege shamelessly. "You never complained before. This is what we like to do. Find a quiet spot, crawl into the bed of the truck and . . . make love under the stars."

His middle finger was still deep inside her body, a fact she hadn't forgotten for a second and which he reminded her of by moving, cupping her mound and driving his finger deeper. "Or we could do it right here in the front seat," he said, leaning over to kiss her, deep and wet.

But this was her fantasy damn it and she wanted it her way. "No. Under the open sky. Trust me. It's what we love to do."

"All right." He eased his hand away from her and they both got out of the truck and went to the back. As he reached to pull down the tailgate she stopped him. "Doesn't work. Gertie backed into a tree years ago and it's jammed shut."

"Bad driving must run in your family," he said as he clambered over the back. Once inside he turned to give her his hand, but what she could have managed in jeans, wasn't going to be easy in a short skirt and no underwear.

She propped her sandaled foot on the back bumper, making the tight skirt ride high. He grinned down at her, enjoying her predicament so much she decided to wipe the grin right off his face. She yanked the skirt to her waist, took his hand and scrambled up giving him a great view which he took full advantage of.

"I'm going to kiss Gertie when we get home," he said.

Oh, she was a wild woman all right, she decided as she pulled the picnic blanket out of the backpack she'd brought along and laid it out. Then she dug back in for a couple of beers and a handful of condoms.

His eyes twinkled down at her. "You got a steak dinner and some candlelight in there?"

"Yes," she grinned, pleased with herself. "Candles, anyway. To keep the bugs away. Why don't you come on down here beside me?"

"Why don't I."

He eased down by her side and kissed her slowly. The bed of the truck was harder than she'd imagined it would be, but the sky was as open-armed, making her feel free enough for anything.

"It's so beautiful," she said softly, listening to the breeze rustling through the corn and the chirping of crickets.

"It's beautiful all right," he said huskily as he swiftly unbuttoned her sleeveless blue shirt and bared her breasts.

They tingled in the still-warm air, her nipples already hard with anticipation, her blood pounding from the teasing he'd subjected her to during their drive here. He cupped her breasts in his big hands and brought his mouth down to suckle.

Her back arched beneath him and her own cry joined the night chorus.

Needing to feel his skin against hers, she tugged at his shirt and he hunched his shoulders to help her pull it off.

She'd wanted to go slowly, to savor the experience of making love in the great outdoors, but Wes had driven her too close to fulfillment and now she ached with a need that was almost unbearable. Her hips shifted and twisted beneath him and the burning between her legs intensified, even though he was only kissing her nipples, curling his tongue around each sensitive tip and then sucking them into his mouth.

Grabbing his belt, she undid it with trembling fingers, then unbuttoned his jeans and eased the zipper over the bulging hardness.

Like her, he'd ditched his underwear and that pleased her inordinately as she encountered his hot, hard flesh.

As though on fast forward, their movements speeded, becoming almost frenzied as the need escalated. He yanked his jeans down. They caught on his boots and so he left them around his ankles.

As he turned back to her, he got tangled in the bunched denim and flopped half on his back. Taking that as a sign, she straddled him, knowing it was time to take matters into her own hands. If she left it to him and he teased her any more she wouldn't be responsible for her actions. Murder was a distinct possibility.

Leaning over his lean and hungry face, she nipped at his lip before kissing him, slipping her tongue in his mouth. Reaching between their bodies, she grasped him where he was so hot and so hard, slipped on a condom, and placed him at the entrance to her body already pulsing in anticipation. Unable to hold back any longer, she slowly sank onto him feeling him fill her, stretching her wide.

With hands splayed on his chest she rocked back and forth, adjusting, but the need for friction was too strong to be denied and she began to pump her hips, finding her rhythm, taking him deep, deeper, and then all the way until her muscles tightened around him and they both groaned.

As she rode him, she stared out at the open road. The air tingled against her damp nipples and she felt as free and connected to nature as the hawk circling high overhead.

Cars could drive by, planes could buzz overhead and she

wouldn't care, in fact the possibility of discovery only added to her excitement. She dropped her gaze to Wes's and felt a jolt of connection so strong she gasped. She was connected to him physically, as close as a man and woman can be, but something outside of the physical zapped between them.

She wanted their lovemaking to last forever; she wanted satisfaction now.

She felt his tension like a reflection of her own, saw the sweat break out on his brow and knew she could no longer hold back. Tipping her face to the heavens, eyes open to the sky, she increased the tempo, hearing the wet slap of her flesh against his, the pressure building in their bodies until explosion was inevitable.

He grabbed her hips and bucked up into her even as her body clenched around him. "Oh, yes!" she shouted out across the whispering cornfields. As the spasms of pleasure took her, she kept her eyes open, feeling as much a part of the universe as the red ball of sun dissolving in a crimson sunset that suffused the sky.

Beneath her, she felt the final twitch as he emptied himself into her.

"Mmm," she sighed, collapsing against his chest. "It was like the three of us came together. You, me, and the sunset."

He kissed her, then swatted a mosquito that had found them. "We'll be covered in bites tomorrow."

"Do you mind?"

He smiled at her, snugging her tight against his chest. "Nope."

Reluctantly, they donned their clothes to protect them from the bugs that had arrived in force, drawn rather than repelled, it seemed, by the citronella candles she'd lit. They sat there, anyway, hands linked, and watched the night sky while they sipped beer.

"Are there a lot of derelict barns around here?" he asked after a while.

"We have our share, I guess. Why?"

He shrugged. "I was thinking about tomorrow night."

She chuckled. "I like the way you think. I don't know this area as well as Gertie. I'll ask her." She tweaked his arm. "Is a hayloft a requirement?"

He gazed over and her face appeared indistinct in the twilight, her eyes dark and mysterious. "You are the only requirement," he said, and was surprised at how much he meant that.

He saw her quick grin acknowledging the compliment, her teeth white in the dim light, her eyes glowing like the early stars.

Why didn't she tell him they hadn't known each other before? They were sleeping together. She was taking him into her body, why wouldn't she take him into her confidence?

Did she have somebody else? Was he a diversion? A summer fling?

He sighed up into the dark sky. He didn't know squat about himself or his past but he knew there was something more than just sex going on between him and this woman. "Not only is my own life a blank, but everyone else's is, too. Tell me about you."

"Tell you about myself?" Nell repeated. What could she possibly tell him? About her breakup? About the way she was searching for herself, for a career that meant something? For a life that made sense to her?

She settled with her back against his chest and his arms came round her, warm and secure. "I was a publicist in LA, which sounds glamorous but basically means I was a combination secretary, servant, and therapist for a bunch of spoiled entertainment types."

"Overworked?"

She chuckled softly. "Yes. And mauled, cried on, puked on, OD'd on until I couldn't stand it anymore."

Wes dropped a kiss on her hair and his hands tightened. So she found herself telling him the rest.

"I was . . . seeing a director. Peter. Very glamorous life, successful, handsome, rich—"

"Sounds too good to be true." The trace of jealousy in Wes's tone made her tip her head back and smile up at him.

"You didn't let me finish. Also cold, calculating, and utterly self-absorbed. By the time I figured out I'd become his unpaid publicist, shrink, and call girl all in one . . ." She stopped as anger punched her in the chest. "I—I realized he was not the man I wanted, my job was not the career I wanted and . . . I guess I just wanted some time off to try a simple life for a while. Gertie's not getting any younger and I decided to come for a visit."

He dropped a kiss on her hair. "Then you met me. Going out with a gang member isn't exactly simple and serene."

She sighed. "You ever think about going straight?"

"I don't remember going crooked."

Chapter Seven

She chuckled. "You seem like too nice a man to be in a gang."

"We were talking about you. You came here for a simple life. Have you found it?"

She let out a quiet sigh. "Okay, I ran. Back to Gertie, back here where there's a connection between planting seeds and growing crops, where life makes sense."

"Are you planning to go back?"

His words were so simple, but she heard the edge to them. "I—I don't know."

"Is Gertie just a place to run to? Somewhere to hide out?"

"No. I love her."

"And what about me?" His hands tightened on her arms. "Am I a handy roll in the hayloft? A quick stress release until you get back to your regular life?"

"No. I . . ." But what had she been about to say? She loved him too? She must be more seriously deranged than she'd realized. Bad enough to fall in love with an amnesiac, but an amnesiac criminal? No wonder he seemed so innocent, he couldn't remember all the vile crimes he'd committed, didn't even know how briefly they'd known each other, and yet she found she trusted him more than any other man she'd ever been with.

Which only showed what bad shape she was in.

"It's getting late," she said. "We should get back."

He helped her pack everything away, then got to his feet and helped her to hers. They were quiet as they scrambled out of the back of the truck, quiet as they drove back to Gertie's.

She turned off the ignition and the old truck rattled itself to sleep. The silence was thick, full of unspoken words, mistaken impressions, and longings.

"Well, I guess—" She never finished the sentence. His mouth captured hers in a kiss full of frustration, passion, and driving lust.

"I can't get enough of you," he whispered. "Can I come to you tonight?"

She licked her lips, tasting him, tasting her own deceit. She should tell him no, but she had no willpower. They had such a short time together, she didn't want to waste a minute. Sometime he'd retrieve his memory and when that happened, this wonderful, magical affair would end. She was realistic enough to know the chances were good he wouldn't be thrilled that she'd pretended to be his lover. If she was going to lose him, she should at least build some memories.

"Yes," she whispered back. "Oh, yes."

He snuck in like the moonlight slipping between the gap in the curtains and found her waiting for him, already naked, already wet.

He wanted to take it slowly, but it was tough when need and desire snapped at him with sharp teeth driving him forward.

It had only been a matter of hours since they'd gone at it in the truck, and already their lovemaking was taking on the quality of myth. Had her breasts really been as soft to the touch? He had to find out, first rubbing his hands over them, then his cheek, making her gasp as stubble grazed the sensitive flesh, then finally his tongue, lapping, soothing, tasting.

Yes, he discovered, she was every bit as smooth there as imagination and memory had suggested.

But surely her belly hadn't quivered when he'd trailed his fingertips down its length. Yes. He discovered, it had and did.

Could she possibly be as open and giving?

He stroked his fingers down her thighs. "I want you to open yourself for me," he said quietly, keeping his gaze on hers.

Her entire body seemed to quiver, her eyes grew dark and exotic, her lips slipped apart in a quiet moan and then her thighs parted beneath his gaze as she opened herself to him.

It was his turn to moan as he contemplated her mysteries. The dewy femininity, petals opening at dawn inviting him toward the dark, hot heart of her hidden beneath.

He touched her, with just one fingertip and was amazed to find himself trembling. Just as she trembled everywhere he touched. He traced each glistening petal, deep with color, opening to his touch as a flower opens to the sun, exposing the stiff nub at its center. He took a quick trip around it, making her gasp and quake, but he refused to rush. He wanted to keep her gasping and quaking all night. He had precious few memories. He wanted to build a few that were spectacular.

Her hips arched off the bed, thighs straining open in urgent invitation and he held back his roaring libido, letting the tip of his finger trace the opening to her body, so slick and hot it beckoned him forward the way a fire draws a cold traveler on a winter night.

He couldn't resist the lure, but hunkered down and replaced his finger with his tongue. Mmm. She tasted juicy and all woman. Only a taste wasn't enough. He pushed his tongue all the way inside her.

Even from down here he could hear her gasping cries and from the wild tossing of her hips, he didn't think she was far from climax. He withdrew his tongue slowly, loving the way her internal muscles clutched and tried to draw him back, then licked his way up to the tightly furled bud that was about to burst into bloom. Ruby red and pulsing, he had only to give it a slow, lazy lick to have her tossing her head and crying out.

Another hit-and-run tongue stroke and she was sobbing with frustrated need.

Did he want to punish her for not telling him the truth? he wondered idly as he barely touched with the tip of his tongue, hearing desperation in her tone. Or did he simply love having her completely, mindlessly in his control?

"Please," she gasped. She was so close he felt the muscles in her thighs tighten, her clit shudder as it prepared to explode. As though not noticing her state, he moved to plant kisses on the soft white skin of her upper thigh.

"Please!" She grabbed his hair in both hands and hauled him back to where she wanted him.

He couldn't keep the smile off his lips as he placed them where she was hottest and neediest and sucked her clit until it burst on his tongue like the ripest berry.

He sucked her sweetness, enjoying the cries of fulfillment she tried to muffle, until she was limp with release, and then, kissing his way slowly up her body, entered her.

He bent his head to kiss her lips and noticed tears on the end of her lashes. He would have asked if he'd hurt her in some way, but then he saw her smile. It was the kind of smile that sniffling women share at weddings or christenings, a teary smile of female happiness and love. For just a second he paused, staring down into her dewy eyes; then he felt his lips curve, returning her smile, before he kissed her deeply, his tongue mimicking the movements of his cock as he drove her up again to bliss.

"Get me a list of derelict barns in the area," he said to Harvey as they met in their usual spot at the back fence.

"Who's going to list crap like that?"

"A map then. Aerial photographs. Find me something. Time's running out."

His partner shook his head. "It's no use. You've been here a week and your memory's still MIA. You've got a brain injury; we'll have to bail."

Frustration, mixed with fury, swept through Wes. "I can't bail. You think they'll let me go so long as a shipment of their coke is missing along with me?"

"I realize your brain is not functioning real well right now, but we are getting you out. They won't be able to track you."

Wes grabbed Harvey by his collar and dragged him forward. "Use your own brain. Who will they go after if they can't find me?"

Harvey's eyes shifted. "She's just using you. For all we know she's helping them."

He pulled his hands off the other man's lapels as though they'd been soiled and stepped back wondering how he'd ever managed to work with such a weasel. "Not Nell. You already checked her out. Right?"

"You don't know—"

"I know Nell. And I'm not putting her safety at risk. I have to see this through with you or without you."

"Stop thinking with your dick. You—"

"I can see the barn in my dreams. I'm sure the drugs are there. I just have to find it. Look, we're partners. You must trust me."

Harvey lit a cigarette and dragged hard on it. "Every time I get shot at it's because of you."

Somehow, Wes believed him. "Come on. I need your help. I made up a bogus story for Louie, wrangled another week out of him, but that's all we have. Get me anything you can on barns in the area." He pulled out the rough drawing he'd made based on his dream.

"This is insane. We're putting government resources into

finding an old barn in the middle of Kansas because you, a man who can't remember his own name, dreamt about it."

"My memory's coming back," Wes said.

"How do you know?"

"I know that every time we get together we argue but we get the job done." In fact, he knew no such thing but it was a safe bet that he and Harvey tweed-jacket didn't have the same MO.

A reluctant grin dawned on his partner's face. "Yeah. And I always end up shot at."

"Well, I haven't gotten you killed yet, have I?"

Harvey pocketed the drawing and turned, already giving in. "Sometime I'll tell you about Mexico."

Wes chopped wood with a vengeance, venting his frustration on Gertie's wood pile. Since Doc had pronounced him physically healthy, and remained placidly convinced that his memory would return in its own good time, life continued day by day while Wes earned his bed and board by doing manual labor for Gertie, and tried to solve two puzzles.

Where was that rickety old farmhouse?

And why was Nell pretending to be his girlfriend?

Wes loved women. Of that he was certain. But he didn't think he could ever have experienced anything quite like what he discovered every night in Nell's arms.

They shared the kind of intimacy that made him want to reveal all his deepest secrets—if he could only remember what those were.

She, on the other hand, seemed not at all interested in sharing the fact that they'd never known each other before he so spectacularly face-planted into the vegetable garden. And, although he'd bet one or two favorite body parts that she wasn't promiscuous, she had slept with him the day after she met him. If you could even call it meeting, when she'd been the one to introduce him to himself.

Puzzles. Did he like puzzles? he wondered. This one merely frustrated him.

What he hadn't bothered telling Harvey or Nell or even old Doc Greenfield, however, was that his memory *was* returning. He was having ... not visions exactly, more like daydreams where people and things appeared in his mind. He had a feeling it was memory surfacing in snatches. As hard as he tried, he couldn't ever drag the whole works up. He had that frustrating feeling of a forgotten word at the tip of his tongue. Except in his case, it was his whole life, hovering there, teasing him, but so far eluding his grasp.

Truth to tell, he wouldn't much care and would be only too happy to follow the Doc's prescription of rest, healthy food, fresh air and his own prescription: sex with Nell in large doses, taken several times daily, and allow his memory to return when it was ready.

Except he had an urgent deadline. If he couldn't find the drugs by next week, the gang would kill him.

As deadlines went, this wasn't one he wanted to screw around with. If it got close to the day he'd promised to deliver the goods and he hadn't yet found the cache or recovered his memory, he'd bail, taking Nell and Gertie with him. But he wanted those drug-dealing assholes busted and jailed. That was his job and he intended to do it.

"Are you planning to keep Gertie in kindling all winter?" Nell's amused voice broke into his thoughts.

Puzzled, he stared at the wood he'd just chopped and saw what she meant. He was turning a healthy wood pile into toothpicks. "Sorry, I guess I got carried away." He stopped to stretch out his back, then propped a foot on the stump he'd used as a chopping block and wiped the sweat off his forehead.

"What's up?"

She ran her gaze down his sweaty body and her expression made the question redundant. In spite of the frequency and intensity of their lovemaking, she only had to look at him and he was rock hard and ready to go.

He'd taken off his shirt a while back, so he wore only shorts, socks, boots and an elastic band holding his ridiculous hair off his face.

"I've got something special in mind for tonight," she said.

"So have I."

Her eyes twinkled as they stared into his. "Another abandoned barn?" Since Harvey had produced a rough map based on some aerial reconnaissance, they'd visited barns night after night. He told her he'd gotten it from a neighbor who'd stopped to chat while he was mending the fence. She hadn't even raised her brows at the notion. Harleyville was that sort of town.

In spite of her groan at his mention of yet another barn, he could see her nipples pebbling beneath her shirt.

He understood the feeling. He didn't think he'd ever be able to look at a barn again without getting a hard-on.

"I can't help it," he said to her, putting down his ax and stepping closer until their bodies almost touched. "There's something about you, naked on a hay bale that does it for me every time."

"This barn better not have bats," she said primly, but she moved in closer as she said it. With a saucy grin, she leaned into his chest and surprised the hell out of him when she took his nipple between her teeth and bit down gently, but firmly.

"Ow," he complained, but it was just for show. He wanted her teeth, her tongue, her whole mouth all over him. "I can't wait until after dinner. Can't we go now?"

"That's my surprise. I packed us a picnic. You remember when you asked me if there were any lakes or a place to swim nearby?"

He nodded. One of the old barns on Harvey's list was near a small body of water, so he'd casually asked Nell about swimming, telling her he hated swimming pools.

"Gertie reminded me of a water hole I'd forgotten all about. I thought we might take a swim first . . ."

"Nell, you are my kind of woman," he said, grabbing her hand and dragging her toward the pickup. If swimming was first, he had a very good idea what was second.

Chapter Eight

The truck bounced over the inevitable rutted road as Nell and Wes tried to follow Gertie's scribbled directions. The wide-open windows let in the hot air and blowing dust, but when they were closed the heat was even worse.

Nell allowed herself a moment to miss the endless California beaches, then glanced sideways at her companion and knew she'd rather be here.

She was beginning to squirm against the seat, and that wasn't because of the temperature outside. In almost two weeks of being with Wes, she hadn't nearly overcome her burning attraction to him. If anything, it grew each day.

"Potholes are starting to make me horny," Wes said.

"You must have read my mind." And she laughed, speeding up a little.

"I think it's down this road," he said, staring at the map in his lap. "What do you think?"

She slowed and squinted at Gertie's artwork. "Worth a try." She turned and they bounced down yet another lane. For several minutes they rode in silence. There was no sign of water ahead, just an old farm with a few big trees guarding its perimeter.

"Do you think this is right?" she asked doubtfully, already searching for a place to turn around.

"I think this is exactly right," he said in an odd voice.

She stared at him, feeling the back of her neck prickle. "You're not even looking at the map."

"The trees . . . the blue door . . ." He stared ahead as though in a trance.

"Are you okay?" she asked him.

"When you get to that T intersection turn left," he said in a voice of command, one she'd never heard from him before. She was so surprised she followed his instructions before realizing he couldn't be correct. "Left? Surely that will lead us away from the water."

He appeared not to have even heard her. All his attention was on the farm. "That's it. That's got to be it," he muttered. "There'll be a lane, overgrown with grass leading round the side of the farm to an old barn. Take it."

Even though they'd made love in countless barns over the last week, she could tell from his tone that he wasn't thinking about sex. He was like a different man, full of purpose and command.

The lane came into view. He said, "Yes!" under his breath and, curious to see what he was up to, she kept her mouth shut and swung the old truck into the lane. Long grass scraped the undercarriage as they jounced toward yet another derelict barn.

"I was looking forward to that swim," she complained. "And I'm not sharing my picnic with rats. Or bats."

She might as well have kept her mouth shut for all the notice he took of her. He was rubbing the back of his head and blinking his eyes as though he couldn't believe what he was seeing. Must be getting another one of his headaches.

"Pull around behind so the truck's out of sight of the road."

"Oh, like anybody's going to steal this old heap."

"Do it."

If he was trying to seduce her he was going about it all wrong, but her curiosity was fully engaged so she did as she was told.

He was out of the truck before it stopped. She cut the engine and scrambled after him. He strode through the open doorway and she watched him. As though he were in some obstacle race, he skirted rusting equipment and a half-rotted wooden wheelbarrow. In a dark corner he dropped to his knees. She thought about scanning the rafters for bats, but she didn't want to know.

What was Wes doing? Hoping whatever creatures called this old barn home were tucked up in bed, she crept forward and watched him lift a floorboard and then blow out a breath. "Found it."

"Found what?"

But he was already pulling out a cell phone. *Cell phone?* Where the hell had that come from? He hadn't had one on him when they found him.

While he punched in a number she stepped forward to peek into the dark space under the loosened floorboard. A group of square, plastic-wrapped packages, each about the size of a small bag of sugar, were down there. Only she didn't think that was sugar. She rubbed her arms against a sudden chill. She'd almost convinced herself he was nothing like the other bikers in town. Now, here he was with a cache of drugs.

Nausea curdled her stomach. God help her. She'd gone and fallen in love with a drug pusher. She rose, knowing that whether she loved him or not, she was going to have to turn him over to the police.

"Harvey," Wes spoke rapidly into the phone, "Wes Doman here. I found it."

"Yeah. Better make it tonight. Right. Meet me at the usual place. Half an hour."

Wes stomped the board back into place and rose. He stepped

forward and noticed Nell cringing away from him looking like the next victim in a gruesome horror flick. Her eyes were wide and her mouth was working. "Who are you?" she asked in a rusty voice.

And, for the first time in more than two weeks, he knew the full and complete answer to her question. It was as though the switch had turned back on in his brain, reconnecting all the circuits. Along with the relief, came the knowledge that he had to handle Nell carefully. Except he didn't have time.

"Wes Doman, US Drug Enforcement Agency."

Her mouth widened and he watched first relief, then anger flash in her eyes. "You're a cop?"

"In a manner of speaking. Come on. I've got a job to finish. I have to help Gertie get rid of the bikers." He grabbed her arm but she shook him off.

"When . . ." She licked her lips: "When did you get your memory back."

"When I saw the road, it all started to fall into place. It was the same road I've been seeing in my dream. Same old farm, same trees outside, same barn. And now my memory's back." He dipped into his past and it was like opening a photo album or viewing random moments of film about a stranger's life.

He could tell her he was definitely single, had parents still living, a sister and a couple of hellions for nephews. He had a criminology degree, friends, an apartment in Chicago. For some reason, he blurted out only one fact: "I was born in Maine."

She dropped her gaze to the ground and even in the dim light of the barn he could see the color deep in her cheeks; hell he could almost feel the burn from her fiery blush. Not that he had a lot of sympathy for her. He'd given her plenty of opportunities to own up to the truth and she hadn't availed herself of a single one. "Then you know we're not . . . you know we didn't . . ."

He could ease this moment for her but he didn't feel like it.

"I've known that for more than a week. I was working with a partner. He told me."

She made a gurgling sound in the back of her throat, almost as though she were choking on something. The unpalatable truth, likely. "I don't know what you must think—"

"It's pretty obvious, isn't it? You're recently single, cut off from sex out here in the boonies and I was handy to scratch your itch." He was suddenly angry. It boiled up out of nowhere and he felt like he'd explode if he didn't spill some of it out.

At his deliberately casual words, her head shot up and she stared at him, eyes widening. "If that's what you thought then why did you . . ." She flapped her hand helplessly.

"Easy," he said, letting the scalding anger out. "I had an itch, too."

Chapter Nine

She would not cry. She wouldn't give him that satisfaction. Was that really all she'd been to him? All he thought he was to her? An itch to scratch?

She recalled the sweet loving man who'd taken her to places she hadn't known existed, who'd helped her discover a new aspect of her own sexuality that she really, really liked.

A glance at Wes's profile as they bumped back toward Gertie's place showed her not the man who'd made love with her the past couple of weeks, but a hard, impersonal stranger. She'd been so shaken by his words in the barn that when he'd headed for the driver's door of the truck she hadn't made a peep. Truth was, this new guy scared her a lot more than the old one.

Swallowing a sob, she realized she wanted her Wes back. The one who didn't know his last name or what state he'd been born in. Or, oh, God. They'd both assumed he wasn't married, but the possibility had flickered from time to time like an incipient migraine. When he'd had no memory, it hadn't mattered. Now, unaccountably it did.

"Are you married?" she asked, the words scratching her throat like the dust flying in the window.

"No."

Well. There was married and there was married.

"Girlfriend?"

"My girlfriend moved out six months ago."

That was a relief. Although the irony wasn't lost on her that she was asking him these questions at the end of their affair rather than the beginning.

Oh, God. The end of their affair. She blinked rapidly and turned her face to the window so the dry wind could dry her tears before they fell. Why hadn't she told him?

She had all night to think about it.

Once they were back at Gertie's, he didn't even stop the truck, merely said, "You and Gertie stay inside and lock the doors. You see or hear anything you don't like, call the cops."

"What are you going to do?"

"My job."

She had the door open and was half out when she turned back. "Be careful."

With a curt nod, he said, "I'll return the truck later." And with that she had to be satisfied. She stood beside the road and watched the dusty red truck disappear while cold fear settled in her stomach.

After spending the evening torn between worry about what Wes was doing and how much danger he was in, and feeling pangs of guilt at the way Nell had deceived him, she was exhausted when she went to bed.

Of course, she didn't sleep. She lay there, recalling the times he'd crept into her room, and wondering if she'd ever see him again. As the minutes dragged slowly and painfully by, she accepted the truth. Somewhere in the last two weeks, she'd fallen in love with Wes.

A man with no past, no memory, whom she'd assumed was

a motorcycle gang member. It hadn't mattered. All he hadn't been able to tell her himself, his body had communicated.

Now that it was too late, she wished she'd told him they were strangers as soon as they became intimate. It wouldn't have mattered then. What a fool she'd been.

She heard the truck engine and stole to the window. He was alone, and there wasn't a second vehicle to whisk him away so he must plan to sleep at Gertie's.

Excitement filled her. In spite of his cold words, she didn't believe he hadn't felt what she had. She refused to believe it when every touch, every glance they'd shared had dragged them deeper into intimacy.

Heart pounding, she heard him creep past her door to the bathroom and then she heard the bath. A while later, she heard him go to his room.

Then nothing.

She waited for the familiar pad of his feet approaching her door, for the stealthy way he'd learned to avoid the squeaking board outside her room, but it didn't come. Sadness turned to frustration. She flipped over in bed and forced her eyes shut. Fine. He didn't want to talk to her? Fine.

She flipped again, almost tossing herself out of bed onto the floor as anger built. Didn't she at least deserve to hear what had happened? She may have allowed him to continue in a misconception, but it was for his own mental health. And she had saved his miserable life, hadn't she?

Flouncing out of bed, she decided she'd better have it out with him. And there was no time like the present.

She happened to be wearing a short silk nightgown with crisscrossing straps that played peekaboo with her cleavage, but she couldn't help that. She certainly didn't have time to change before giving DEA Agent Wes Doman a piece of her mind.

Barefoot, she slipped out of her room, stepped over the squeaky board and crept soundlessly to his room.

Well, not soundlessly enough, apparently, for when she got there, he was raised on one elbow, staring at the doorway. And a black, deadly revolver was pointed right at her.

She squeaked in alarm. "Where did you get that gun?"

"It's for protection." Was it her imagination or was there a thread of humor in his tone.

"Well, I don't need protecting, so you can put it away," she said with all her bravery pushed forward to shield the fact that he'd be scaring the pants off her if she were currently wearing any.

"I think I might need protecting," he said, his eyes glowing in the moonlight that streamed in the open window. The heat of his gaze had her nipples tightening until they poked through the strappy gown like blueberries through a lattice piecrust.

"I . . ." She cleared her throat and began again. "I wanted to know how it went tonight."

His lips parted in a quick, satisfied grin. "Mission accomplished."

He shifted to shove the gun under his pillow and she saw him wince. "You're hurt," she said, rushing forward, everything else she'd planned to say forgotten.

"It's nothing"—he waved her away irritably, then running his gaze down her body said—"nothing that a kiss wouldn't help."

"Where does it hurt?"

He glanced at his lap. "I don't suppose you'd believe me if I told you—"

"It looked like your arm to me," she replied, trying to stifle her grin. Maybe it was simply the aftermath of a successful bust, but it seemed as though the Wes she knew and loved was back. Settling herself beside him on the bed, she reached for his arm, but with his good one he held her off. "Strained my shoulder is all."

Seeing no blood or obvious bruising, she said, "Then you should lie still and rest it."

"Maybe you could take my mind off the pain," he said, his good hand palming a nipple.

Warmth streaked through her at his touch. She'd begun to believe she'd never feel it again. But if she thought he was going to ignore her deception, she was wrong.

"Why didn't you tell me?" he asked, even as his hand moved to the other breast.

"I didn't mean to deceive you. You woke up while I was reviving you . . . I did bring you back from the dead you know," she said indignantly, just so he'd know she wasn't planning on a big grovel-fest at his feet. "Then, when you woke again, you seemed to think I was your girlfriend. The Doc said I should let you go on believing it since it seemed to soothe you."

He snorted, changing his movements so he was plucking at her nipples as though they were ripe berries. "Nothing about you soothes me."

"Well, that was the doctor's advice. And then, when you . . . when we . . . I didn't know how to get out of it." He raised a brow and she shook her head. "No. I didn't want to. I . . . I . . ." He was doing that incredible twisting, pulling motion that sent sparks shooting straight to her core. "Oh, God. I liked it too much," she admitted.

She was squirming against the sheets, and he knew it. If he was planning to punish her for her deception he couldn't go about it any better. She was restless, burning, needy and all he'd do was toy with her breasts in that maddening fashion.

Enough already. She was only human. "I did what I did and I'm sorry if you didn't like it," she gasped, "but damn it I'm going to do it again." She flipped back the sheet to find him fully aroused and gorgeous.

She straddled him, already aching to have him inside her. She lowered herself slowly onto him, taking him so deep into her body that she purred, head thrown back. Perhaps she'd concealed too much before. Now it was time to rectify that by revealing everything. She rose slowly over him, stared deep into his eyes and took the biggest risk of her life. "I love you."

The words seemed to glavanize both of them; they bucked and rocked, drove and thrust until starbursts danced before her eyes. "I love you!" she shouted as she exploded.

When she awoke, with a sleepy, satisfied smile curving her lips, he was gone. In seconds she realized that not only was the bed empty but for her, but that his things were missing.

She dashed back to her own room and threw on jeans and a T-shirt, then ran downstairs, but the kitchen was as empty as the bed they'd shared last night. She tracked Gertie down out back where she was hanging washing on the line.

"Did you see Wes?"

"He left early. Said to tell you good-bye."

That was it? A second-hand good-bye?

If he'd wanted to punish her for pretending to a past they didn't share, he couldn't have struck truer. She'd bared her most intimate feelings, said the words she'd never said to another man, and he'd left her without so much as saying good-bye to her face.

As the blistering heat of summer faded to fall, the corn ripened and the pumpkins turned color. Gertie's chrysanthemums and dahlias burst into orange and purple and yellow bloom.

"What are you going to do now?" Gertie asked as they dug potatoes out of the garden. Without any will of its own, her gaze wandered to the spot where Wes had landed head first, changing her forever.

"I'm not going back to LA. I might look for work in a PR firm or an advertising agency." She didn't mention Chicago, but it was in the back of her mind to start her job search there. It was a good-sized city where there was lots of work and it was only a day's drive from Gertie. She knew from the newspaper reports of Harleyville's biggest-ever drug bust that Wes worked out of the Chicago office, where the trials had been held. Not that them being in the same city would matter. She hadn't seen or heard from him in a couple of months.

Her great-aunt was no fool, and her gaze shifted to where the beans had stood proud and bountiful before Wes headplanted into them. "I thought that man had ruined my whole crop of beans," she said with a sidelong glance at Nell, "but I propped them back up again, fussed with them a little and they came back better than ever."

Nell's smile quivered at the corners as she wrapped her arms around Gertie. "Sometimes it happens that way. He did the same thing to me."

"The beans are stuck here. You're not."

A laugh was surprised out of Nell. "Are you suggesting I go chasing after him?"

Gertie grunted as she attacked another potato hill with her shovel. "I'm saying if a man like Wes landed head first in my lap, I wouldn't hang around moping after he left."

"I was not . . ." Gertie's raised brows had her petering off. "Well, maybe a little." She shoved her own shovel into the rich dark earth as she voiced her greatest fear. "What if he doesn't want me?"

"Boy's been busy. You read in the paper like I did about the trials. They're all in jail now and this town can get back to normal. I'm thinking Wes won't be so busy now."

Nell sniffed. "Who's too busy to make a phone call? Or send a postcard?"

Gertie straightened, her lips already pursing ready to answer; then she cocked her head, looking so much like a robin listening for worms that Nell smiled fondly at her. It took her another minute to realize it wasn't worms Gertie was listening to, but the low, unmistakable roar of a motorcycle.

"Now that's a sound I haven't heard in a while." Gertie shot a sneaky glance at Nell. "Wonder what I did with that speed bump."

"Gertie, don't even think about it." The motorcycle came into view.

Her heart sank when she saw the helmet on the lone rider and noted there was no hair flapping out the back. Of course it wasn't Wes. Unable to watch, Nell turned away. "This bucket's full. I'll go get another."

Gertie grabbed her arm. "Not just yet. I think we have company."

Sure enough the rider slowed and pulled up in front of them. Even before he'd pulled the helmet off his head she recognized the lean planes and arrogant angles of his face. His hair was short but even short it had an unruly curl that she bet drove him crazy.

"Wes," she said, since it was the only thing she could think of.

"Hop on," he said, giving her a grin that spoke of wrinkled sheets and long nights making love under the stars.

She licked her suddenly dry lips. "Why?"

His grin ought to come with an age-restricted warning label. "You know why."

" 'Bout time you showed up," Gertie said behind her. "Your intentions honorable?"

"Gertie!" Nell all but shouted, the blush already rising.

"I plan to marry her," he said over her head.

"Well, of all the high-handed . . . You might ask me!"

"Nell?" he said.

"Yes?" she replied with haughty dignity.

"Get on the back of the bike."

Her jaw dropped. "Gertie, can you believe—"

"You heard the man. Go on. Git."

She narrowed her eyes and stalked up to him. "Where are we going?"

He grabbed her and kissed her until stars danced before her eyes. Then he stared at her and she saw every one of her fantasies staring right back at her.

"Honey," he said, "I'm going to take you on the ride of your life."

Please turn the page for an exciting preview of
THE FOREVER KISS by Thea Devine.
A summer 2003 paperback release from Brava.

It was the blood. That gypsy blood pounding through her body that would never let anything go. And it was the house, Ducas's house, a magnet, with the gas and candlelit windows that beckoned deep in the night, especially when the Sangbournes were entertaining.

They were always entertaining. Lady Sangbourne had an insatiable need to surround herself with people all the time, with fascinating people. People about whom you could find out things if you were clever enough and if you followed the lure of your gypsy blood.

Oh, there was something about the way it thrummed deep within her, blotting out her mother's every attempt to turn her into the lady her father wanted her to be.

But then, her father didn't know that her mother was a frequent visitor to Sangbourne Manor, because he himself was such an infrequent visitor to the house in Cheshamshire.

And this he didn't need to know—that his exotic, alluring Gaetana was frequently the entertainment. They feasted on her, the wild gypsy dancer, as they gossiped about her, she who had enticed an earl and held him still in her thrall. They paid her to come to the Manor and dance for them, and she went, following the call of her nature, and in spite of the fact the earl kept her like a queen.

It was the blood. It could not be denied. Not in her mother, not in her. And so Gaetana danced, giving herself to whatever voluptuous pleasures were on the menu on any given evening at Sangbourne Manor, and giving herself to the earl at his command.

Gaetana on the inside and Angene, her changeling daughter, on the outside, looking in, squirreling away secrets.

So many secrets. Her gypsy blood reveled in the secrets. Secrets were knowledge, secrets were power, and Angene knew someday the power would come in very handy.

And besides, what else had she to do until Ducas came back from the war? Dear God, Ducas, throwing himself in harm's way in a godforsaken country thousands of miles away for no reason she could ever understand.

Ducas, with his persistent tongue and honeyed promises.

Her body twinged just thinking of it. It was the blood; no decent woman would even conceive of doing what she intended to do when Ducas returned.

And he would return. There was not a doubt in her mind. And then . . . and then . . . She would become his mistress and enslave him forever, the way her mother had captivated the earl.

The thought made her breathless.

How stupid of him to go to war. It wasn't his war. And it was so far away that it could take him years to return. The idea of it yawned like an abyss, dark as the night that enfolded her. Perhaps that was why she so loved the night: there was always the promise of a new day, and with it, Ducas's return.

But until that day, it was the house that drew her, and the sense that at night she could be close to him by just touching the cold stone walls, and by learning everything she could about those who peopled his life.

By lurking in the shadows . . .

It was the blood: there was a turbulence in her that could not be tempered by all the good breeding of the man who had sired her, nor by a hundred lessons with the best tutors in deportment and manners her mother had employed.

She was what she was: daughter of a gypsy dancer and an aristocratic earl, and the fact she was creeping along the outer walls of Sangbourne Manor was proof enough which part of her held sway.

And then there were the secrets, the delicious sensual secrets about the games that adults played.

Games that quickened her blood, because she and Ducas had played at playing those games, had skirted the ultimate conquest and surrender, with the full understanding that someday, somehow, it would happen.

But for now, she moved noiselessly through the trees and into the bushes that fronted the windows of the grand parlor where the games would begin.

The dining first, hours of it, with five or six courses of elegantly prepared food and the best china and silver; they began early in the country, on the evenings when they played their games. After dinner, the men would retreat for port and polite conversation as the tension and anticipation escalated to an unbearable degree. And finally the men would join the ladies for the evening's entertainment—this night, Gaetana, the gypsy, well-paid for her sensual dances, for her time, for her body.

A never-ending fascination, watching the aristocracy as they ate, drank, eyed each other, flirted, paired off, disappeared; sometimes they imported girls from the village to service the gentlemen while the ladies went off with the goat-boys and shepherds into the fields.

Or they would hire high-priced courtesans for a more elegant and willfull seduction.

Or they took each other up and off in private rooms in a variety of interesting combinations.

All of this, Angene knew. And the the queen of all this rampant lasciviousness was Ducas's mother.

Gaetana would not talk about her, nor anything that went on at Sangbourne Manor. Secrets were safe at the Manor, kept beyond the grave in a devil's bargain. No one would tell, ever, about the things that went on there, weekend-long things, forbidden things.

Things, perhaps, Ducas had been a part of. Things, because of that, Angene had to know, since she was certain they were things that would give her the power she needed to convince him to become her lover, forever.

She was a bastard child; she wanted nothing more.

As she peered into the tall, multipaned windows of the dimly lit grand parlor, she saw her mother dancing to a wildly strumming guitar, her skirts held high, her feet and legs bared to all. And the look on her face—the transcending look of joy that she could finally be herself, even among these heathens who had no idea of her life, her lore, her heritage.

It didn't matter. She did not need to pretend in these wild hours. She could follow the dictates of her heart, her blood, and no one would tell.

In that curious honor among deviants, her mother's secret was safe.

Angene was the only one who knew—and even she harbored a tumultuous desire to be among these libertine people, her hair, her skirts, her desire flowing free.

If only Ducas would return; Ducas understood her. Handsome, reckless Ducas with that irresistible combination of haughty aristocrat and primitive stable boy—and that tongue, that insatiable, demanding tongue . . .

But wait—her mother's voluptuous dance was finished, and the guests—four couples in all, excluding Lord and Lady Sangbourne, were clapping loudly and appreciatively.

She knew what came next in this sexual quadrille: every

country weekend almost seemed to be a set piece. In tonight's little play, the lights would dim, a gentleman would rise and select the lady of his choice, who was not his wife, and away they would go into the shadows to explore the unfettered nature of men and the naked response of women.

Lady Sangbourne directed the scene, standing tall and slender in the center of the room, dressed in her habitual green, with her long thick hair that deliberately grazed her waist bound away from her narrow face; did she not know how much men loved long hair to curtain their sins? But she was always the last to go into the shadows.

She knew everything, Lady Sangbourne, and didn't blink an eye as her husband chose his companion for the night . . .

Gaetana?

Angene's heart sank. This she had never witnessed before, this wholesale taking of her mother, in spite of her allegiance and her love for the earl. But none of that ever counted here. And certainly not tonight, if her mother's expression were any indication.

The air was thick with expendable lust, and every last guest only wanted that evanescent moment of surrender. Instinctively Angene understood that the crux of the evening was the pleasure point, nothing more, nothing less, and not even her mother was immune to the call of her blood.

She sank against the wall, her heart pounding painfully. This reality was not pretty. But then, wasn't it what she wanted for herself? To give herself wholly and completely to Ducas, and to live, outside constraints, as the love of his life forever?

Was there a forever when it came to the nature of men?

Would *she* entertain Ducas's friends and companions, and would he just as cavalierly hand her over to whoever wanted her for a night? Was this the life she wanted to commit to, in her overwhelming desire to possess Ducas?

It did not bear thinking about . . . She couldn't. He might be dead for all she knew, on some foreign battlefield, dead with no remains to be buried and mourned over . . . and this was worse than anything that might come of their life together.

Oh, dear Lord—Ducas . . .

Silence descended, the curious silence of the deep dark night, where the merest rustle of a leaf could set the blood thrumming. Not a star burned; the moon drifted behind a tail of clouds; every detail of the landscape merged into another so that there was only the flat black of nothingness around her.

There was nowhere to move, nothing to see that could guide her back home. She was a prisoner of the dark, caught in that abyss of emptiness, that cold black hole she so feared, and there was nothing she could do but curl up against the cold stone walls of Sangbourne Manor until daylight.

The howling of a dog awakened her.

Dawn. Cold. Wet. Dank.

Jingling. A rasping, rolling sound. Horses. A carriage emerging out of the fog that hovered just beyond the drive in front of Sangbourne Manor.

Dreaming. Too early in the morning for visitors . . . and besides, they were all still tumbled in their ruttish rest.

If she moved quickly, she could get back to the house before her mother returned.

Only, limbs stiff from the cold. Can't move. Not yet. Slowly, slowly . . . no sound—if anyone caught her here, her mother would abandon her to the wolves . . . the carriage door opening—who . . . ?

A stranger. Wait—someone leaning on him . . .

Slowly easing out of the carriage—was it? The stranger, giving him a cane. A familiar stance, a bend of the body, the rumble of a word, a familiar voice . . .

Oh, God—Ducas . . . *Ducas?* As if she'd conjured him with her thoughts. Injured? Maimed? Oh, mighty Lord in heaven, he must not see her here, not like this, not now . . . There could be no explanation, ever, for her skulking around his house.

She ducked into the bushes, watched him walk slowly and painfully on the arm of the stranger up to the front door.

A jangling bell in the distance. Scurry of footsteps. The door opening. She couldn't see anything—it couldn't be him, could it?

But it must be . . . a word, a welcome, and he entered the house.

Thank heaven there was fog—while they were all occupied by the surprise of his return, she could slip and slide away without anyone noticing.

But dear heaven, this was so unexpected; she didn't know what to think, what to do.

But you don't have to do anything.

Ducas is home . . .

And here is a seond preview that will whet your appetite
for WILDE THING by Janelle Denison.
A July 2003 release from Brava.

He had *bad boy* written all over him, and Liz Adams wanted him in the worst possible way. From his rumpled sable hair and striking, seductive blue eyes, to that lean, honed body she'd imagined naked and aroused, he exuded raw sex appeal and brought her feminine instincts to keen awareness like no other man had in a very long time.

And she was completely and totally in lust with her gorgeous, head-turning customer who'd recently started frequenting her cafe, The Daily Grind, in the evenings. He'd become a pleasant, visual distraction to other responsibilities and worries that had been weighing heavily on her mind lately.

He lifted his head from the latest best-seller he was reading, and from across the room their eyes met briefly and she caught a glimpse of the to-die-for grin that lifted the corner of his sensual mouth. An undeniable warmth and excitement stirred within her, and she had to resist the urge to close the distance between them, rip his black T-shirt and tight jeans off his long, muscled body, and have her wicked way with him. On the countertop, on one of the couches in the sitting area, or even the floor. She wasn't picky about the *where* part of her fantasy.

Picking up a damp towel, she wiped down the stainless steel espresso machine and let out a wistful sigh that conveyed two long years of suppressed desires. She'd recently turned thirty-one, and she swore she was hitting her sexual prime, because for the past few weeks she'd been *craving* sex. Ever since *he'd* strolled into her coffeehouse and jump-started her libido and fueled her nightly dreams with carnal, sinful fantasies.

Undoubtedly, it had been too long since she'd felt the exquisite caress of a man's mouth sliding across her sensitized flesh. Too long since she'd experienced the delicious heat of a hard, strong body covering hers, the silken texture and erotic friction of him sliding deep in a slow, grinding rhythm. Those realistic sensations were something no artificially enhanced sex toy could duplicate, and she missed that kind of physical connection with a flesh and blood man.

But as much as her fantasy man tempted her, everything from that black leather jacket he wore, to his come-hither eyes and self-confidence, screamed rebel. And she'd vowed after her marriage to Trevor she'd never fall for another man who was wild and reckless and had the ability to leave her devastated in the process.

Unfortunately, despite being burned by one bad boy who'd turned out to be bad to the extreme, she couldn't help her attraction to the kind of man who had a bit of an edge to him. A take-charge kind of man who was decisive and straightforward, yet unpredictable, with a sense of reckless adventure. That Harley-Davidson motorcycle *he* rode told her a lot about the man, that he was secure in his masculinity, didn't like to be constrained by rules, and was untamable, intrepid, and daring, as well.

Even knowing he was most likely all wrong for her, that those qualities could only lead to trouble and heartache, she still wanted him. *Badly.*

"Mind if I make myself a chilled mocha before you finish cleaning up?"

The sound of Mona Owen's voice snapped Liz out of her private thoughts and jolted her back to reality and the stocking and cleanup still awaiting her attention. She glanced at her good friend and owner of The Last Word, a new and used bookstore that directly connected to her café, and caught Mona eyeing the last of the drink mix in the blender.

Liz grinned, having grown used to Mona's tendency to mooch off leftovers near closing time. "Sure. Help yourself."

Mona tossed ice into the concoction, switched the blender on for a few seconds, then poured the icy drink into a plastic cup and added a straw. "I've been meaning to ask you if you've heard from your cousin Valerie yet?"

The reminder of Valerie's vanishing act tossed everything else from Liz's mind except worry, and a helpless feeling that had grown with each passing day without any contact from her cousin. "I haven't heard a word from her since she left me that vague note Friday night." And all the message had said was that she was going to a weekend work party with a new boyfriend who was a client she met through The Ultimate Fantasy, the phone sex place where she worked.

While Valerie had always possessed a wild, reckless streak, and it really wasn't out of the ordinary for her to do something as frivolous as to take off with a boyfriend for a getaway, Liz found the whole situation too disturbing, and worrisome. It just wasn't like her cousin to go so long without getting in touch, especially since they shared an apartment together, even if to leave a brief message on their phone recorder. And here it was Tuesday evening, and Liz had yet to hear from her.

Liz knew Valerie enjoyed her unconventional occupation, but there had been other aspects of her job that her cousin had mentioned that concerned Liz, and made her fairly certain that the phone sex business was a front for a much larger operation dealing in prostitution and other sexual escapades. Her biggest fear was that Valerie had gotten herself involved in something illegal, or even dangerous, with this man she'd taken off with.

"Are you thinking about contacting the police?" Mona

asked, apparently sensing Liz's distress over her cousin's disappearance.

"I already tried that." Grabbing the steaming pitcher, she dunked it into the hot, soapy water in the sink and took out her frustration in scrubbing the stainless steel pot. "I spoke with an officer, but once I told him about the note Valerie left stating she was off on her own free will, he said at this point there wasn't any evidence of foul play to warrant an investigation, and all I could do was file a missing person's report on her behalf."

And with every day that passed without a word from her cousin, Liz's desperation grew. So far, she'd been able to keep Valerie's vanishing act from her aunt and uncle who'd moved from Chicago to Southern California a year ago and had asked Liz to look after Valerie. The last thing Liz wanted to do was apprise them of the sort of career their daughter had chosen, but if her cousin didn't show up soon, she'd have no choice but to inform them of the less than ideal circumstances.

Not wanting to shock her aunt and uncle with the news that Valerie indulged in phone sex for a living unless she absolutely had to, Liz had opted to pursue her cousin's absence herself, in the only way she knew how. And knowing she needed to tell someone of her plan, she decided to make Mona that person.

She bit her bottom lip and gathered the fortitude to spill her secret. "I applied at the same phone sex company where Valerie was working," she said, the reasons for her actions self-explanatory. "I have an appointment for an interview at The Ultimate Fantasy tomorrow morning at eleven."

Concern creased Mona's dark brows. "Do you think that's safe or smart?"

Liz didn't want to directly respond to that question, because she knew the answer would be a resounding *no*, and she wasn't about to give up on the idea. "It's the only way I can think of to get inside information on Valerie or where she might be and with whom."

Mona shook her head, her expression adamant. "I don't think this is something you should do on your own."

Liz dragged her fingers through her hair and sighed. "The police aren't willing to get involved, so I don't have much of a choice, not if I want to find Valerie or get in touch with her."

Her friend was quiet for a few moments while she considered Liz's idea, her gaze focused on something out in the lounge area. Then a bright smile spread across her face. "Why don't you hire Steve Wilde?"

Liz frowned in confusion as she filled a basket with scones and another tray with gourmet cookies. "Who?"

Mona pitched her empty plastic cup into the trash and hooked her thumb toward her fantasy man. "Steve Wilde. The guy you've been lusting after for the past month. And don't bother denying it. I've been watching the two of you, and when you're not ogling him, his eyes are following you. And from my astute observations, that lingering gaze of his is hungry for more than just your pastries." She gave Liz a playful but encouraging wink.

Wilde. God, even his last name insinuated trouble of the most sensual variety. Her gaze strayed back to the lounge just as he unfolded his big, lean body from his chair and shrugged into his well-worn leather jacket, causing the muscles in his arms and across his chest to shift temptingly as he moved. Her pulse quickened with female appreciation. He was so compelling, his magnetism so potent, she couldn't help but respond to his stunning good looks.

He picked up his book and keys from the coffee table and glanced up, his disarming gaze locking with hers—as bold, direct, and unapologetically sexual as the man himself. He tipped his head in acknowledgment, causing a lock of unruly sable hair to fall across his brow, accentuating his rakish appearance. The private, sinful grin he graced her with literally stole her breath and sent her hormones into an overwhelming frenzy of sexual longing. Her breasts swelled and tightened, her nipples tingled, and a surge of liquid desire settled in intimate places.

Oh, yeah, he was most definitely trouble personified.

He exited the cafe, leaving her with more than enough new stimulating material to fuel another night of erotic mind candy. She returned her attention to Mona. "So, tell me, how do *you* know his name?"

Her friend snagged a biscotti from the glass jar on the counter and munched into the baked treat. "He's come into The Last Word to purchase a few books, and we've talked a time or two."

Which essentially meant Mona not only knew his name, but his age, marital status, and occupation, as well.

Finishing off her cookie, Mona licked the crumbs from her fingers. "And knowing the attraction between the two of you is mutual, I'm thinking it's time you took off that gold band you wear on your finger that makes men think you're taken, and take a walk on the *Wilde* side."

"Ha-ha. Very funny," Liz said, though the idea was one she'd already considered . . . in her fantasies.

"I'm being completely serious." Mona's tone reflected just how resolute she was. "At least about taking that ring off your finger and putting yourself back on the market. There's a time and place to shed everything . . . your ring, your clothes, your inhibitions . . ." she added meaningfully.

The lights overhead glimmered off the gold band Liz had worn since Trevor's death, mocking her solitary, abstinent lifestyle—of her own choosing, she reminded herself. She was still struggling to dig herself out of the financial mess her late husband had left her in when he'd died two years ago, and she didn't want or need the complication of a binding relationship. Not when her focus was on her café and seeing her savings account back in the black again.

Feeling useless resentments clawing their way to the surface, she redirected their conversation back to their original topic. "You mentioned hiring Steve Wilde. What for?"

"Because while he might have all the markings of a bad boy, he's definitely one of the good guys. He's a private detective with his own agency, and I'm betting he can help you out with Valerie." Excitement infused Mona's voice. "At the very least, he can offer advice or follow up on your cousin's disappearance without you putting yourself at risk."

So, he was a good guy with a bad boy demeanor, a combination Liz found much too intriguing. "It's not like I have a lot of extra money to pay a private investigator. You know that." She'd spent the past two years on a tight budget while Trevor's debts had drained a huge portion of her savings. "I could barely afford to have the alternator on my car fixed, let alone a PI's professional services."

Mona seemed undeterred by her lack of funds. "Maybe Mr. Wilde would be willing to work out a payment plan of some sort. If you're really lucky, he'll take his services out in trade," she offered with a sly smile, leaving no doubt in Liz's mind what her friend meant. "I have his business card back in my shop if you're interested."

Interested in his services or paying him in trade, Liz wondered wickedly. She shivered, unable to stem the fiery sensations rippling through her at the thought of being a slave to Steve Wilde's every sexual whim. Not that she believed he'd agree to such a shameless proposition. But it did make for a nice fantasy to add to her growing collection.

On a business level, she supposed an initial consultation with Mr. Wilde couldn't hurt, and any free advice he might impart could only help her in her search to find her cousin.

"I'm interested," she said to Mona, and realizing how

those simple words could be misconstrued, she followed that up with a quick, "In his business card."

"Of course." Amusement and satisfaction flashed in Mona's eyes. "I'll be right back."

Liz watched her friend trek across the short distance to her bookstore, anticipation making her heart pound hard in her chest. She swore that contacting Steve Wilde—the object of her fondest, most carnal dreams—had nothing to do with her attraction to him, and her interest was strictly professional.

Her mind accepted the lecture. Unfortunately, her neglected body wasn't completely convinced.

Steve Wilde wasn't a man easily shocked. Yet he couldn't have been more stunned when his secretary, Beverly, announced that Liz Adams was there at his agency to see him. Seconds later, the woman who'd occupied too much of his thoughts lately appeared in his office, her vivid green gaze tentatively meeting his from across the room.

She looked incredibly sexy. He'd only seen her in her work uniform of jeans, T-shirt, and a bib apron that tied around her neck and waist. Nothing overtly suggestive or clingy, but he'd seen enough of her coming and going to know that she had the kind of full, luscious figure he liked on a woman. And the thigh-length, form-fitting cocoa colored skirt and matching blouse she was currently wearing confirmed a knock-out, head-turning shape he couldn't help but appreciate and admire.

Unlike his brother Eric who was drawn to a woman's derriere, and Adrian who went for long, shapely legs, Steve was first and foremost a breast man; he liked them full and firm, and preferred more than a dainty handful to fondle and play with. The "V" neckline of Liz's blouse dipped low, giving him a glimpse of an ample amount of cleavage that made his mouth water and his fingers itch to touch. He assumed she was wearing a bra with no padding, because he could see the faint outline of her nipples pressing against the silky fabric of her top. He imagined the velvet texture of those stiff crests in his mouth, against his tongue, and felt a rush of pulsing heat spiral straight to his groin.

He gave a barely perceptible nod to his secretary, and Beverly quietly closed the door as Liz continued to walk into his office. The skirt she wore accentuated the indentation of her waist and the provocative sway of her shapely hips. From there, he took the liberty of continuing the sensual journey, taking in the curvaceous outline of her thighs, and long, lightly tanned legs designed to wrap around a man's hips and clench him tight in the throes of passion.

God, he just wanted to eat her up, inch by delectable inch— from her soft, glossy lips all the way down to those pink painted toenails peeking from the opening of her heeled sandals, and everywhere in between.

Much to his delight, there was nothing dainty, delicate, or petite about her. No, she was a well-built woman with a voluptuous body made for hot, hard, lusty sex. Which was just the way he liked his physical encounters, though it had been too long since he'd been with a woman who matched his sexual appetite and could fulfill his needs and demands in the bedroom.

Shaking off his surprise at Liz's impromptu visit, along with the thrum of arousal taking up residence within him, he stood and casually rounded his desk to greet her. "You're Liz, from The Daily Grind." He held out his hand and waited for her to acknowledge the gesture.

"That's correct." With a slow, sensual smile that made him feel sucker-punched, she slipped her palm against his, allowing his long fingers to envelop her hand in the superior strength of his grip.

Her flesh was warm and soft, but her handshake was firm and confident. As for the instantaneous chemistry that leaped between them at first touch, well, that was nothing short of a simmering heat just waiting for the right flame to ignite their attraction into a blazing inferno.

She didn't try and tug her hand away when he lingered and brazenly brushed his thumb along her skin. Rather, she maintained eye contact and waited until he chose to release her, confirming his first impression of her at the café that she was a strong, independent woman who was secure in her femininity and had no problem giving as good as she got when it came to the battle of the sexes.

He liked those unique qualities about her, and knew he'd found a woman with enough tenacity and daring to keep him stimulated physically, as well as intellectually. A rare feat and challenge he'd more than welcome, if it wasn't for the ring encircling her left hand finger that gave the impression she belonged to someone else.

As soon as he let go of her hand, she said, "I hope you don't mind, but Mona gave me your card."

Ahh, Mona, the chatty, albeit friendly woman from The Last Word who enjoyed prying information from her customers. "I'll have to thank her for the business." Though he'd always thought of Liz in terms of pure, unadulterated pleasure. The kind that made him wake up sweating in the dark of night, his muscles rigid and his cock granite hard from erotic images of Liz beneath him, her body soft and inviting and just as tight as his own fist stroking his erection.

Before his libido reacted to the nightly, obsessive dreams that plagued him, he leaned his backside against his desk and crossed his arms over his chest. "What can I do for you, Mrs. Adams?"

"Actually, it's *Ms.* Adams," she clarified.

He glanced at the ring she was absently twisting around her finger. Since she'd come to him and was in his territory, he figured he had every right to ask frank, personal questions. "So, you're unmarried and single?"

She nodded, causing her silky, shoulder-length blond hair to brush along her jawline. "Yes, to both."

She didn't give an explanation for the band she wore that indicated otherwise, but he'd just learned all he needed to know to give him the incentive to pursue her on a more intimate level. With less than two feet of space separating them, there was no denying the awareness between them, and their attraction was something he had no qualms about using to get what he wanted.

And what he desired was *her*.